THE EGG OF THE GLAK
and Other Stories

THE EGG
OF THE GLAK

and Other Stories

by
HARVEY JACOBS

1817

HARPER & ROW, PUBLISHERS
New York, Evanston, and London

The author gives grateful acknowledgment to the following magazines in which many of these stories first appeared: *Cavalier, Cosmopolitan, Fantasy & Science Fiction, Midstream, New Worlds, Mademoiselle,* and *Playboy.*

FIRST EDITION

LIBRARY OF CONGRESS CATALOG CARD NUMBER: 75-81874

To the memory of Lou and Laura Jacobs

CONTENTS

THE EGG OF THE GLAK
and Other Stories

EPILOGUE

MY NAME IS HARRY LUB. I AM THE AUTHOR OF A NOVEL CALLED *Wandertime* that is a song of myself. The book concerns my passionate journey across the American continent. It is a chronicle of my pleasure and pain, of my greed for life and of my unsuccessful, clumsy attempt to touch the body of everything.

Wandertime was written ten years ago, yet it is not in the Modern Library. Since its creation in the distant past, and since its rejection by seven reputable publishers, *Wandertime* has commanded a small, loyal audience consisting of myself. Even that audience is losing interest. The manuscript rests in my bookshelf beside the Chalon Edition of the *Works of Rabelais* and a morocco-bound copy of the Holy Scriptures. Several volumes to its left there are *The Golden Bough, Introductory Lectures in Psychonanalysis* and *Ulysses*. Four volumes to its right are *Don Quixote, Grimm's Fairy Tales* and *The History of the World in Two Hundred and Forty Pages*.

For several years I have been an instructor of English Composition at a certain Eastern university. When I first came here the university had very little prestige. Due to the foresight of the chancellor and due to an active alumni fund and due to the dedication and faith of eleven powerful youths, it has since achieved some fame in athletic combat. Tradition here has it that a bell on top of an old tower is rung at each football victory. As the bell has been ringing regularly this season, my stature has grown, together with that of Alma Mater.

I live by myself in a small clapboard house a few short blocks from the Hall of Liberal Arts. The Hall was donated to the uni-

1

versity fifty-two years ago by an industrialist who manufactured a
well-known line of glassware. The products he originated are still
very much in use and bear his name. The Hall of Liberal Arts, in
the Georgian style, was built for his lasting monument. A small
replica of the building serves as the family vault in a little cemetery a mile out of town.

I can see the Hall from my living-room window. It is illumi-
nated by colored spotlights that are placed around campus during
Winter Graduation Week. It snowed this afternoon, and tonight
the pastel lights reflect from pure white walls. Actually, the stone
is a deep gray. The snow and the lights have effected a miracle of
decoration.

Though it is past midnight, I am fully awake. By nature I am
a nocturnal person. The early morning hours give me a sense of
intense isolation. My head clears and my thoughts come like cool
water. I have no thought of sleep. This evening I have gained
what is said to be the highest fulfillment for an instructor of English Composition, and I face a terrible loss. My day has been full
of emotion. I have smoked more than forty king-size cigarettes.
My throat is as dry as straw. A nerve is twitching over my left eye
with an irregular pulse of its own. I am afraid of the next hours
because I know that Rachel Ashgren will come here asking me
to help her. I will not answer the bell. She will go away full of
raging pain and hate.

Outside, it is a clear blue night. A crescent moon rests on its
curve and seems to rock cradlelike in the blowing gray-blue clouds.
The night is alive with ivory light. Gusts of powder snow swirl
phantoms around the street lamps. Chimes mark the half-hour.
The heavy bell sounds absorb like thick syrup into the snow. Past
a bank of houses I can see the neon glow of Hilson Street, where
the restaurants and coffee shops provide a student oasis. The street
shines like a separate city.

In front of the fraternity and sorority houses stand the frozen
snow statues that decorated Winter Carnival. The theme for this

year's celebration was Fairyland. An elfin population—the snow prince and princess, the pumpkin coach, the smirking dwarf—stand icelocked in the street. Their painted snow bodies are luminous in the moonlight. Last year a premature storm ruined our festival. The statues were wiped out in a single turbulent night of lightning and rain.

Perhaps I am wrong in being so certain that Rachel will come here. I am neither wizard nor magician. How then can I predict her thoughts? She had her first triumph tonight and who can say how she feels now? I sat with her in the theater while they gave her play. All during its performance she said nothing. The actors, although nonprofessional, did well. The audience of faculty and students and visiting parents seemed to enjoy themselves. They gave the production heavy applause. Do they know what they experienced? The program mentioned that Rachel Ashgren is twenty years old, the daughter of Professor and Mrs. Martin Ashgren. They shouted "Author! Author!" when it was over and she went up on the stage to bow.

She stood surrounded by the characters she had created. The leading man and the heroine stood next to her. The boy who played her hero was slender and dark. The girl, who had cleaved to him moments before in the final scene of young discovery, had an abundant fresh beauty, her rich black hair falling over her shoulders. Her body, opulent and ripe, had a dancer's grace. As the curtain fell, when the actress yielded in fear and expectance to her lover's pleading, she had succeeded to believable, deep emotion. Rachel Ashgren shared their bows. She wore a simple white dress with long sleeves and high neck. The dress hid her body, but still she seemed a skinny, fragile thing. Her severe boyish haircut made her face tiny. She did not know what to do with her hands and folded them in front of her. Someone rushed up with a bouquet of chrysanthemums for the leading lady. The actress, embarrassed, gave one flower to Rachel Ashgren. She held the flower like a pole. Its enormous bloom hid half her face. The flower was a great comfort to her, almost a shield. I could not help but laugh at how she looked. She was Charlie Chaplin standing between Pan and Jehovah.

Rachel dislikes her looks and her body. She inhabits her shell with a militant fatalism and reacts to it the way a brilliant and cynical ghost might react to spending eternity in a Levittown house on Long Island. She is familiar with the geography of her frame the way a very tall man or a midget is, and she knows all the things that people say or think about her flat-chested, straight-hipped figure. She collects references to herself in a mental scrapbook that dates back to the first boy in public school who christened her a "skinny-marink."

As yet, no man has taught her pleasure. Rachel resents her skimpy flesh. She punishes it with drab, concealing clothes. Since childhood she has gone garbed in perpetual sackcloth and ashes, mourning the loss of something she never possessed. Her usual costume is a denim jacket and pants in faded blue of the kind that laborers wear. She has always felt herself apart and different.

Like all outcasts, she regards herself as someone enchanted into ugliness. To feel enchanted is not entirely unpleasant. If she despises her loneliness, she also adores it and treasures a covert, tenuous egotism. I have sensed her secret many times in the evenings when we worked together on her play, in the classroom during discussions, even during casual conversation. I have seen her look at me with a tiny smile that says: "We are tuned to a special music."

Her separateness has been her salvation until now. A thin protective glass covers her like a sarcophagus. Tonight the glass will begin to crumble.

She will come here begging me to glue her together. She will expect me to supply her with the magic adhesive as I have done for a year now. She has no reason to suspect that I will deny her. I have helped her build her walls.

I do not know if I have sinned against Rachel. If I did, it was because I had no choice. I do not know if I will have the strength to send her away tonight. When I think of her coming here to me, my impulse is to run to her and to welcome her, to tell her, "Rest! Rest! You are home!" To make love to Rachel tonight would be like creating a sun.

But my name is Harry Lub and I have already written a novel called *Wandertime*. I have read my Rabelais, my Scriptures, my Frazer, my Grimm and my Joyce. I have read my Cervantes, my *Introductory Lectures* and my *History of the World in Two Hundred and Forty Pages*. I know many things. I know also that my greed for Rachel Ashgren is enough to dry my throat and to make a nerve twitch over my eye and to make me sit here in the dark. My greed for Rachel Ashgren, my love for Rachel Ashgren, my love and greed for Harry Lub, my mind as clear as water, my eyes watching the snowy street and the syrupy bells from the tower marking time—all this on the night of my great fulfillment as an instructor of English Composition, and the night of my great loss.

I found Rachel's talent and I recognized it at once, and for this I congratulate myself. When she gave me her poems and stories, written in pencil on lined copy paper in a child's notebook, I knew it then. I courted her and made love to her in words. Gently I fastened her to me. From the first hour I had a premonition of tonight. But there was nothing else for me to do, so I taught her and urged her on.

Tonight, after the performance, I went up on stage to congratulate Rachel Ashgren. She was still holding her flower. I said simply, "You have written a beautiful and important thing." I spoke with sincerity, in a slow voice. My words were not spontaneous. I had rehearsed them all day. I was careful to take no credit. I deserve no credit. She said to me, "At last I have done something they can understand." I left as Professor Martin Ashgren and his wife came backstage to pay tribute to their daughter. Professor Ashgren is a short, slender man who has been with the university for thirty years. He is an expert in the Romantic Period. His wife,

slightly taller than her husband and with a tendency to over-
weight, has been with Professor Ashgren for twenty-seven years,
and she is an expert in self-denial.

They approached Rachel with marked caution. Their hesitation
was the result of many years of warfare. Their impulse to cross
the barrier was accompanied by automatic awareness that they
would be trespassing in their daughter's kingdom. Rachel tensed
to greet them. I could sense her ordeal. She had given them something to understand: they understood that three hundred people
had applauded their daughter's play. They did not know exactly
why. The play itself was surely a mystery to them, a puzzle in
modern verse. Its language concealed the violent attack that had
been made on their lives and their daughter's wail of pain at her
escape. One virtue of modern poetry is that its enemies are often
spared the pain of recognition. Even Rachel does not yet know
what she has written.

As I left the stage, Professor Ashgren nodded to me. He has no
idea of my feeling for his daughter, or of hers for me. He does not
know that I have been a guest in his house many times in the
past year. He does not know that I have risked my position of
respectability by visiting his virgin child in her bedroom. He
knows only that often he has heard sounds from her attic apartment, and that he then wondered who was with her. His wife
wondered too and feared to imagine what might be going on
above their heads. Never once did they call upstairs to ask who
the visitor was. The attic was accepted as Rachel's fortress.

She had taken over the huge unfinished room when she was
still a child. There she played, and listened to the rain, and
dreamed and planned. She consolidated her hold on that part of
the house with its separate staircase, issued her own declaration
of independence and set the attic off-limits to her parents.

She fought their intrusion in the living room and the kitchen
through endless serious talks—"now that you are not a child,"
through her mother's excruciating headaches and her father's at-

tempts at anger. Her strangeness and their fear of it won for her. They retreated and waited for her to outgrow the angry worm. I am sure the professor and his wife did not accept their child as peculiar and never considered her moodiness or isolation as malignant. Perhaps they were sorry to see their dreams for Rachel alter—the first blushing boyfriend, her first poem, the evening gown in peach and silk lace, pleasures that the Ashgrens had come to expect and anticipate from movies and magazines and from the everyday talk of the families on Beach Street. These things were denied them, yet they were patient, waiting for the change, the inevitable conversion to sobriety for their girl.

Rachel refused to be a teenager dreaming of film stars and asking mommy for advice. She developed a terrible temper against the life they wanted and expected for her, and turned away toward other lands. She agreed to live in the house by her own rules. When her parents tried to force the doors of her personality, their forays were met with Rachel's temper, leaping like an animal for the throat.

Rachel walked in the little university town exploring and mapping the borders of her world, returning with trinkets and prizes to her attic. She made pets of her finds, arranging them in the huge room, slowly filling that immense space with bits and pieces that meant something to her and nothing to anyone else.

When I first saw Rachel's room, the size of the place made me blink. I am accustomed to small defined rooms closed in by papered walls. This room stretches like a corridor. There are small windows on the far end that let in two squares of color-fractured light. The walls are lined with wooden shelves. Packing crates stand in a chessboard pattern, painted red and black. The shelves and crates are filled with books and objects—a glass statue, a Mexican doll, a bit of driftwood. The room is crowded with a cluster of cloth hangings and prints. Puppets dangle from one wall. A clown and a girl hang near a savage mask. A bullfight poster shows the bull with his head low, charging to meet the sword. Cups and bowls, old jewelry, pictures of medieval angels, abstract wandering designs, photographs that Rachel has taken, bits of colored paper, sea shells, a beach ball, a Japanese kimono, the model of a clipper ship, apothecary jars, hundreds of accumulated objects share the room. The cluster of things holds together somehow, like a living swarm of bees. Through the discord I felt some strand of order, as if the smashing of one tiny figurine would cause the room to tumble. In the center of the room, Rachel's bed is set on a small platform. There is a work table near the bed, completely empty of litter. Her desk is kept in perfect order.

On the last night of our collaboration, when we knew that the play was finished, Rachel brought out a bottle of wine. We drank the warm wine out of old beer mugs and sang drinking songs from a book of ballads. I sang softly. I was self-conscious in her room and always afraid that I would be discovered there. She sang loudly and began to dance.

"You are worried, Harry Lub," she said. "Because I am making too much noise. You are convinced that they will find you here spooning alcohol to a minor. You are terrified that they will take away your tenure and march you through the streets yelling, Seducer! Seducer! You are apprehensive because they will throw you to the football team and you will be gobbled up. I will tell them how you tricked me into swallowing the juice of the grape. I will tell them that you told me you had concocted a brew that would transform me into Sappho. I will tell them you said you used a formula of quatrains and iambics and Rice Krispies and Arpege. You have reason to worry, Harry Lub. You are the cause of my cloven hoof."

"Rachel," I said, "your elephant dance is shaking these venerable timbers. Honor thy father and thy mother."

"My dance expresses myself," she said. "Notice how I contract and expand. The navel is the center of life and the core of expression. Everything happens out from the navel. What happens if the little bellybutton knot comes untied? Will my skin fall off?

Everyone has a tragic flaw, Harry Lub, and mine is in my navel."

"Rachel," I said. "You are a magnificent athlete. You will represent our Republic in the all-girl Olympics. Now sit down and be quiet."

"I will, Harry Lub," she said. "I will amuse you like a geisha. First I must tell you a story. Once upon a time there was a princess who had a small wet frog that she played with. One day her frog behaved very humorously. It stood on its head and sang a wedding march. She was so delighted that she kissed it. Her emotion transcended a natural fear of green and goo. Poof! The frog turned into a prince. He was a prince of tremendous proportions, and nothing like you, Harry Lub. He was woozy and dizzy, having just come out from under a spell, but he introduced himself to the princess. She looked at him and began to cry. 'What have you done with my frog?' she said."

"Rachel," I said, "that is a completely believable story."

"I only tell the truth," she said. "Here is another story from the life of Rachel Ashgren. Last night after you left I took off my clothes and fell asleep naked on top of the blanket. You know I am a very skeletal type, all bones and angles. My breasts are something like paper drinking cups upside down. I woke this morning with my mother standing over me. She was looking very sad and probably wondering if a body like mine could have normal children. I pretended I was sleeping. She shook me.

" 'Rachel,' she said. 'Get up.'

" 'Get out,' I said. I turned over on my stomach and made myself into a hill.

" 'Rachel,' she said, 'Rachel, Rachel! Is that a way to talk? Don't provoke me. I want to discuss something with you and I want you to behave like a mature person.'

" 'Mother dear,' I said, 'I will behave like a fantastically mature person. I will behave like Lydia Pinkham.'

" 'Why won't you take a graduation picture? Why? You know how much it means to your father and me. Is it too much to ask after what we've done for you? Please be a normal person. Please be a human being.'

" 'Mother,' I said, 'cameras are dangerous. Do you know that thousands of natives and Chinese and Mongolians believe that a camera steals away your soul? Suppose they are right?'

" 'Rachel, I never before asked you for a favor. Please take a picture. Please go to graduation. It's one day out of your life. Don't hurt us, Rachel darling.'

" 'Get out of here,' I said.

" 'My God, how are you talking!' she said. 'Are you a mental case? Do you think you're talking to your stinking friends?'

" 'Go away, Mrs. Ashgren,' I said.

" 'Rachel, I'm pleading for your father.'

" 'Go away. Go downstairs.'

" 'Rachel, cover yourself.'

" 'Go away. Go downstairs.'

" 'Will it kill you just to take a picture? Please. You owe us that!'

" 'Leave me alone,' I said. 'This is my room. You have no business here. Get out of my room.'

"She went away crying, Harry Lub. Sometimes I think I'm a creature with hundreds of legs that lives in a bog. What do you think of me, Harry Lub?"

"I think you are a petulant child who should take a graduation picture and attend the ceremonies," I said. "You should do it for your parents."

"Thank you, Harry Lub," she said. "Thank you for your kind advice."

She drank more of the wine.

"Harry Lub," she said, "am I very ugly?"

"No," I said. "You are beautiful."

"Thank you, Harry Lub," she said. "Harry Lub, do you know when my mother saw me naked I cringed under her eyes? I felt on trial. I flunked. Do you know what I mean?"

"It doesn't matter," I said.

"Thank you, Harry Lub," she said. "Harry Lub, do you know that a boy in my Citizenship class asked if he could take naked pictures of me? Did you know that?"

"No," I said. "I didn't know that."

"Yes," Rachel said. "He asked me if I would pose. Should I take a naked graduation picture, Harry Lub?"

"No," I said. "That is not dignified."

"Thank you," she said. "You know everything. I went with him. I got as far as his room. He even had the camera out. Are you jealous, Harry Lub?"

"Yes," I said. "I am jealous."

"Thank you, Harry Lub," she said. "You are a second Othello. I didn't go through with it. I was ashamed. I told the boy I was all tattooed with flowers and that I would come back when he had Kodachrome. He was very angry with me. Am I a coward, Harry Lub?"

"No," I said. "You are not a coward."

"Thank you, Harry Lub," she said. "I want to be the kind of girl who tames stallions. Really, that is the only kind of girl to be."

"I wish you many stallions," I said.

"Bless you, Harry Lub," she said. "If a girl is old enough to vote she is old enough to tame a stallion. Do you see it that way?"

"Absolutely," I said.

"Harry Lub, I am graduating from college," Rachel said.

"I know," I said.

"I am going out into the world."

"Yes," I said.

"Do you wish me fair weather?" she said.

"And plums," I said.

"How beautiful," Rachel said. "How beautiful. Will you put me to bed tonight?" she said.

"No," I said.

"I think I want you to see me naked," she said. "Is that shame-
less?"

"I'm leaving now," I said. "It's very late."

"I sincerely mean it," she said. "I want to be naked for you.
But I don't think you would like me. I'm very skeletal. Medical
students follow me home."

"Good night, Rachel," I said.

"Please put me to bed, Harry Lub. Please tuck me in."

"No," I said.

"I'm a poet," Rachel said. "You told me I was a poet. I need
experiences. Please."

"Good night," I said.

"Kiss me good night," she said.

I kissed her good night.

"Harry Lub," she said, "I have known girls who have had their
noses reshaped and girls who have had their breasts made smaller
and girls who had their ears pinned back. I have heard of girls
who had their hairlines changed and their teeth capped and their
chins altered and their bosoms filled with liquid wax. There are
girls who have their skins scraped and their spines straightened
and girls who have superfluous hair removed and superfluous fat
redistributed. There are all kinds of girls who have had something
new from the factory. What should I have new from the factory?
I have so many moving parts, Harry Lub. Maybe I should take an
x-ray graduation picture. Show the whole girl. Martha Bodley
from Anthropology got engaged for graduation. She showed me
her ring. She is getting married before Christmas and is going
away to the Virgin Islands. Do you know, Harry Lub, her lover
is from New York and he never even asked her for an x-ray?
Would you believe such a story in this day and age? Do you
think the marriage will last? Harry Lub, I am sure I should have
something changed. I need somebody with a surgical outlook.
Should I get psychoanalyzed? Doctor, I am afraid of the little

numbers in the financial section of the *Times*. Harry Lub, please put me to bed and tuck me in. Please look at me naked and smile warmly and banish all my fears. I want to lie on a beach and fill myself with sun. Why should I go out into the world? When the dramatic society does my play they will all look at me with awe and wonder because I am such a dark star. They will touch me with rubber gloves. Harry Lub, please put me to bed. Please. Please. Stay with me in my own little room and share my animal crackers."

"Come to the door with me," I said.

"My play is finished," Rachel said. "You can go now. Thank you for coming into my living room. Be careful of the snow. The snow is very deep and something might happen. If you freeze over and they mistake you for a fossil, don't worry because I will come and visit you in the museum. Good night, Harry Lub. Sweet dreams."

"Sweet dreams," I said.

"Listen," she said, "before you go I'll tell you what kind of a girl I am. In elementary school they made us sing a song 'O do you know the muffin man?' Then we sang, 'Yes! I know the muffin man, he lives across the way.' Well, Harry Lub, I never knew the muffin man. Do you know who lives across the way? Mrs. Mitchlanger lives across the way. That's the kind of girl I am, and you might as well know it."

"I forgive you," I said.

"I feel better now that that is off my chest," Rachel said.

"Good night."

"Good night, Harry Lub."

"Go to bed now."

"Yes," Rachel said. "I am so tired. You have no idea."

"Sleep now," I said.

"When Halley's Comet comes around," Rachel said, "I'll meet you at the American Express in Lhasa. Is it a date?"

"Yes," I said. "And be on time."

"I will," she said. "Depend on it. We'll tap-dance in the streets."

Once, as a young man, I went through the West. It took me many weeks before I could believe the scenery. I had never before seen a mountain or a forest as old as the earth. Once I rode on the back of a truck, through the redwoods, along the ocean toward Oregon. The driver took time out to stop at a shack on the beach. He blew his horn until a man came out to sell him a fresh crab. He threw a piece of the crab to me and I could taste the salt water and iodine in its meat. Once I went to fight a forest fire. The fire burned an orange crescent over the land. With farmers and soldiers from the National Guard we rode into the fire and came out again for coffee and food. The fire left us dirty and smelling of burnt wood. A waitress in the diner sponged my back and chest with a damp towel.

You can read about all this in Wandertime. I kept a careful diary.

Somehow, between then and now, I have grown more conservative and careful. Perhaps there is a physical explanation. Does a sheath form to protect the nerves? I do not regret the change. If I were required to pick my favorite self of all the selves I have been, which would I choose? I am not even certain of that. Tonight, under my nervousness, there is a feeling of tranquillity that I cannot deny. Though I am still embarrassed to admit it, lately I find the Hall of Liberal Arts, with its gray stone, a comforting building, for all its obsolescence. Ding dong bell. Is this my sea change into something rich and strange?

They say that the highest fulfillment for an instructor is a student whom he can love with a saintly love. They say it is a sin, as incest is a sin, to keep such students with you once they have grown wings. The old professors sit and remember how hard it was to let them go free. Do they lie?

When Rachel Ashgren comes trembling to Harry Lub, he will sit in the dark and ignore the knock at his door. What are his motives? Why does he close his eyes to her? Does he give her back her life, or does he preserve his own? If he touched her, what unrest would his own flesh remember?

The bells have rung again. It is much too late to look for truth under rocks.

Only this: night after night I stayed with her in that room while she searched out the words for her play. I was with her when her mind went prowling through frightening valleys. When she exulted, I brought her back to earth. When she despaired, I joined in her chorus of self-pity, soothing her, making her aloneness and difference into a diamond. If I confused her life with her talent, it was the only road to follow. If I was cruel to Rachel Ashgren, if my encouragement was its own curse, I hope that one day she will forgive me. I could not help taking from her. In her frantic birth as an artist, I found a birth of my own. Had Rachel been arrogant or strong, I would have hated her. I am not old enough or mellow enough to smile down on all youth and growth. I am a jealous man now that my own dream of success is fading. I am loath to let it go, as who is not? Rachel came timidly to me, and afraid. Her gift, if that is the word, was forced on her. She is condemned to it; for better or for worse, Rachel must sail strange, emerald seas.

If she is fortunate, a figurine will smash and her attic will crumble. She will learn to live in the world. A man will take from her in lust and hunger, and she will find peace in the yielding. Her art will become a communication, itself an instrument for giving and not a cloak for her mysteries.

If she is unlucky, her sensitivity will choke her like quicksand. I have seen Rachel wandering through museums, waving her hand to music, walking through hostile streets, tasting vagueness on her tongue and glorifying her own enchantment.

As for Harry Lub, he turns his back on her. He will never again go seeking himself in those wild nights when winter turns to spring. He will never again confuse himself with a priest of the temple. He will never again become the flesh umbrella protecting an exotic bud from storms of fire and ice.

Outside, in the blue night, the wind has stopped. The streets are deserted. I thought for a moment that I saw a figure move, but there is nothing now.

REASONS OF HEALTH

I know I never saw that man before.
But where?

—Oliver Dragon

HILTON LAMB, PROPPED ON PILLOWS, SIPPED THICK COFFEE AND watched snow fall on the Elburz Mountains. The mountains struck him as sad, like the humps of mangy camels.

It rained in the city of Teheran. Hilton watched it rain down below and snow up above, a rare sight.

The miserable day was welcome. There was no need to do anything. Hilton's business was finished. He had until the next morning to catch his plane. He could write some postcards. Later he would go down to the bar off the hotel lobby and drink Scotch while they lit little lamps on every table. Hilton liked the little Persian lamps, carved brass globes on brass sands, curving and coming to a point like young breasts. The young breast shape was everywhere—in the architecture, in the furniture, everywhere.

In the bar he could watch olive-colored, hawk-nosed Iranians come and go whispering in Farsi, a secret code developed over millenniums by traders with shifty eyes. Farsi never gave you so much as a familiar sound. It was like a tongue exploring your ear, pliant and moist, then snapping like a whip.

When the telephone rang, Hilton coughed on a cracker. He

knew no one in Teheran, in all of Persia for that matter. He knew no one for at least a thousand miles in any direction. The delegation from Lebanon and the representatives of Israel with whom he had met to talk about licensing rights to his company's device to simplify the construction of concrete structures had gotten the facts and gone their ways. There was absolutely nobody.

"Hello."

"Hello. Mamoud here. Good that you are in your room, sir. I am coming right up."

"You must have the wrong . . ."

"Mamoud from the Public Health. Wait now."

"My name is Hilton Lamb. This is room 788. You must be . . ."

The connection was broken. Hilton jumped off the bed and grabbed for his bathrobe. On the bureau was a strand of Japanese pearls he bought in Tokyo for Ruth, his wife. He put the pearls into their red velvet case, then hid the case in his airline carry bag. He heard a tap tap tap.

"Yes?"

"Mamoud. Mr. Lamb?"

Hilton opened the door.

"Some terrible day, eh?" A man stood dripping in the doorway, wiping his hair with his hand. He wore a thin raincoat with a rust stain on one shoulder and heavy army boots. He carried a green umbrella and a battered attaché case. He reminded Hilton of a pencil stub. A river trickled from his scalp.

"Excessive wet, eh? Excuse my condition. If it is permissible I will go to the toilet and dry."

"Of course," Hilton said. "Come inside."

"Plenty courage to use a strange facility, eh?" Mamoud said, coming out, wiping his head with a towel.

Mamoud threw the towel on Hilton's bed and put his wet

attaché case on top of it. Inside Hilton saw a folder thick with
official documents. Mamoud thumbed the folder and removed a
page.

"Lamb, Hilton, U.S.A., eh?"

"What is this about?"

"Not much. Life and death. You are visiting here on business?"

"Yes."

"The extent of your stay?"

"I came Sunday. I leave tomorrow morning."

"For which destination, please?"

"Geneva."

"Very nice."

"I must ask you to explain . . ."

"Cholera. I am in the cholera business at the moment. Don't
worry yourself. I am so sure of your health I used your toilet first
thing, eh? Tell me in a list what countries you came through and
show me your international health certificate."

"Japan, the Philippines, Vietnam, Thailand, India."

"Air France. Very popular. Nice trip, eh?"

"Fine."

"The certificate?"

"I showed it at the airport."

"Good," Mamoud said, examining the book. "You got your
shots."

"Yes, I had the full complement of shots. Thank God there's
no problem."

"No problem except the shots are no good. Maybe twenty,
thirty percent statistical. Practically useless, eh?"

Mamoud swiped at his hair and pushed it sideways. Hilton saw
how thin his skull was and that his skin had a bluish tint. He
had a kind of transparency.

"I am saying Iran is clean and we keep it clean. No cholera.
But the places you have come through are bad news. Very bad
outbreaks. We look to catch the ones like you, Mr. Lamb."

"Frankly I doubt if the places I went and the people I associated . . ."

"Naturally. There is such a small chance of your infestation as not to bother with. But Iran is strict. In five days we will know you are clean. Does your belly or head pain you? Dizziness? A few cramps, maybe?"

"Absolutely not."

"Absolutely, eh? I am certain you are telling the truth. Do you mind giving me your pulse?"

Mamoud held tight to Hilton's wrist. Hilton was surprised at the power in his spider fingers.

"Nice. Regular. A little rapid but that is understandable. The chances against you are so slight I would use your toilet right now."

"Good. Now what was that nonsense about five days?"

"Mr. Lamb, excuse me but you are on cholera control. If nothing develops by Thursday you are liberated from concern."

"Impossible," Hilton said. "I leave tomorrow morning for Geneva."

"Mr. Lamb, your reservations are cancelled. Your embassy has been informed. Think of yourself on forced vacation."

"This is ridiculous," Hilton said.

"Just keep in contact with me, Mr. Lamb, especially if there is severe cramping of the bowels, head pains, or any agonizing sign of attack."

"Why me?" Hilton said.

"Nothing special points to you, sir. But you passed through epidemics, eh? Better to precaution."

"The American Embassy is completely aware of your visit?"

"Totally," Mamoud said. "I am totally authorized. We are grateful to you for cooperation. You are a sensible person. You see what we face. So I am the law for a few days, eh? I will see a lot of you."

"Well, I don't feel very sensible or cooperative," Hilton said. "I feel pretty damn mad about all this."

"Who likes inconvenience? Do I? Eh? I mean, I get no bonus if you have cholera, Mr. Lamb. I am here to help you and my country and other nations of the free world."

"I don't consider myself a danger to the free world," Hilton said.

"Where did you get that haircut?"

"Haircut?"

"Yes, that one, up there," Mamoud said.

"At the hotel barbershop. Yesterday."

Mamoud wrote something in a little pad.

"Time and chair?"

"It was three o'clock," Hilton said. "You want the chair?"

"The chair, eh?"

"I think it was the third chair in from the door. Why?"

Mamoud shrugged. He went to the telephone and dialed an outside number. This time Farsi sounded like running water to Hilton, who watched Mamoud's face turn from blue to purple.

"What was that about?" Hilton said when Mamoud hung up.

"Routine. The service will consult with the barbershop. No harm will be done to anyone. Surveillance is all. Sanitation is an art, Mr. Lamb. In this part of the world it is a dedication. I reiterate to you, you are most likely clean. Notice I did not take the effort to wipe the telephone mouthpiece before speaking. I would surely have done this if my suspicions were aroused. I spoke normally, as if you were in perfect health. A barbershop is an intimate place. You comprehend that a barber can be a terminal for plague."

"Plague?"

"I spoke generally. Don't think any more about it. We will not boil the barber who served you. It's not like the old days, eh? I must go now. There are others to see. I will call you later."

"Suppose I'm not here," Hilton said.

"I will leave a number you may call. It is desirable that we speak in a few hours, eh?"

Mamoud took his belongings.

"See how I grasp the bare knob," he said, "with no glove or handkerchief. Believe me, if you were a lady I would kiss your hand. I have no qualms that the odds are with you, sir."

"Let's hope so. Let's just hope so."

"And Mr. Lamb, for our sake, stay removed from crowded places. Maybe watch the television, eh? It would be very much appreciated."

"I see."

"Again, thank you for receiving me with such grace. Some are more violent and abusive."

"Thank you for coming."

"Adieu, now."

The snow had stopped on the mountains but the rain came harder. Dark mist blew from the east. It filled the air like poison gas. Hilton turned on the room lamps. The young breast globes glowed ivory white.

Hilton showered and shaved. He put on his best suit, rubbed instant polish on his shoes and lime cologne on his face and hands. He poured himself a drink from the flask he carried for emergencies. Braced, refreshed and more optimistic, more himself, he went down to the lobby.

He considered wiring his company about the unavoidable delay. He decided against it. There might be a way out. He could telephone the embassy, but if they refused aid it would be too official a refusal to countermand. There might be other roads to follow.

Hilton found a table in the lobby bar and ordered a double Scotch. It was still early. Only one other table was occupied. Two stewardesses sat with a bald man in a striped European suit.

When he spoke, the girls giggled and one, a slender blonde, kept pinching his double chin.

Hilton finished his Scotch and ordered another. He doodled on a napkin, drawing mazes. The more he thought the more things cleared. If he could convince Mamoud that he was in excellent health and that it was essential to the company that he leave on time, there might be a chance. But Mamoud had the smell of the determined and dedicated. Naturally there was always the bribe. That was a dangerous route. Hilton did not relish spending a month or even a year in a Persian prison as an example of Yankee corruption. "Everything is politics," Hilton thought. "An individual is caught like a bug."

Sudden music alerted him. He looked up. Several tables were taken now and there was Margo the resident belly dancer standing in a spotlight waiting for the record that played her tune. She began to swirl inside a costume of lavender gauze. The flames had been lit in the young breast lamps. The room was warm and pleasant.

Margo discarded a cape of gauze and then threw off another layer. She was down to essentials, rhinestones on her breasts and bikini pants of black lace. Hilton stirred the ice in his drink with a finger while he watched her twirl. He had seen her before and was getting familiar with her body. She was a fine dark color, soft and firm, with a shyness Hilton liked. She kept her eyes half closed and averted, moving as if she were alone in her bedroom rolling her belly in a slow circle just for the fun of it. Her rhythm was celestial. It reminded Hilton of the planets circling on the roof of the Hayden Planetarium. The music hit a peak. Margo shook her breasts for change of pace and Hilton blinked. In the moment of darkness Mamoud appeared at his table.

"Good evening," he whispered. "May I join with you?"

Hilton motioned him to sit. He pointed to his drink.

"Thank you, some orange only," Mamoud said.

While the orange was being ordered, Mamoud found Hilton's wrist.

"Nice, but strong. Very strong. Have you been smoking?"

"Moderately."

"Then please permit me. It is something I should have done before."

Mamoud took a thermometer from a black case and put it in Hilton's mouth.

"It is oral, not rectal," he said. "An attempt at humor."

Hilton sat with the thermometer inserted under his tongue watching Margo move faster. He had his elbow on the table, one hand over his mouth so the thermometer was concealed. Margo was working toward the climax of her act. She danced among the tables. She stroked heads in the audience and leaned from time to time to kiss a cheek.

"Mmmmm," Hilton said as Margo danced at his table. He moved to take the thermometer out but Mamoud restrained him. Margo bent, then pulled away and veered off like a vessel in a gale. Hilton blushed.

"Two minutes more," Mamoud said. "I am sorry, Mr. Lamb."

"Mmmmm."

"Let me tell you now of some psychological traps to which you are vulnerable," Mamoud said. "You are not the first man to face this kind of crisis. To be forearmed is to be forewarned, eh?"

"Mmmmm."

"A Catholic of my acquaintance became so alarmed of his death that he telephoned home collect to confess the most obscure infidelities. The tragedy was he survived. I believe he would have given his savings to be injected with some fatality. You are not a frightened person, Mr. Lamb, but should the impulse arise, resist the urge to unburden yourself until the last and final moment. That is wise advice, eh?"

Hilton pointed to Mamoud's watch.

"Let it be for another minute. Is it not true that Americans respect the sanctity of a confession? You are a forgiving man. Here we brood for centuries."

Mamoud took the thermometer, read it by candlelight, then shook it down.

"So," he said. "That's that."

"Was it normal?"

"Near enough, Mr. Lamb."

"You might have let me look."

"For what conceivable reason?"

"Simple decency," Hilton said.

"Ah, I detect hostility," Mamoud said. "How I hate this job. I know that I represent a sewer to you, a diplomat of death. The second psychological pitfall to which you may yield is hatred to me. So be it. Vent your spleen with impunity. You cannot help yourself. But know that there are certain areas of insult I will not tolerate. I cannot abide attack upon members of my immediate family or derogatory references to this nation or the Public Health."

"Listen," Hilton said sincerely, "I have no desire to antagonize you, Mamoud. Quite the contrary. There is something I want to talk about, cards on the table."

"Continue."

"About the embargo on my leaving. My job depends on a schedule. Any delay . . ."

"Stop. Please do not fly in the face of the health organizations of the world. We will speak of your exit permit when the time comes."

"Then there *is* a chance."

"Mr. Lamb, let me say that you should not kindle hopes. Think of yourself as participating in a crusade for the elimination of a dread pestilence, eh? Now watch that Margo. She is something marvelous."

"I intend to bring up the subject again," Hilton said.

While Mamoud drank his second orange and Hilton nursed his

fourth Scotch, Margo spun like a top under changing colored
lights. She began a long backbend that took her hair to the floor,
and when it touched she thrust her pelvis up and down in the
blue bar air. Her music reached an Oriental crescendo and the
record stuck. Margo kept thrusting as if she were trying to launch
a rocket, then the record continued.

"Imagine the power of her spine," Mamoud said. "Imagine the
level of destruction that girl could commit. One feels that one's
own needle is making her music."

Margo had collapsed on the floor in a total bow. Hilton applauded with the rest.

"For the sake of my curiosity," Mamoud said, "tell me if you
are thinking now of your wife's entrails."

"What the hell kind of remark is that?"

"The most innocent kind. I was not implying anything com-
parative or pornographic, sir. It is just that you seemed in a state
of trance, far away. I sensed that you were experiencing pleasant
lust and nostalgia."

"Bad taste," Hilton said. "Bad, bad taste."

"There was no malice intended. Excuse me, Mr. Lamb. Let us
drink to a much better rapport."

"Agreed," Hilton said, draining his glass while Mamoud finished
the orange.

"You like our women, eh, Mr. Lamb?"

"I would say so. Yes. Especially that Margo. I was wondering,
Mamoud, if you might know the girl personally . . ."

"I interject," Mamoud said. "Forgive me in advance. Mr. Lamb,
I am aware that in moments of threat the whole idea of fornication takes on huge importance. Fornication is affirmation, a yes
to life, eh?"

"Fornication?"

"You were asking me to ask Margo to join us for a little drink."

"Well, yes I was. But fornication was the last thing . . ."

"Mr. Lamb, I do not question your intentions. The fact is it is better to say quickly, no. Coldly speaking, sir, you may carry great contagion. Margo appears in the public eye. She kisses upon the hands of her audience. You begin to understand my position?"

"Jesus God."

"Or take that girl over there, the airline stewardess. Often in situations like yours, airline ladies become objects of unbridled desire. Their loveliness notwithstanding, sir, they represent flight. Their very bodies take on wings. Many of my people endure torturous cravings for them, Mr. Lamb, believe me. But those are the very persons who serve foods and drinks, who fondle babies and so forth, eh? Deny it."

"Boy, you don't pull punches, I'll say that, Mamoud."

"Get some dinner, Mr. Lamb. Eat lightly, go up to bed. You will be a new person. Forget the entertainers. Forget the airline ladies. Forget our women. They are good women. Forget them."

"Your women? What is this, Yankee go home?"

"Nothing personal. The onset of distress increases lust."

"What lust? You're the one foaming about lust."

"Show your rage, Mr. Lamb. Good. Gratify yourself by nourishing meals, by smoking, by drinking. Remove the focus from your genitals."

"Mamoud, you are psycho," Hilton said, suddenly conscious of warm pressure between his legs. "You are what we call a character back home. Well, I could use a few laughs. Have dinner with me. Let's have a bite right here in the hotel. What do you say?"

"You are a forgiving person. I accept your invitation. It is best that you have company tonight. In any case, I would need to return later for your checkup. Thank you, Mr. Lamb."

Outside, in the lobby, Hilton reeled. His eyes went out of focus, then popped back.

"What is it?" Mamoud said urgently, and the urgency made Hilton's stomach contract.

"A little tipsy is all," Hilton said. "Don't call the ambulance yet."

Hilton rested against a railing, a great curved arc of chrome that led to basement pleasures. In the stairwell hung a long tubular sculpture of burnished copper carved in the local manner. It terminated in the young breast shape, a huge young breast of hammered metal that reflected light so strongly it hurt Hilton's eyes.

"The time capsule," Hilton said. "We bury them back home at World's Fairs."

"My association has always been phallic."

"Naturally, Mamoud. You have a one-track mind. By American standards, that is a time capsule."

"I know about your time capsules," Mamoud said. "They could only happen in a young industrial society. Such a feeble attempt at immortality."

"Let's talk about life and the living," Hilton said. "Let's put on the feedbag."

Mamoud negotiated a table in the hotel dining room. Hilton ordered a double Scotch. Mamoud consented to a beer.

"Better days," Hilton said and downed his whiskey neat.

"You are drinking much too fast. You must be under enormous strain. Enormous."

Mamoud said this in a voice so tender, so sympathetic, that it struck an astonishing chord of response. Hilton began to cry. Tears welled in his eyes. He blotted them with a napkin.

"Oh Lord," Hilton said.

"You are confronting a specter. Fear is no cause for shame."

"I was thinking about . . ."

"The things undone, the words unspoken, the touch untouched."

"On target," Hilton said. "You know something, you're a fine speaker."

"Thank you."

Mamoud ordered shish kebabs. They came on flaming swords.

Hilton ordered Tattinger champagne. It came swaddled like a baby in a cradle of ice.

"This is more like it," Hilton said, raising his glass.

"Salud."

They ate their way through the main course, a salad and a pyramid of lemon sherbet. Hilton sent for cognac. Mamoud protested but accepted a snifter. Glowing, Hilton stood and proposed a toast to the Shah.

"Shanshah," Mamoud said.

"Whatever the hell," Hilton said. "Shahshahshah."

"You are speaking very loudly, Mr. Lamb."

"To hell with them," Hilton said, gesturing a bow to the other diners. "Besides, I'm drinking to your Shachacha. Long may he wave. Mamoud, you can't begin to imagine how funny it is to a person like me to read in your papers how the Shasha said something big about farm problems or Commies. Back home where I come from we call him Shah, like that, once. And you think of him as somebody in the movies, maybe. When he dumped Sonya or whatever her name was because she couldn't get pregnant I'm telling you his image suffered. But we still like him."

"Mr. Lamb, maybe we better get some air, eh?"

"I personally don't hold it against him for dumping Sonya. But it was rotten. The new one is OK though. She's a real piece. And I read the old one is in the jet set. He's got a good image in America, the Shashasha. We don't begrudge him his personal life. Did you ever see the crown jewels in the bank downtown? Christ, when you think what you could buy with . . ."

"Excuse me," Mamoud said. "I'm going to the men's room. Can we meet outside?"

"I'm not embarrassing anybody, Mamoud. I'm drinking good brandy to your Shashashasha. There are plenty I could drink to. Plenty."

"I am a government worker," Mamoud said.

"Jesus, that's right," Hilton said. "I get the whole picture. But how come you say Shasha twice?"

"It means the emperor of emperors, something like that. Respect."

"Right," Hilton whispered. "Double or nothing. Shashashashasha."

"Make sure they do a job on those utensils," Hilton said on the way out; and the waiter said something to Mamoud in Farsi. Hilton remembered that the name for Farsi was Farsi. He laughed out loud. He kept laughing all the way to the postcard rack out near the front desk.

"Sit a minute," Mamoud said. "Regain your composure."

"You think I'm doomed," Hilton said, sitting in a great mothering chair. "You think this is last rites. I see the way you look at me like I was turning to garbage. The words unspoken, the things undone, the touch untouched. Shashasha."

"Easy, Mr. Lamb."

"Oh Lord, I will never see my kids get married. I will never see man land on the moon. I will never see the gross national product top a billion. I will never see Ruth's birthmark or play jelly with her. That's a game we have. These are supposed to be my prime consuming years, Mamoud, but I am one of the losers."

"You are a curious mixture of sentiment and business, Mr. Lamb. I can't keep up with you."

"Mamoud, everything in this crazy country you should excuse the expression is shaped like a teen-age tit. Why is that?"

"If you are speaking now of our architecture . . ."

"The bugs have me, Mamoud. I feel them. I can't look the other way anymore. Mamoud, I want to get laid."

"Mr. Lamb, please."

"Help. I must get laid. I forgot what it feels like and I have got to get one more chance. As a fellow human being, Mamoud . . ."

Mamoud sat closer and shielded his mouth with his hand. Hilton noticed that he looked very well in the position.

"If it were possible to accommodate you, Mr. Lamb, it would have to be, how shall I say, with an expendable woman. You understand that?"

"Disposable. Oh, yes, I understand."

"You are in terrible mental condition and I feel responsible. Perhaps it would be a positive thing."

"A positive thing. That's it, bull's-eye. God, you turn a beautiful phrase. I want a positive thing."

Mamoud had words with the doorman, then excused himself. He returned with a package of prophylactics.

"Fantastic," Hilton said. "Persian rubbers. Look at the writing on the box."

"Take the preventives," Mamoud said. "Though there is probably no need."

"It'll fall off by itself, right?" Hilton said.

"We are a neat people, Mr. Lamb."

"Now I know that, Mamoud," Hilton said. "Don't be so touchy. How much do I owe you for these?"

"A gift from me to you," Mamoud said. "Brothers, eh?"

"That's fine of you. But you shouldn't spend . . ."

Mamoud waved Hilton away. They stood under the hotel canopy waiting for a cab. The wet air made Hilton tipsier than he was before, as if the drops were alcohol. He put out his tongue and caught some mist. It tasted fresh and cool.

"Mr. Lamb," Mamoud said, "I hope you are aware that this is highly irregular activity. I am indulging your need because the welfare of two humans is involved."

"How come two humans?"

"Yourself for reasons that you already know. And a lady by the name of Pivi. You are in tragic need. She can use the commerce. Times are hard for her due to the competition of normals."

"Normals?"

"This weather is a foul thing, eh?"

The doorman began to whistle and wave. A gray Mercedes with a blue bulb on its roof stopped in the driveway. The car sprayed mist and Hilton sneezed.

"You are sure you would not rather rest?"

The idea of being alone with the terrific sex of multiplying viruses racking his body made Hilton shudder. The thought of lying on his bed with the Elburz Mountains glowering in through the picture window was impossible.

"Nasal drip," Hilton said. "Sinusitis. It's a family curse."

Mamoud gave the driver an address. The driver didn't seem to believe him. Hilton listened to the words slush past his ears. The driver gestured in his direction. For a moment Hilton believed he was being taken to the hospital. The car started.

"Idiot," Mamoud said.

"What's the matter?"

"Never mind."

"Out with it."

"Ah, he said you appear peaked."

"Peaked?"

"Not exactly. It is difficult to translate. He said you look the color of canned corn."

"He didn't want me in his cab, is that it?"

"He knows who I am," Mamoud said. "These drivers are superstitious beasts."

Hilton sat cramped in the back seat. He made an island in the fog on the window glass. He secretly felt his pulse. It was racing, the thwok of the windshield wipers was slow counterpoint. The cab went fast on Pahlavi Avenue. Hilton saw thousands of lights along the road and up onto the mountains. Then a great gash of darkness marked the end of life.

Hilton saw a Pepsi-Cola sign. With a Persian label it was like a CIA agent in partial disguise.

"You hear a lot of jokes about good old soda pop around the world," Hilton said, "but you have got to hand it to them."

Hilton saw the driver's eyes in the rearview mirror. They were focused dead on his own. He felt the bottom of the valley rush under him. He had a sudden longing to climb the snowy cliffs, stand for a second at the top, and jump howling into the Caspian Sea.

Fifteen minutes later the cab turned off the highway and headed up a cobbled street. Hilton's insides rattled. He felt as if his private parts detached and clashed. A hard bump threw the Mercedes and sprawled Hilton against Mamoud. Mamoud put his hand over his mouth.

"It's all right," Hilton said. "I was on an inhale."

The cab turned again into a lane where the houses were less opulent, and again into a row of broken cottages. Hilton flexed. His travels had shown him poverty. His skin no longer crawled with automatic guilt at the spectacle of the hopeless in cities far away. But he still felt a combination of compassion and revulsion. It was a confused and confusing response. There was something tantalizing about having new shoes in a place where they would slit your throat for a lace. It released a feeling of personal rottenness that wasn't all bad. You could kick a beggar in the belly or give him a U.S. dime and somehow either action was identical. The problem was Hilton didn't know what to feel. Nothing had replaced his former horror.

"This neighborhood has become run down," Mamoud said.

Then Mamoud pointed to a tiny house painted green. He told the driver to stop and wait.

Hilton and Mamoud got out separate doors. They met in front of the cab. Hilton saw the driver still watching him through a pie-wedge of glass already half-covered by raindrops.

"The face of the left-behind while others go to pleasure, eh? Don't let it bother you, Mr. Lamb."

Hilton pulled his coat around him. He took a giant step over a puddle the size of an inland sea. They went up three steps to the door.

"Listen. Already I am breathing like a locomotive," Mamoud said. "I am glad we came despite the risk to my career. There is nothing like the act of love to clear a man's chest. For my money every cemetery should have a brothel adjoining, both for the dying and the surviving."

Mamoud pounded at the door with an iron knocker shaped like a blackjack.

"Open the gates," he said.

The door was opened by a lanky, dark girl with long straight hair and a hook nose. She wore a red kimono covered with flowers and belted with a thick black sash.

"Hello, Jap," Mamoud said as she backed inside. "Is Pivi here too or is she up at the Palace?"

"Pivi is home."

"Thank God, eh? Come in, Mr. X. This is Tama who thinks she is a Nipponese."

"Good evening," Hilton said holding out his hand. Tama looked at the hand and nodded.

"Look at her, miles from earth. Look at the glassy eyes, eh? Tama is a simple mind but she is sweetness itself. And I am crazy for her string-bean body. You could cut yourself on her bones. I have strange tastes, eh? Well, do we stand here forever?"

Tama led them down a short hallway through a curtain of beads. On the other side of the beads was a little room with a table, four chairs, a couch covered in red velvet and a radio shaped like a church arch. Hilton had not seen a radio like it since his childhood.

"Cozy. At least it's warm and dry in here. Sit down, Mr. X. Tama, get something to drink."

"I'll get."

"Where is Pivi?"

"Washing herself."

"That's good, eh? See the carpet, Mr. X. Always that. The famed Persian carpet."

Hilton looked down at the remnants of a carpet. It pictured a battle scene between soldiers on horseback.

"Who knows where that came from," Mamoud said. "The work is first-rate. But it can't be seen here. The light is terrible."

"It doesn't bother me," Hilton said. He looked into a light bulb on a hanging wire. It swayed like a snake with an electric head.

"You are not here for the lights, eh?"

Hilton heard the sound of glasses clinking.

"No mixing, no cubes," Mamoud yelled. "The water down here is sure death, Mr. Lamb."

Tama came with four glasses filled with a brownish liquid. Hilton took one and Mamoud and Tama joined him.

"Down the hatch," Mamoud said. "Cheers."

The brown liquid filled Hilton and took his shape. He held the blazing sculpture inside him, then it cooled leaving a residue of ash.

"Nice," Mamoud was saying. "Now Tama, be a good Jap and tell that Pivi to get in here. She is not being paid for bathing herself. What is she washing, eh? An ox?"

Tama got a slap on the tail that Hilton could feel.

"I know," Mamoud said. "Like a rock. Yet I am already experiencing tumescence. Go understand these things. There is something about that girl. Helplessness. Familiarity. It is a muff I have known since early youth. Ah, how do you feel, Mr. Lamb? I should be taking your pulse and temperature but the thermometer is hotter than the patient, eh?"

Hilton took another drink of the brown juice. He felt as if somebody had slipped sunglasses over his eyes. His head solidified above the ears. Was it the liquor or the cholera? Or both? The room oozed. Hilton thought it might be his last moment on the planet. Had Mamoud conspired to simply put him out of his misery? No, it was only that Mamoud was granting him a reprieve from the grave and training in oblivion at the same time. Mamoud was a good soul. He was the Elsa Maxwell of the incurable. Poor Elsa. She was dead too.

"Elsa Maxwell is gone," Hilton said.

"Ah?" Mamoud said. "And who was she? Memory is delicious, eh? A delicious thing. She is gone, sure, but I would bet plenty you can remember her naked and warm as honey on the stove. I am excited myself."

"I hardly knew her," Hilton said.

"Who knows who it is we remember as life's door shuts. Maybe a face from the streets seen no more than an instant. The human mind."

"Look," Hilton said, "no matter what happens I want you to know that I fully appreciate your . . ."

"Nothing. I want you to keep your mind off yourself. Let yourself go, Mr. Lamb. Think only of pussy. It is a month's vacation. Meow, eh? Pussy, pussy. Let me see you smile."

Hilton drained his drink.

"Pivi will assist you enormously. She is a girl who gives beyond necessity, a woman of nutritious qualities. A creature of great yield like a butter churn. Even the risks she takes give her pleasure. She will open her mouth and such to you, Mr. Lamb, with as much ardor as she would to . . ."

"Say it. Go ahead."

"Ah, who is in good condition these days, eh? If I was in the business of insurance I would destroy myself."

"Mamoud, I feel like a time bomb. Really, it bothers me to think of infecting . . ."

"Don't I know the impulses of the germ-riddled? Some take satisfaction in keeping the germs within themselves knowing that the victory of the microbe is its own defeat. They are the true misers. You are another sort, a better man. You worry yourself about a Pivi. Between us, you honor her to come here with

American business. She will boast for a century. If you are in-
clined, give her an extra hundred rials."

"Does she know that I . . . am suspected of . . ."

"She knows my job," Mamoud said. "It is nice for Pivi to worry
more about what she is getting than what she is giving. Not that
she is corrupted with Biblical afflictions. She glows with vitality.
Now, we find you another drink, Mr. Lamb. Where the hell are
the girls? It is provocative to think of Pivi washing so much her
snatch and putting on perfumes and cosmetics, eh? They are
all alike."

Mamoud called Tama. She came through the bead curtain like
a phantom walking through a wall.

"This important person has no drink," Mamoud said. "And tell
your friend if she cannot come to send her organ. We don't have
a whole day."

"She is ready soon."

"Plenty rust, eh? That of course is just a phrase. Pivi is as clean
as a spring."

Tama filled Hilton's glass.

"Pivi," Mamoud roared, "what is this? Is the store closed for
a holiday?"

Hilton heard from far away. He perked to the voice of an animated mouse from a movie cartoon.

"I am making ready. Control yourself."

"What is that speaking?" Hilton said.

"Pivi is making ready," Tama said.

"Was that a person speaking that way?"

"I should have enlightened you about Pivi's entrances," Mamoud said. "That one has a vast sense of drama. It makes for
additional entertainment if you can stand it."

"The light," said the movie mouse. "Extinguish the bulb."

Hilton tried to construct a person from the voice, building on
it like an anthropologist builds from a chip of nose bone. He
could form no image. The brown liquid made a rejecting sea of

his mind. Nothing would float long enough to be recognized. He managed to think of a furry creature that sat in his palm and blinked.

Tama walked to the light cord. She tried to smile but the smile failed at her mouth. Then she reached for the switch as precisely as a general reaching for a trigger at a routine execution. The room blacked out.

Hilton sat stiffly. A piece of the mountain night slid in avalanche and poured through the windows.

"Come on, you crazy hole," Mamoud said. "Or we run out of here."

Hilton heard a record start to play. It turned too slowly. Its music didn't form. Then the record gained speed and Hilton recognized the song.

"That's the 'Star-Spangled Banner,' " he said.

"Why not?" Mamoud said.

A candle moved into the room. Hilton's eyes fastened to the flame. An American flag moved with the light.

"What the hell," Hilton said.

"Fantastic," said Mamoud.

The flag stopped in the room's center. It was an astonishing flag. Hilton saw that it was patched with large squares of alien cloth.

"She throws these things together," Mamoud whispered.

Hilton's vision spread and fused. He saw that the flag draped from a huge bosom and fell to the floor. The candle rose. A round face appeared.

"Gimme tireds," it said from a somber expression. "Gimme homelesses."

Hilton began to shake. He was outraged there in the dark.

"Gimme tired, gimme homelesses."

"She is the Statue of Liberty, eh?"

"Now look here," Hilton said, rising from the couch.

Like Francis Scott Key, Hilton stood reeling with emotion, re-

garding the banner. What battle could have done all that to Old
Glory? Then Hilton began to sing. ". . . *thro' the perilous fight,
O'er the ramparts we watched, were so gallantly streaming; . . .*"

"*Ramparts streaming.*"

"Bravo," Mamoud yelled, stamping his feet. "Unbelievable."

"*Oh! say, does that star-spangled ban-ner yet wave . . .*"

"*Yet wave.*"

"*O'er the land of the free and the ho-me of the brave.*"

"Ya, ya," Mamoud sang, jumping up and applauding.

Hilton ignored him. He reached for the tattered flag. It squirmed
away. He chased it and caught it. The candle sputtered. Hilton
held his ensign in the dying light. He saw a naked body leap at
him with open arms. He was smothered in flesh. He fell backward. Faces of soldiers and sailors passed across his eyes like the
last scene in many films.

"Kelly, Birnbaum, Jackson, Washington," he said.

A lovely patriotism shot through his body. The war rushed over
him. He crawled along a beach of skin toward an unknown but
necessary objective. His heroism was extraordinary. They pinned
medals on him.

"Ruthie, Ruthie," Hilton said.

"Sure, sure. Some Ruthie." It was the mouse, talking softly.

"Water, water," Hilton said.

"Hello, darling. Here is water."

Hilton was covered with wet kisses on his lips and cheeks, on
his hair, chest, arms, legs, on his sex and shoulders, then back to
his mouth.

"I can't breathe," he said.

"Artificial respirations courtesy of Pivi."

She climbed on top of him and began pumping his ribs.

"In goes the good air, out goes the bad air. How about that?"

It occurred to Hilton that he might be encased in an iron lung.
But why would it talk to him? He was slapped on both cheeks.
His eyes opened.

"Sleepy beauty."

Hilton saw the flag face looming over his own.

"Darling, I love you. Say hello."

"Hello," Hilton said.

For that he was rewarded with more kisses.

"So good, so good."

After a quick experiment with his hands, Hilton certified that he was holding a naked lady, naked himself, lying on his back in a bed like a slab of iron.

"Do me again. Please. One more time, generous man."

"Wait a minute," Hilton said.

"Why?"

"I'm not ready. I'm thirsty."

"You have a thirst?"

"That's it. I have a thirst."

"You wish a beverage."

"Yes. I wish a beverage. That's it."

The lady rolled off Hilton. He was catapulted upward by the bedsprings. His back arched, then settled. He propped himself on an arm. He saw the lady's rear vanish through beads. It was an ample rear, large and rounded, attached on the one hand to a broad back and on the other to short heavy thighs and legs.

"What are you in here for? Are you some kind of barbarian?" Hilton heard Mamoud's voice, then a giggle. The giggle must have come from Tama, the Jap. It sounded as if it had traveled through a long, narrow straw.

"He has thirst."

"Get your bottle and get the hell out, you animal."

The beads rattled and Hilton saw Pivi holding a bottle and a glass. The brown liquid. Hilton winced but he wanted some.

"Hey, Mr. X," Mamoud yelled. "How are you doing in there, eh?"

"Fine," Hilton said.

"She treats you well, the fat one?"

"You damn right," Pivi said. She filled the glass.

"Cheer," she said, drinking off a few sips. Hilton took the glass and swallowed hard.

"Sex makes thirst for some," Pivi said. "For me it makes my head itch. I am always scratching my scalp after. Did you ever hear such a thing from anybody?"

"I don't think so."

Hilton felt the brown liquid settle and take hold. It was like being grabbed by a magnet. Pivi crawled into the bed. She kissed him on the navel.

"Cuddle me. Lay back. Relax, baby."

Pivi put one of Hilton's hands on a breast. She massaged his middle.

"Give me something nice," she said.

"I can't," Hilton said. "Not yet."

"Worry and booze. OK. Don't push it. You are the absolute boss. When you want, tell me. I am here. Then talk to me. What are you doing in Iran?"

Hilton told her about his company's cement construction process and its potential benefit to clients. After the first sentence she began a slow stroking of his nether regions, and he had the feeling she was not listening. She blew warm wind over his chest. She was listening, though, and he told of his meeting with Israelis and Lebanese and of his long travels around the world.

"I love tales of business," Pivi said, breathing hard. "Business is wild as an animal."

She rolled onto Hilton and bit his ear lobe. Hilton rolled her off and wrestled on top of her. She threw her head back and smiled. "Hello, darling ceiling," she said. "Fill me up, baby."

Hilton felt as if he were being seduced in the middle of an office debriefing. Pivi climbed him with her legs.

"Do me."

"I'm trying," Hilton said.

"Wake up, member."

"Shhh," Hilton whispered.

"I upset you?"

"I think we should rest a little longer."

"All right."

"I'm sorry," Hilton said.

"It is of no consequence. You are the boss. I shouldn't rush you anyhow in your condition."

"What condition?"

"It reasons that if you come with Mamoud of the Public Health there is a condition."

"I should not have exposed you to danger."

"Nah. I am all immunities. Nothing can hurt me. All my life I have been open to everything. Do you want another drink?"

"Yes. Thank you." Hilton finished the glass of brown liquid.

"You don't like me," Pivi said.

"I do. Of course I like you."

"You would rather be with Tama."

"No. I never . . ."

"It is the markings. You with no scars on your American body. You hate my markings."

"What markings?"

"You really wish to examine them?"

"I suppose so. If you want . . ."

Pivi reached for a candle standing in a saucer. Hilton saw that there were pale black lines sectioning her off like the drawings of steers in butcher shops. There were Persian inscriptions in each section.

"I never even noticed those," Hilton said.

"My shame," Pivi said. "Years ago I was with a man who tattooed me so. It was his plan to rent me to the college of fine arts and to the school of medicine for classes in human anatomy. He promised to draw in each space the thing that was underneath as if I were of glass. It was an idea worth trying. But we fought and now I am a freak show."

"Believe me," Hilton said, "if you hadn't made an issue of it I would never have noticed."

"How could you not notice? Be honest. So you see, you are not the only one in this room with troubles."

"I know that," Hilton said. "I'm sorry about your markings. Still, you shouldn't expose yourself to . . ."

"I have lived so long I will live forever. I have been with every kind of man of every description and quality, all but a Yemeni. I have never had a Yemeni and hope it will continue that way. For me a Yemeni is especially attractive. God knows why. I am saving the Yemeni like a last pocket to look in. But, darling, I like you too and you worry about me. Come, wake your member. I want to give you one just for love."

From inside Tama whooped. Mamoud made a sound like the end of a drought.

"Come on," Pivi said. "Everybody has a good time here."

Hilton was too full of thoughts. The brown juice had contracted his mind to a pin of light like the dot on a television screen when the set turns off, but the dot would not fade and release him. Hilton thought about the great power failure that plunged the Eastern United States into darkness. He could hear a Consolidated Edison apologist explain about grids and trip switches while people hung in elevators and waited in stalled subways. He was about to tell Pivi about it but it struck him that it was too foreign an experience to sum up quickly.

"Boy you are plenty sick I guess," Pivi said. "Nothing turns you on."

"Try to understand . . ."

"What's the matter?" Mamoud yelled.

"What you bring me here?" Pivi said. "A dead body? If I had a brother you would suffer a decapitation. What a lousy life this is."

"A sudden inhibition of the ability to fornicate, eh?" Mamoud said running into the room. He put his hand on Hilton's head. "Hot," he said. "Steaming."

"Steaming?" Hilton said, covering his genitals and feeling for fever.

"Mr. Lamb, do you feel an irritation near the prostate?"

Hilton leaped up. He shoved Mamoud toward the curtain.

"I knew it. He is a crazy," Pivi yelled.

"Mr. Lamb," Mamoud said. "Calm down."

Hilton groped around until he found the light cord and pulled it hard. The cord came off and wound around his arm. The room blazed. Mamoud and Pivi covered their eyes. Hilton rubbed his own, forcing them to see. He saw the bottle of brown liquid on Pivi's bureau. Next to it was a bottle of aspirin. He took two pills and washed them down with brown rage. Pivi grabbed at his shoulder.

"Go away," Hilton said. "I am steaming . . . steaming . . ."

"My birth controls. The crazy is taking my birth controls. Disaster."

"It was not a suicide attempt," Hilton said, holding a wet towel to his head.

"Sure not."

"What idiot keeps that stuff in an aspirin jar? The damn Shah . . ."

"Please. The driver has ears."

"Driver?"

"We are in the car. We are going home, Mr. Lamb."

The sound of the windshield wipers and the feeling of motion was definitely there.

"My stomach feels terrible. What did that bitch charge us?"

"A nominal thirty American dollars plus a few cents for the lost medication and the towel. You gave her American Express checks."

"That covered both of us?"

"Yes. I want to thank you."

"Was I very bad? I can't remember."

"A little delirious but not disgusting. I mean, sir, there can be no real sin in a junkyard, eh?"

"Jesus."

"You called for a tape-recording machine to send messages for your wife and children. It was touching. Even the girls said so."

"I am spinning in circles. Mamoud, can that driver speak English?"

"Who knows? My intuition is no. He seems an uneducated type."

"Mamoud, please, I have got to get out of here. I have got to get out. I don't care anymore if the whole world gets rabies. There has got to be a way to get me on that plane tomorrow morning."

"Impossible."

"Mamoud, I am speaking from the heart. I deserve to make that plane; I'm trying to say, Mamoud, I'm going to crack. I feel it. You're going to have a real jellybean on your hands. And maybe some kind of international incident. That's a lot to carry on your conscience. And there will be questions, Mamoud. Let's face it. The American influence is strong here. Plenty of questions."

"Are you threatening?"

"Never. Never. I'm being realistic. I'm battling for survival. Mamoud, let's face things squarely. There is always a way."

"Mr. Lamb, your record is on file with . . ."

"Files are files. Files are just cases. What goes in can come out."

"Are you suggesting an assault on the files?"

"There are occasions when anything is justified. Now, dear friend, in simple numbers, how much?"

"One cannot measure a life's dedication . . ."

"Numbers. Please, Mamoud. Please. Numbers."

"There is the inspector, the second inspector, his superior, the clerk and assistant clerk . . ."

"And you. Let's not forget you. Incentive, Mamoud, motivation. I believe in that, I really do."

"Alas, Mr. Lamb, it is all beyond possibility. It is not as if you have committed a crime. But for you, even to mingle is a sin."

"I won't mingle. Personal quarantine. I won't even put a cigarette in a public ashtray."

"Ah, years ago I had one like you. He was a hysteric."

"And? What happened to him?"

"I confess, an arrangement was made."

"Were there repercussions?"

"Things were done with discretion. That gentleman preferred to expire in Paris. He expired in Paris."

"And no heads tumbled, right? No one was the wiser."

"If he left a trail of destruction it never became obvious."

"You said it, Mamoud, I didn't. See, there is a way."

"You are prevailing on me to go against my own grain. To take a risk of everything."

"I know that, friend, I know that."

"Mr. Lamb, I have continually demonstrated my sympathy toward you."

"Numbers, Mamoud. This is the hour for numbers."

"I would calculate the cost of a quiet exit to be in dollars three hundred."

"Three hundred? It's high. I'm not a rich man. It's astronomically high. But not impossible. Three hundred is the final figure?"

"I think yes."

"Mamoud, we have an arrangement. You will leave me broke, but it's all right. I'm more than satisfied."

"I am obliged to caution you that the odds are by the morning you will be . . ."

"Some kind of mush? I'll go with the deal. What the hell."

"Then I wish you luck, Mr. Lamb."

"Amen," Hilton said. "Amen, dear friend."

"They should show more like you on American television programs," Mamoud said. "Instead of the cowboys."

In his room at the hotel Hilton gave Mamoud six blue checks signed and dated. Mamoud gave him a string of large yellow beads. Tied to the beads was a blue ceramic eye.

"Worry beads," Mamoud said. "I got them from a Greek, rest in peace. Take them as my token, Mr. Lamb."

"Mamoud, what can I say to you that I haven't already said."

"May your antibodies be sufficient to the challenge before them."

Hilton saw that Mamoud was crying. He watched as the figure in the raincoat walked to the elevators. Mamoud turned and saluted. Hilton returned the salute.

Alone, Hilton stood near the door with his pounding head resting against the cool wood. Then he got his suitcase out and began to pack.

When he was done, Hilton took his flask of Scotch from the young breast table. He swallowed a deep drink, then went to the window. Rain still pelted the glass. He could not see the mountains but they were out there, the mangy humps of unforgiving clay. Beyond, sturgeons spawned and Russia began. What an ancient land, a boneyard as old as history, a marketplace where the oldest disease and the newest cement construction process cast equal shadows in the street.

"Shahshahshah," Hilton said.

At the airport Hilton looked quickly at each official face but they were unreadable. He paid his exit tax, went past customs and paced in the duty-free area. There was no trace of Mamoud, which was to be expected. Mamoud was probably tapping on someone else's door. He had a quota to fill.

The plane was late by a half-hour. Finally Hilton sat inside the silver tube and buckled his safety belt. He chewed gum the stewardess gave him to open his ears.

The plane taxied onto the runway. Its motors powered. A jet of pressurized air cooled Hilton's face. He inhaled, then exhaled at the plastic window. It pleased him that the lady who sat beside him was easily in her seventies and had surely lived well. She had serenity about her.

Hilton rose above the city of Teheran, the Elburz Mountains, the world. The plane cut clouds. At thirty thousand feet there was nothing to see except a blue shell of space.

A month later, Hilton found time to write Mamoud. The letter detailed his good luck, affirmed his good will and remembered old times. He mailed it care of the Public Health.

It was returned a month after that, stamped with strange symbols, marked *unknown*. From his office in Manhattan, Hilton smiled warmly at the incompetence of the underdeveloped. He re-posted the letter in a fresh envelope.

This time he wrote the address in huge, clean childlike letters.

THE GIRL WHO DREW THE GODS

MY NAME IS OLIVER AUGUST.

I am friendly, a Moose. I try to believe in disarmament. I cook for a hobby. Every seven years my cells change. But each new cell sings of health and well-being. No matter how often I am replaced, I remain formidable.

Compare me with the rest.

In my city, in my time, half the people I meet live in their own suburbs, far from the energy of heart and the steam of bowel. The other half, with pinched lips, breathe their own smoke.

Am I apart, the only one with balance? If so, why so?

Look into my eyes: rain puddles rich with life. My story should be told.

When Oliver August, formerly passive, girded his valuable loins, then charged like a unicorn—there was cause.

The cause was war.

War is a time for attack. But I did not rattle my saber at the common enemy. I had a private skirmish.

The war I speak of was a small war. Not World War II, which moved millions, but the Korean war, a bubble of violence off to the left of the world's population centers.

I was out of college less than a year when the Koreans stopped sharing rice. My full-time job was soul-searching. I was taking the internal grand tour. I resented interruption.

Suddenly the leisure of self-discovery drained away. Because of someone else's history, the focus of my life was blurred.

My parents talked sense to me. They suggested that I go back

49

to school. They regarded this move as wise and patriotic. The whole idea has firm roots in tradition.

It is considered a richer experience to give blood if a boy has his master's degree.

After hesitation I agreed. My reasons were personal. I had just finished four hundred dollars' worth of dental work. My mouth was a wet Fort Knox. In dreams I saw Communists mining my head for gold.

So, not eager to break goal posts, I entered a convenient university. I readied for conflict in the Department of Philosophy.

The Department of Philosophy was a great, protecting bird. Under her thick wings, small groups huddled together.

English Literature was my major. Myself and others like me were assigned a place near the bird's big chest. We took comfort in the regular blood thumps. The hot juices of scholarship kept each feather warm.

At first it was not so bad. After half a year of job hunting and the look of deep fear in my parents' eyes, campus life was pleasant. College was as good a place as any to wait for my war.

I was deeply involved in a thesis on Chaucer's symbolic animals, for exactly one month. The news from Asia got worse. I worried with Douglas MacArthur. Chauntecleer, the old cock, laid eggs of anxiety.

The thing is, I was overly concerned with my own symbols. Every night, my book by my bed, I dreamed about inlays, crowns, and unnatural bridges. With the equipment I used for chewing, a family in Peking could live like mandarins.

Oliver August grew restless, logy, irregular, ill at ease. Most of the day I spent sitting in the library smoking room, which is a huge, rancid lung. When you open the door to that chamber of gas, blue ooze filters out. I am sure that smoke from students long dead is still imprisoned there.

I sat, hour after hour, pooling my gray breath with the rest. I tried to read classics, but the words were wooden. For the first time in my life I gew jumpy. My belly housed an imp who churned and cursed fate. My palms gave salty sweat.

To pull myself together, I shopped for new involvements. Desperately, I looked for some subject to lure my response. The Eighteenth Century, the Nineteenth Century, Shakespeare's Minor Plays, James Joyce, John Donne, Art in the Modern World, the Middle Ages—name it, I was there. I listened. I heard. I heard. I heard soldiers marching. I heard the lap of the Yalu River. I heard Oriental dentists sharpening their burrs.

Finally, thank God, something caught my attention. The course that won me the minute I read its abridged description was Know the Navaho II.

Why?

I have since learned that many eminent persons, to keep their sanity, involve themselves with a universe far from their daily experience. They become experts on the Civil War, on Henry Adams, on the Estonian Uprising of 1236. It is not too different from collecting stamps or coins. I needed something to keep my brain intact. I needed Navahos badly.

There was a problem. I should explain here that the university was divided genitally into a brother and a sister school. Usually, students were not permitted to cross this simple sexual barrier. But exceptions were made in cases of hardship. Know the Navaho II, a course for ladies, was given Tuesdays and Thursdays at ten. I read about it on Wednesday. By Thursday at nine, I was waiting at the proper room, signed dispensations in hand.

At nine-thirty, the instructor came. Her name was Miss Sydney Luptik. According to her biography in the catalogue, Miss Luptik had lived for years among assorted Indians. She was the author of two books, *They Dined on Buffalo* and *The Laughing Waters*, and she served as an adviser to the Bureau of Indian Affairs.

Miss Luptik walked along the corridor—a thin, dynamic soul

who accomplished motion in a barrage of baby steps. It was easy to see her walking right up to a Geronimo or the Great White Father himself.

We met head-on outside her classroom. I told her how much I wanted to audit her. She refused me the way she would have refused the Union Pacific permission to build its track over her grazing land. She refused me for the logical reason that I had not had proper preparation.

"Without Know the Navaho I," Miss Luptik said, "how could you expect to jump into Know the Navaho II? My course builds. You wouldn't understand subtleties. It would not be fair to you, Mr. August. Come back in September."

I swore I would bone up. I promised to devote myself. She could not be moved.

"Look," I said, "by September, I'll probably be in the U.S. Army, and remembering back to the way I played stickball and ring-a-lievio. I'll most likely be dead on an alien shore. Give me my chance."

Miss Luptik considered my unusual circumstances.

"Welcome to the tribe," she said.

The course itself was beautiful, exactly right.

We met in the basement of a building whose first female students were rebels against the tarantella. The walls were tooth yellow, stained with brown. The blackboard was cracked down the center. The wooden chairs, which had had flat seats, were actually worn down into small valleys through the attrition of thousands of impatient rumps.

Each chair had one flat arm for book resting. The arms were covered with initials, dates, and names. The place was full of nostalgia. Only a bank of fluorescent lights intruded, and a sprinkler system.

As might be expected, Miss Luptik had triumphed over her environment. Everywhere there were pictures of Indians at work and at play. A table near the window held a jar of seeds, samples of

wampum, a necklace of clay, arrowheads, a drum, a pipe, a feathered headdress, and a tiny model of a village complete with inch-
high figurines.

Our group was small. Besides myself, there were six girls. Miss
Luptik had given them names. I became Blue Bear, according to
the custom. Miss Luptik taught her section in semidramatic form.
We acted out brief dramas of Indian life. In our impromptu
playlets, a kind of group therapy with moccasins, Miss Luptik's
names added scope and dimension.

I, for example, might be asked to describe a day hunting buffalo. As Oliver August, I would have been paralyzed. As Blue
Bear, out of Shaking Cow by Great Grizzly, I felt right at home.

Pale Moon, a chubby girl to my left, might tell of her be-
trothal. Green Tree, a Bostonian, would hash out her weaving
problems. Waterfall, Bending Willow, Sipping Deer, and Wild
Bud might sing a fertility song while beating their feet.

So the days went. On Mondays, Wednesdays, Fridays, Saturdays, and Sundays I read the papers, listened to the radio, watched
television and did push-ups while waiting my call. Tuesdays and
Thursdays, I put on gaily-colored clothes and concentrated on
the antelope situation.

As the only eligible brave in Know the Navaho II, I became
aware of the maidens who shared my hogan. The girls divided
into notetakers and knitters. I watched them note and knit, with
paternal tranquillity. In our dramas it was I who brought them
fresh meat and supplied protection against everything but the
flow of history. Even Miss Luptik spoke to me with special respect. I knew my responsibility and its rewards.

Which brings me to Marilyn Mayberry.

Of the knitters, Sipping Deer (Marilyn Mayberry) was the
most chronic. She made mufflers—long, roadlike mufflers with
fringes at their beginnings and ends. She knitted the way a spar-
row pecks, in frantic flurries. Miss Mayberry was blessed with
huge energy.

I noticed her the way I noticed the rest. No more. No less. She was pretty enough, a medium-sized girl, nicely built, short black hair, pleasant lips, nothing special except for fine breasts. She dressed well, much like the others, in thick sweaters and plaid skirts.

To comprehend the passion that developed between us it is necessary to understand Miss Luptik, a superb storyteller, a marvelous creator of mood, a lovely builder of climaxes, a born inciter to riot. Had Miss Luptik come along in the 1870s, there would be only red faces on the North American continent. General Custer would never have got past Jersey.

Miss Luptik introduced us to the ebb and flow of Navaho life in easy stages. As the term moved on, according to her master plan, she lifted us along the way like canoes in the Panama Canal.

From digging for roots and grubs, we came to the spring feast. From swatting flies, we progressed to the shrieking hunt.

Together, in a group as tightly knit as Sipping Deer's mufflers, we achieved new levels of insight. Never suspecting, we traveled from fact to poetry.

With her wise face, her bouncy body, and tinkly voice, Miss Luptik carried us. I, her enraptured papoose, went willingly. Strapped to her bony back, Blue Bear was happy. The fluorescent sun and the sprinkler-system rain bordered a terrific cosmos. Tender Tuesdays. Tremendous Thursdays.

Yet all this was only overture. As it is with all instructors, Miss Luptik had her specialty. When she finished teasing us with trifles, when she reached the purple gut of her course, then Know the Navaho II ceased to be an experience and became a trauma.

Her specialty? Direct from life's cellar, Myth and Magic, the elemental sisters.

Miss Luptik began her lectures on what she called "the creatures of the wind," on a fine May morning. A puddle of yellow lit her desk. Our room glowed like the inside of a brown egg. Miss Luptik cleared her throat and found her start. From her purse she produced a wooden doll with a feather on its head.

The doll was a squarish fellow, something like a B-picture robot, but decorated in the Indian manner with slashes of white and red. Miss Luptik held him at arm's length, silently. Then, from the floor of her soul, she screamed, "Make rain!"

Until that moment, our instructor had talked of migrations across the Bering Strait during the Ice Age. She had talked of Mongoloid traits, of longheads and roundheads, of layers of piled life, of seed gatherers and grinders, of modified basket-making peoples of the Anasazi—the ancient ones.

I listened, satisfied, studying the markings carved on the arm of my chair.

That day, Miss Luptik shed her skin. She added the dimension of horror. She connected up with eclipses, council fires, coyote howls, time itself.

"Make rain!"

It did not rain immediately. There was a drought that month. But my skull flooded. I nearly drowned in joy.

There was no question but that Miss Luptik was about to give beyond the demands of tuition. "The higher tribes," Miss Luptik said, still holding her powerful didy doll, "believed deeply and devoutly in the Great Spirit, Father All Father, the Universe Man."

Her voice, as she spoke, took on a singsong, like Carl Sandburg's when he falls into his democratic trance. But it was not the shoes of industrial workers that sparked the instructor. It was bare feet on hot land.

"Say after me," she semisang, "Great Spirit, Father All Father, Universe Man."

We made a good chorus. And we liked the tune. Trained in the monotheistic manner, we felt a kinship—knitters, notetakers, and Oliver A.

"Ambiguity," Miss Luptik said. "Paradox. Along with their

faith in a single moving power, the dynamo of creation, our Indian brothers took an animistic view of daily life. Wakanda—life
energy filled everything. Everything. People and rocks. Flowers
and sky. Day and night. Wakanda."

Nice, nice. Good, good. That was our reaction. For wakanda,
the life energy, had also visited the Bronx. Here was another idea
that was familiar, therefore friendly.

"Say after me."

"Wakanda."

"Again, once more."

"Wakanda."

Wakanda was generally something to feel warm about. Why
not? The smallest bug, the weest pebble had its chip of spirit.
But the concept had its nasty side. Wakanda Good, Wakanda
Evil. Mr. and Mrs. Navaho had their bogeymen, too.

A knitter laughed. Miss Luptik frowned.

"Wakanda Good. Love. Babies. Corn. Wakanda Evil. Dwarfs.
Ogres. Underwater people. Thunder people. Maize blight. Sick-
ness. Sterility. Death."

A notetaker coughed. And coughed again. Miss Luptik was patient. She wet her upper lip with her tongue. The doll had not
moved from her hand. Like the carving of a figurehead, it gave
dignity to her prow.

When the coughing spasm had subsided, Miss Luptik raised
her second arm and held it suspended at an angle of roughly
ninety degrees to its companion.

"What a treasury of lore sprang from this simple belief. Epic
poems, Greek tragedies have nothing on the creations of the first
Americans. Oh, Red Man, how inspired you were in the naked
days before we brought you smallpox, measles, syphilis, and gold."

Miss Luptik upped her voice an octave. There was something
in her manner that made me twitch. I could feel her accelerating.
A vessel in her neck swelled with pressure. My left eyelid jumped
in response.

"Children of the land, what have we done to you? Today, the holy Shaman watches Ed Sullivan before conducting his rites. Our cancer culture presses in like fingers on a throat. Rice Krispies and insecticide stifle the Star Maker and the Animal Wife."

"Who?" said a notetaker. "Animal who?"

"Shoosh," a neighbor whispered.

"Think back!" Miss Luptik said, in her "Make Rain!" tone. She conducted with her free hand.

"Think back," we said. "Think back."

"Think back many moons," we said, an obedient philharmonic.

"Think back to the time of rich earth, clear streams, pure sky, steaming beasts, sharp teeth. Think back to the time of strong medicine."

"Strong medicine. Strong medicine. Strong medicine."

"Medicine made from the human heart and the human head. Not cheese mold. No hypodermic remedy injected into the tushy. Medicine catapulted into the bloodstream by lightning in the navel, by the shaft of fear."

Miss Mayberry dropped a plastic needle. It bounced, rolled, and ended up at my feet. I let it lie.

"Medicine of flesh and for flesh. Medicine to make vegetables grow. Medicine to fill squaw belly with kicking sons. Medicine to rip the enemy. Medicine to chase blood-drinking ghosts. Medicine for fire, for water, for sunrise. Medicine for resurrection. Think back to the time of magic. Back, back, back. Let your brains be the land in a world of wakanda."

Miss Luptik dropped both arms to her sides and stood rigid, like a palace guard. She began to chant. Then she moved in a kind of religious box step. With a quick wrist motion she told us what she wanted, and we gave it to her. We stood in our places, duplicating her sounds, and moved our feet. It was like singing a national anthem for a faraway flag. Again she stopped suddenly and covered her face with her hands. Then she kissed the little doll and held it to the girl sitting nearest to her desk. The girl kissed the doll and passed it along. We all kissed the doll and it was returned, smudged with lipstick, to Miss Luptik's right hand.

By the last and final kiss, we were had. With glazed eyes and open ears we entered the time of magic. As a dentist tests his Novocaine, Miss Luptik tested our involvement by dropping the doll. Nobody moved.

How can I tell you what happened next? I can only describe the skeleton. You must add the nerves and tubes.

Miss Luptik introduced us to the workaday gods and devils of the Navaho. She knew them so well, she could show us, in words, how they looked, what they wore, what or who they ate, how they played, how they were calmed, what they controlled, who they rewarded, who they destroyed.

For some reason, possibly because Miss Luptik was then into a malevolent chapter of her Ph.D. thesis, she ran through the Wakanda Goods in three minutes flat, then swung over to the other camp. Here, in the kingdom of open sores, many legs, fuzzy bodies, and pincers, Miss Luptik seemed curiously at home. Each creature Miss Luptik dragged up from the swamp was a separate Hitler, a swirl of claws and gore. Miss Luptik brewed bitter herbs. We sank in her soup—ankles, knees, thighs, middles, chests, necks, chins, mouths, noses, eyes, hair. We simmered together in an old clay pot. Miss Luptik ran around the room begging for plants to grow, calling to the heart of each seed, begging the thunder people to rumble the world's ovaries, fighting off demons, raising the dead, harvesting beans, butchering birds, cursing age, sucking at youth, licking strength from the fiery sun, then tonguing the cold moon for relief.

I stared down at the fallen doll. It grew, a tidal wave of sour protoplasm, slashed in color, its fat feather a weapon. I, Oliver August, who lights three on a match, was frightened half to death by the skinny instructor in the tight girdle. Miss Luptik was some new kind of ventriloquist. She spoke through the doll. And she, in turn, was someone else's puppet.

Wakanda Bad rolled into a snake, crept like warm ooze into my head through the ear. And a strange and secondary magic occurred for me. The slap of red hands on stretched hide, the tom-tom throbbing of Miss Luptik's voice changed to another music. Yellow hands beat drums of human meat. Chow mein mixed with feathers. Wakanda Bad developed an urge for gold fillings. He wanted mine, and my bellybutton for a nose ring.

All fear has one mother. My mouth dried. My armpits were drenched. My neck tingled. I couldn't breathe.

Slap! Miss Luptik clapped her hands. I fell five miles, breaking to pieces. Talk about timing! One minute before the bell, Miss Luptik returned us to the world.

In epilogue, a changed Miss Luptik, the familiar Miss Luptik, said in a chatty summary, "The dear Navahos knew their gods the way we know our own moles. They talked to them, prayed to them, made offerings to them. But they never never never drew them. It was an inconceivable act, the worst imaginable sin. Think on that. Isn't it the perfect testimony to pure horror? Isn't it the essence of belief? They felt, with wisdom handed down through millenniums, that if the gods were depicted, the image would leap up and devour the artist. Crunch. Fini."

The bell rang. Miss Luptik asked me to hand her the doll. She took it, dropped it into her bag, and left the room with gorgeous poise.

Later, Oliver August lay thinking of dark forces. Our apartment was on the second floor. The neon sign from the candy store downstairs flashed on and off, a green guardian through the troubled nights of my childhood. That night I noticed the sign again after long years. I was glad to have it. I lay in bed thinking how shrewd were those Indian gods to avoid too much exposure. How much worse is the *imagined* avenger. The Shadow who knows. Pictures or no, the peculiar truth is that if the Rain God came walking on the Grand Concourse, I would recognize him instantly.

Some miles downtown and east, where the island of Manhattan begins to narrow, Marilyn Mayberry was also awake.

"Good morning," said cheerful Marilyn Mayberry on the following Thursday.

She came late, dressed for a party in a soft pink dress, a pink hat with a wide brim, white alligator shoes and bag, and long white gloves. Under a chubby arm she carried a leather portfolio.

"Good morning, Sipping Deer," Miss Luptik said.

Minutes before, I had blushed when the teacher arrived at class. After Tuesday's experience there was an intimacy between us. The night of her epic lecture, I had her three times in a series of greedy, protective dreams. Since then, this was our first daylight encounter.

When Miss Mayberry entered, I was sadly accepting the fact that Miss Luptik would never again duplicate the Tuesday emotion. Her old self, she was telling us about ceremonies of initiation. She was strong but not possessed. Facing the truth was difficult.

"I drew the gods," Miss Mayberry said.

"Beg pardon, dear."

"I drew your big old nasty gods. I drew them as an extra term project."

"Ah?"

"I think they would look nice hanging around the room."

Miss Mayberry pulled the zipper that held her portfolio together. She lifted out a pile of drawings. In living color, before our eyes, she displayed her gallery of gods. Each drawing bore a legend:

WE ARE OF THE FIRE

I MAKE THE SUN TO BURN

GIVE US CORN, O CORN SPIRIT

I AM BLACK DEATH IN THE STORM

BOW LOW TO ME, BRAVE HUNTER

et cetera, et cetera. All the gods, sneering, grimacing, or passive and smoldering, bore a striking resemblance to Robert Mitchum.

Miss Mayberry beamed. She positively beamed.

"I brought wall tacks," she said.

"How creative," Miss Luptik said.

Then Miss Mayberry tacked up the gods. Miss Luptik worked along. She had been taken completely by surprise. Miss Mayberry won the day without losing an arrow.

As I sat watching, in the greenhouse of my heart a simple hatred bloomed—a clean, neat hatred for the pink, ripe, bitchy, muffler-knitting, big-knockered, tight-assed Marilyn Mayberry. Instantly, easily, absolutely without anger, I swore vengeance on her for this fantastic act of total blasphemy. Without ado, the gods appointed Oliver August as their ambassador in this matter of honor. I accepted the job without hesitation.

To this day I can only speculate. Perhaps because I had only recently learned about being afraid. Miss Luptik allowed me to see something of dignity and beauty in that dirty emotion. The darkness is *real*. The Wakanda Bads are a bopping gang. There is reason for shakes during new moon and, therefore, real reason to huddle together. Having learned about fear, I learned about need. But all this was new and vulnerable insight.

Miss Marilyn Mayberry, on the other hand, was impatient with unseen phantoms. Undoubtedly, she too had been disturbed by Miss Luptik's doll, but she refused to nurse its ugly hunger. Her mother had warned her not to play jacks with the Wind People. There was too much going on, hope chests to fill, the promise of weddings and babies. So, a true child of science, she drew the gods and nearly killed them all.

The girl came close to wiping out all of Hell. That, of course, was really the terrible penalty the Indians suspected—that the evil gods would die, leaving not a stain, but only tepid paradise.

I screamed for blood. I swore to drill Marilyn Mayberry to

some carpet, somewhere. That was the way it had to be, the only way to save the universe.

Imagine, I of tender passions, Oliver, the lonely dreamer, the nibbler of rose petals. I had grown feathers. I painted my face. Miss Mayberry was my buffalo. I wanted a coat made of her.

The pictures were hung, the class went on. I heard Miss Luptik's voice, but not the words. For the first time in my life, I had a single purpose. Already I was busy with blueprints.

After class, looking eager, I invited Miss Mayberry for a Coke. She thought things over. I had a difficult moment. Did her antenna pick up static?

She said yes.

From then, to the end, it was a quaint courtship.

In the early phase my biggest problem was to conceal my red identity.

There is a story about a lonely prince who wanted a certain, tender maiden, so he saddled his white horse and galloped to where she was picking strawberries.

Around and around he rode, but the maiden never looked up. So back he rode and fell into depression.

The prince slept and dreamed he rode a green horse. When he woke up, the message hit him right away. He ordered his groom to paint his stallion green.

"Green?" the groom asked.

"Uh, huh," answered the prince. "Get the picture: I ride down to the field where this maiden is picking. She sees me on a green horse. Then she says, 'Heavens, sire, your horse is green.' And I say, 'Yes, beautiful lady. I am the prince.' In a week, I send her flowers. In two weeks, I send her jewels. In a month, I grant her daddy a fief. In six months, I take my pleasure."

"Great," said the groom, and painted the horse green.

Later, the prince saw the maiden. He jumped on his green horse and went flying down to the field. Around and around he rode, but nothing happened. He rode faster, the horse snorting, the prince in a lather. Finally, the maiden looked up from her strawberry patch.

"Heavens, sire," she said in a golden voice, "your horse is green."

"Yes, beautiful lady," said the prince, "and in six months we're going to have sexual congress."

My situation was similar. The important thing was to go slow and steady. Dressing for dates, I used my sister's deodorant. I chewed Dentyne and gargled with Lavoris. I trimmed my pointy nails. Nothing should offend. No jagged ends should telegraph jagged intentions.

I followed a perfect timetable, forcing my mind to think like a German. It was two ballets at City Center, an Italian movie, and an Off-Broadway revival of *The Tempest* before I even touched her hand. When I touched, she pulled away. I did not pursue with reckless fingers. I made a fist, as if in suffering, and rested the fist on the arm of my seat.

No need to give you every detail. A human totem pole, with all the faces mine and smiling, I took Marilyn Mayberry into various worlds.

What did she like the best? Art? We went to the Museum of Modern Art, where she showed a taste for Edward Hopper's picture of an usher in the movies.

"I like films," she said. "And not only uptown. Right in the neighborhood is just as good."

I took her to the movies.

"I like foreign," she said. "But I think people who criticize Hollywood are artsy-craftsy snobs."

Remembering the Mitchum-faced gods, I confessed a long-standing love for the Warner brothers.

Books?

"I read and read," she said. "And read and read and read. Do you enjoy Thomas Wolfe? I do."

"I do."

"Look Homeward, Angel."

"Oh, yes."

Food? She loved Chinese, a touchy subject in those days, but I went along.

"You order from Group A."

"No, really."

"Go on. I'll order from Group B."

"Let's start with won ton."

"Won ton is lovely. Two won-ton soups, please. And chopsticks. We'll eat with chopsticks."

"I couldn't. Olly, I just couldn't."

"You can. Sure you can. I just know you can."

Meal after meal, I grappled with stilts. A winner down the line, Marilyn Mayberry never dropped a grain of pork-fried rice or a single snow pea.

How I hated that girl.

Gradually, I got to know her. So comfortable within her healthy skin, Marilyn Mayberry was absolutely without pangs. She had never felt hunger. The few appetites that stirred in her were appetites for future feeding, and she was calm and confident that her table would be set in due time. This was not a girl who would sleep with a frog on the chance of morning metamorphosis. There was enough in the world to keep her happy. Why gamble when it is so much easier, and safer, to simply be cautious?

She liked everything about the twentieth century, from the Double-Crostics in the Sunday *Times* to Jackie Gleason. And she seemed to like them equally.

Oliver Chameleon, camouflaging his secret heart, took on painful coloration. When Marilyn Mayberry bought *The New Yorker*, we went to little theaters where they served coffee in cups designed for thin lips. When she wished to rest from the better things, she would tell me about "when I was a little girl," and we would end up watching that mighty millipede called the Rockettes at Radio City.

Music was important too. So, many of our evenings ended with Marilyn tapping her glass with a swizzle while five obsolete Negroes and a sprinkle of middle-aged Caucasians belched Dixieland. "When the Saints Go Marching In." I sang along all right, but with my own words, celebrating my own dream of entrance.

We came closer. Close enough to discuss the great controversy between square-cut and pear-shaped diamonds, the need for adequate insurance, the matter of discipline in the raising of children and how weddings were made for parents and grandparents. We talked about D. H. Lawrence, for whom we felt sorry, and Joe R. McCarthy, for whom we did not.

And we came closer. We held hands on campus. We kissed in her hall. By the end of May, outside her door, while she fumbled for keys, I pressed her breast and she bit my cheek.

On the bus going home, I rejoiced.

Around that time, I can't exactly remember dates, the gods began visiting me each night. They looked harried.

"White Boy," said the fellow in charge of Household Misery, "hurry yourself. We're fading fast. Necessity is the mother of redemption."

"I'm doing my best," I said. "I'm keeping tight lines of supply. Positions must be consolidated."

Marilyn Mayberry retreated suddenly. Was it her intuition? For a week she wouldn't let me near her. She skipped our Tuesday class, and on Thursday she sat near the door. She broke our Wednesday date. I saw her walking on Riverside Drive eating ice cream with a total stranger. Thwarted love is bad. Thwarted vengeance is awful.

Each night, the gods tch-tched.

Marilyn and I made peace. I doubled my efforts. Desperately, using everything I knew or suspected, I sought to fill Marilyn Mayberry's life with aphrodisiacs.

Based on a magazine article I had read, I encouraged Marilyn to eat spicy foods.

"My upper lip is sweating, Olly."

"Have more sauce."

"No. I'll dehydrate."

"Curry is supposed to punish. That's the gourmet's way."

"No, Olly. No sauce."

To stimulate her mentally, I spent twenty dollars on a copy of the *Kama Sutra* and followed with *A Doctor Looks at Sex*.

"The first book was terrible. They spend so much time thinking about new positions it's no wonder their gross national product is way down. They need construction manuals, not marriage manuals."

"Whoever said the *Kama Sutra* was a marriage manual?"

"Well, people sleep together. The second book was sensible. I lent it to my mother."

I took her to the Persian Room to watch Hildegarde.

I championed the wearing of loose-fitting garments.

I planned picnics in Central Park, where we watched the seals.

I took her to the American Museum of Natural History to feel the great presence of dinosaurs.

We went to the Hayden Planetarium to watch stars being born and nebulae whirl.

"Someday man will probe the mystery of outer space."

"Olly, do you believe that? Why?"

"The sun will enlarge and burn the earth to a crisp. We'll have to venture into new worlds if the human race is to survive."

"When?"

"What difference does that make?"

"When?"

Only one thing kept me going. Every Tuesday and Thursday I saw her pictures hanging on the wall behind Miss Luptik, and my diabolical battery recharged. I saw the pale and beaten Miss Luptik sink into predictability, and I raged freshly.

Then, of course, there were the dreams. The poor gods, cling-ing to existence, were gasping for a hero. One even suggested that my cousin Marvin, whom I saw on major holidays, might do a better job.

The thing that brought Marilyn Mayberry into contact again was the bell at Riverside Church.

From a Juilliard student who lived on my block, I learned that every Saturday at noon there is a concert in the church tower. High above the city, in a small glass room, a bell ringer comes to play the carillon.

For twenty-five cents, visitors are welcome to take the elevator up, walk two additional flights, stand on a landing enclosed by stone arches, and listen.

The main bell hangs in the tower's center. It was designed to rouse spirits as far away as Teaneck, which is across the Hudson River.

When I heard about it, I conceived a scheme so basically rot-ten that I hesitate to give a description. My plan was to vibrate Marilyn Mayberry into submission. Thinking like the Old Testa-ment, I believed that if she were exposed to *total* vibration over a sustained period of—say—five minutes, from her arches to her scalp, her defenses would crash like the walls of Jericho.

It came to pass.

We went, innocently, to the church. We paid our quarters. We breached the tower.

At twelve, they began.

They boomed gobs of sound so rich and full that we did not hear them; they *hit* us. Up there, with the city on one side, the river on the other, we drowned in bongs. It was fearsome.

I had neglected to consider my own reaction to the massed decibels of Bach. Quasimodo would have lost his pants. Marilyn Mayberry started to cry, and despite myself, I joined her.

We held on to each other, shaking, while a tone-deaf pigeon

watched. The bells went on and on. When a man and a woman vibrate so thoroughly, something changes between them.

When we came down, I knew from Marilyn's expression that my conquest was no longer a matter of Will she? but When will she? It was time to think of time and place. This can be a real problem for city youth.

A friend of my family's was leaving for the mountains. It became my responsibility to water their plants. I asked Marilyn to come with me. She did, and she didn't. In the shade of the window garden, she told me the story of a "fellow" she knew who had violated a woman's confidence in a similar situation. I looked down at the African violets and lost the urge for cohabitation.

The gods chided me that night. I hardly recognized them. They were fatter, more confident, ready for deliverance. I warned them about premature optimism, but they laughed anyhow.

Marilyn had to baby-sit for her aunt. We sat on a soft couch that was made up for the night since Marilyn was to stay over. We lay side by side for two hours without movement, like members of the Young Communist League on bivouac. I went home in a crouch.

Even then, the gods cheered the minute I closed my eyes. It took some time for me to get the message. Through the Western Union of sleep, it came to Oliver August that Marilyn Mayberry, not I, would pick the time and place. A girl who drew gods would certainly want to design the stage set for her own greatest moment.

I waited. Days passed.

About a week later, I got a letter from the draft board. They wanted to examine my body. I was no longer worried about the legions of Mao. I was worried about the legions of Mr. Rain, Mr. Sun, Mr. Corn, Mr. Buffalo, Mr. Forest, Mr. Fire, Mr. Death, Mr. Birth, Mr. Pain, and Miss Moon.

The letter was a catalyst. I showed it to Marilyn Mayberry. She invited me out to dinner on the night before my physical.

We went to a French restaurant called the Fleur de Lis. Marilyn kept her eyes on me while eating snails, filet of sole, and an éclair. I ordered an artichoke. Peeling the leaves, revealing the heart, smothering it in garlic butter, I was the soul of seriousness.

After dinner, still on her allowance, we rode in a hansom cab through Central Park, then sat by the bird-sanctuary lake at Fifty-ninth Street watching a matted swan and talking about destiny until the police chased us.

During our hour on the park bench, Marilyn told me many things, but the one that especially impressed me was the revelation that she had planned her wedding at the age of ten.

She described it down to the point where a line of waiters carry flaming Baked Alaska into the dining room while she squeezes her husband's leg under the table.

Her apartment had been mentally furnished a year before first menstruation. She wanted white French Provincial. She was on her way. Her mother had bought her a hope chest the size of a cave, and, since she was "weensy," uncles, aunts, cousins, friends, and acquaintances had been stocking it. With her head on my shoulder, Marilyn informed me that she was indeed a girl of property.

In a soft voice, she asked me about careers. I was ready for her questions.

"A man needs direction," I said. "I have my goal. If I am fortunate enough to leave the Army in reasonably good condition, I'm going into corporation law. You may not think that a dramatic occupation, Marilyn. But that's what I want. And it's not only the money, which is substantial. The organization of business has always intrigued me. And, on the higher levels, a businessman can share his career with his woman."

I looked up. The gods were sitting in a row on top of the Plaza Hotel just behind me. I saw them eating an antelope hock and generally carrying on.

Late, very late, Marilyn Mayberry and I went home.

She lived with her mother and brother in a solid apartment house on Lexington Avenue. Until that night, our farewells were said outside her door. I had never crossed the threshold. The brother, a teenager, slept in an alcove and was trained to bite the ankle of any stranger.

When we reached her apartment, I took her in my arms. She pushed me away. My temperature dropped sharply. I was confused, but not for long.

Marilyn beckoned. She led me to another door down the corridor. And from her evening bag she produced a key with a new set of teeth.

"My sister Betty and her husband Irv live here," she said. "They have darling twins, Jerome and Charlotte. I want you to see the babies."

"It's three-thirty," I said.

"Betty and Irv don't mind. The kids' room is off the foyer. Come on. Nothing wakes them. Nothing."

I went.

We unlocked the door, clicking as quietly as possible. Marilyn took off her shoes. Me too. Like burglars, we entered the dark apartment.

Feeling her way, Marilyn took me to a room. Inside, a night light burned between two cribs. Two children were scrunched under blankets, one pink, one blue.

"Sweet? Yes?"

"Yes."

"Milk and cake?"

"If nobody minds."

We tiptoed again through darkness and found our way to the kitchen.

"Hush! Be a mouse."

Marilyn turned on the fluorescent. It flickered, missed, ignited, blazed. There we were. But where?

That kitchen was like nothing I had ever seen. I enjoy the stamp of domesticity. But such a stamp.

The scene in brief: Dirty dishes filled a table. Bottles of half-eaten baby food sat on the sink. Boxes of cereal, a bowl of fruit, wet towels, drippy Brillo pads, pans, a pile of chicken bones, and other testimonials to life lived, covered every surface.

And the wash. The wash.

There was wash every place. Steel ribs on the ceiling were full of wash. A straw basket, of the modified Navaho type, was full of wash. A machine with its door open had a clump of wash hanging out, and a portable rack near the stove hung wash like a willow.

Food, dishes, bones, soap pads, the fantastic dangling wash, merged in the brittle light. We stood in a tree house, engulfed in the foliage of an active marriage.

Marilyn grinned.

"Betty is such a slob," she said.

At three-thirty-six, Eastern Daylight Time, we stood on blue linoleum. Dew from a turkish towel, or was it a diaper, fell on my forehead. Did Marilyn mistake it for a tear?

The drop ran down my nose, in business for itself, seeking the way to the universal ocean of human misery. And I saw a drop on Marilyn's cheek take the same journey.

"Are you crying?" I said.

The fluorescents blazed onto the blue linoleum. Like bathers testing the water, we stood together and shivered. I heard the gods howl from behind a Sanforized housedress. Mostly I heard my heart. I looked at my wrist watch. The second hand flew.

"Why are you crying?" I said.

Marilyn shrugged. She played with my tie. I kissed her on the neck.

"Are you crying because this is Army Physical Eve?" I said. "Is that it?"

"I don't know," she said.

"Well stop, please," I said. "You're confusing me."

"I'm sorry."

"I think we'd better say good night," I said.

One of the gods coughed up phlegm.

"Here we are," Marilyn said.

"Good night," I said.

"No," Marilyn said.

She opened two buttons of my shirt and slipped her hand in. Her hand was cool, a delicious temperature.

"I know how much you want to make love to me," she said.

"Someday, dear," I said. "Tomorrow we'll find a place. I'll rent a car. We'll drive to a motel on a mountain."

"I've known," she said. "Don't you think I've known?"

"I knew you knew," I said.

"Take off your stupid jacket," Marilyn said.

"It's late as hell," I said.

She took off my stupid jacket.

"I want to feel your chest against mine," she said.

"Look, dear," I said. "Your sister is inside. Your brother-in-law . . ."

Marilyn took off my shirt. First she worked on my cuff links and dropped them into the little pocket, then she did the rest.

"No T-shirt?" she said. "Unzip me."

Marilyn turned around. I unzipped her. She pulled her dress over her head. Then she reached behind herself and unhooked her bra. I slipped the bra off her soft shoulders.

Her breasts tumbled out like children at recess. We pressed together. Marilyn kissed my ear. It occurred to me that Oliver August, the vengeful seducer, had never opened a single button.

"Make me naked," Marilyn said.

I made her naked. In the Garden of Lux, in the oilcloth pool, she looked remarkably fine.

"Be naked with me."

I was naked with her.

"Hold me."

I held her. The cool sweetness of her hand was total. I think I moaned. My moan set the gods cheering. Marilyn heard music.

Oliver August and Marilyn Mayberry fitted beautifully together. Together, we marveled at the coincidence.

Standing, grasping, moving slowly, in time's own kitchen, under an umbrella of laundry, we made love.

"Go away," I yelled to the gods.

"Oh," Marilyn said, hugging tighter.

"Not you," I said. "Oh, sweet, not you."

We made too much noise.

Her sister, a light sleeper, was attuned to all city dangers. For years, with the acuteness of those suspicious of fire escapes (every exit is an entrance), she rested with an open ear. Our tender battle in the place where she cooked for her own was enough to wake her twice. Like Betty, Irving came awake clear-headed and primed for attack.

Bravely, Marilyn stood with me. For some time, two couples stared at one another. Then Betty hollered, and Marilyn turned to the stove. Irving went back to get me his bathrobe.

I grew quickly engaged.

Shortly thereafter, I was allowed a glimpse into the mouth of my fiancée's hope chest. I saw treasure that would have shamed Captain Kidd. Material things meant little to me then. I was young and foolish.

Our engagement did not last long. We were, it seemed, very different. Before choosing our bedroom set, or even our silver pattern, we began to drift. After all, we were total strangers. Once, in Tanglewood, we fell asleep after Stravinsky and never woke to each other. Unprepared for such relaxation, we said goodbye.

Oh, yes. The draft board rejected me for nerves and a bent knee.

In September, Marilyn was wed to an accountant. She invited

me to the wedding. I went. Even Betty did a cha-cha with me, and the Baked Alaska was indeed hot and sweet.

The gods left my dreams. I assume they returned to Arizona. Our parting was friendly, but I am convinced that their immortality was diluted by the whole experience.

Wakanda Manhattan is its own strong medicine.

Time advances. After heavenly vengeance, reality is a warm shower.

Miss Luptik is now Dr. Luptik. She spends summers with such corn grinders as remain. We correspond.

As for Oliver August, I founded my own tribe.

Today I have a store. I give green stamps with pleasure. I sleep beside a mountain of heat.

"Come back inside," she always says.

Three kids ask me questions, and the smell of me gives them security.

You know my hobby? I take pictures. I snap my Polaroid and flash my flash and fill albums by the pound. I take so many pictures the druggist asks if I am some kind of Jap.

It is not that I am a tourist on my own street. My pictures are pieces of a jigsaw. When it is finished, I believe I will have something to look at.

The druggist, a philosopher, says picture-taking is for idiots. He says time should not be saved except in the heart.

"All we need," he said this morning, "is a picture of God. The rest is a waste of clicking."

"God wouldn't pose for a picture," I said. "He doesn't need publicity."

"Sure, He would pose," said the druggist. "He would love it. He could look on Himself and feel impressed. Take Him a picture, Oliver. Be a sport. It would do us all good. Probably nobody asked Him. Maybe He has a shyness."

"All right," I said. "I'll take Him a picture."

"Take two," said the druggist, "in case He moves."

Tonight in the tub I noticed a gray curly hair float like a gondola of nostalgia. It drifted to the drain. I watched it swirl and go bubbling down.

Then I heard myself say out loud to the tiles, "Dear Marilyn. Dear Book of Knowledge. Marilyn *knew!*"

IN SECLUSION

JASON BRIAR AND MONICA PLOY MET ON THE SET OF *Beowulf* and the hairs on him crackled with healthy electricity while she took in air like a vacuum cleaner and held it. He, the handsomest and the most virile; she, the softest and best curved, a vessel brimful of estrogen. "He is the very best," thought she, and "She is the tiptop," thought he. *Beowulf* was being shot outside London "where it really happened," so the climate gave them no encouragement. But they needed none.

They became lovers. LOVERS! L*O*V*E*R*S* for themselves, for their fellow players, for the director and the producer and the staff, for the press, the public, for you and me. Their waking lives were gorgeous, working together and all that. To think of them at night running over moors where blue-painted Angles and Saxons once ran was overwhelming. It was like looking with naked eyes at a fleshy eclipse of the sun, of the moon, of the entire physical universe.

He was married, she was married and they became unmarried and blended. Their exes gave interviews to the papers, wishing them "the best," but theirs were rusty words. Ex-Mr. Her and ex-Mrs. Him rattled like empty old scabbards. Who listened? Nobody. Even other empty scabbards turned away. For Jason Briar and Monica Ploy cuddled and fondled and tumbled for everyone. All cells rang like bells.

The trouble was, their affair was ill-timed. *Beowulf* ran into production problems (something about fog). So the celluloid climax occurred later than the lovers' hottest heat and by the time the movie was ready for selected premier showcase theaters, millions of ingrates were thinking of other jangling thighs, of other midnight panting.

The studio sent them into California seclusion. It was announced that they were going to be secluded like monks. They were going away to pure isolation, to a place of meditation and cold stone, to a place by the salty sea.

The studio found an abandoned abbey near an ocean. It was fine. There was no furniture even. Not even a bed. NOT EVEN A BED. All the windows were broken. The garden was like a crazy man's lair. Ooze made lines on the thick, thick walls. There was, of course, no telephone. Wind from the waters whistled in the halls. You could hear spiders skitter.

The point? The point was peace. The lovers were going to find peace and repose. They were going to discover hidden flavors far from the candy store. With a few cans and bottles, an opener and a busload of photographers, Jason Briar and Monica Ploy set out to heal themselves in double solitary.

The concept got banner headlines right away. The story grew. The studio was pleased. Even the exes gave interviews again. On the fateful day that Beowulf opened across the nation the lovers said goodbye to civilization. Their abbey was on a cliff jutting into the brine. There was only one road for access. Guards were placed where the road joined the rest of the American continent and away they went carrying provisions in canvas sacks.

The lovers wandered wistfully. It was late afternoon. A pink cloud covered the sea. The sand was red. Bits of shell reflected sun like broken pieces of an urn. Jason Briar and Monica Ploy retreated into this magnificence. Even they were impressed.

They had never been to the abbey before so first they explored. The old rock house on an ancient hump of land teetered on the edge of Earth. There was a ribbon of sand separating them from the fishes, nothing more. The house itself was a thick cool egg, a ponderous thing with a hundred tiny rooms and one huge cavern downstairs. Jason Briar and Monica Ploy rattled around the premises.

"You know, Jay," Monica said, "I think I actually *like* it."

Jay looked at her and noticed that her lips were wet. Her lips were always wet. She licked them.

"We might as well, puss cat," he said. "Let's go for a swim."

Monica dropped her clothes where she stood. Jay too. Monica was brown as a nut except for two bikini lines. Jay was brown as she except for one bikini line. Monica ran a finger along his appendix scar. It was a shame, that one flaw. The doctor had shaky hands. The scar rambled. He might just as well have been nibbled by a lion.

Off they went to the ocean. The water was chilly but welcoming. They swam and splashed. Monica, lips wetter than ever, got hungry and thirsty. Jay, dripping puddles, pushed back his hair. He peed.

"Why do you have to do that here?" Monica said.

"Why not?"

"I don't know. You pee in the shower too, don't you?"

Jay slapped her gingerly on the can. Monica yelled. His hand etched on her bottom. She pulled a hair on his chest. They went up to the house.

"This is really fun," Monica said, and made her little noise, a gargled, swallowed purr for which she was justly famous.

In the cathedral of a living room, if that is what it could be called, Jay rummaged through the provision sacks. He found two cans of beans, a fifth of Beefeater and a long spoon. There was a can opener too, with a bottle opener on the back. Jay opened the beans. Sitting on canvas bags, he and Monica ate. Then they drank down the gin. Soon both felt a glow.

"Watch yourself," Jay said. "I think I'm in the mood to stimulate a certain party's erogenous zones."

Monica stood up.

"Not on the stone floor," she said.

Jay unrolled their sleeping bags.

"How do you do it in there?" Monica said.

"I don't know," Jay said. "But we can find out. Thousands of people do."

Monica wriggled into a sleeping bag.

"I feel like some kind of product," she said.

Jay got in with her after some difficulty.

"How come your navel is kind of a football shape?" Monica said.

"What makes you say that?"

"It is. Not that it's important. But it is."

Jay could not see his bellybutton in the bag but he wondered about it.

They made love sideways, then squirmed out of the bag. Jay checked his button. It was mostly circular, not at all football shaped. Monica was holding a mirror while she put on lipstick.

"A mirror? Cosmetics?" Jay said.

"I smuggled them in."

"Well the whole point was a kind of enforced austerity," Jay said.

"Who'll know?"

"Nobody. Unless some reporter gets by the guards. It's a matter of keeping faith. Not that that means much to some people."

"Some people are not hypocrites like other people," Monica said.

She put on a sack dress. Jay put on Bermudas.

"Where do we wash up around here anyway?"

"Pump outside," Jay said.

Monica went out and found the pump. She worked the handle. A trickle of rusty water dribbled out.

"Is that a pump or an infection?" Jay said. He had come up behind her.

"Help me."

Jay pumped. The rusty brown water turned gray.

"I think that pump is connected to the sky there," Monica said.

A heavy cloud covered the ocean and it was indeed the color of the water.

A wind blew from out at sea.

"Brrrr," Monica said. "I'm starting to freeze."

After the wash Monica and Jay went to get more clothes. A storm was blowing in, no question about it. Jay found some logs and kindling. He made a fire, using a copy of *Harlow* to prime the flames.

"Cozy shmozy," he said.

"What shall we do?" Monica said.

"Scrabble," said Jay.

The Scrabble board was set by the fire and the tiles distributed. Jay watched Monica's face change. She loved competitive games. He hated them. But he liked to watch her love competitive games because he fancied that her true self emerged when she played them.

Games were a kind of Sodium Pentothal to Monica. After an hour or so of combat Jay knew he could ask her anything and get a quick, straight, honest and therefore cruel answer. Her answers always hurt Jay in his middle. They clashed with his convictions about what a woman should be. Despite that, he enjoyed the whole process. Monica knew what he was about but she enjoyed it too. And she actually did get carried away with the old team spirit.

"Strap on your phallus," Jay said. "The game begins. And remember in this one you don't collect two hundred when you pass Go."

"Ooooo, you're going to get it," Monica said, and proceeded to give it to him.

Monica could not concentrate on anything for more than a whisper, so Jay opened with a spurt. He strained his head from the first gun. Monica came on like thunder too. It was a healthy, absorbing contest. Jay and Monica, huddled over the board, made great shadows as the flames jumped.

Outside the weather congealed to a murky soup. The cloud grew until it covered everything. The water moaned and churned. The wind whiplashed at waves and rocks. There was no more light.

At the root of the road leading to the abbey the guards looked toward the ocean and saw nothing but fog.

"How'd you like to be stuck out there with that broad?" said one.

"Oh yeah, yeah," said the other.

Then they went into a little shack that had been built by the studio for their comfort.

So turbulent evening settled on Jason Briar, Monica Ploy, the old stone castle, the ocean, the beach, the road, the guards and the little shack.

It was at about this time that the creature moved.

The creature was so big that it really had no exact sense of its parts. In fact, it had no sense of anything at all except hunger and wakefulness. It was awake and hungry so it moved.

For breakfast it had eaten a whale. For lunch some dolphins, porpoises and sharks. Fish, fish, fish. The creature was sick of fish. So it moved itself.

The thing on its head signaled meat. Somewhere, nearby, meat. Yum yum. It moved along the ocean floor, tons and tons of it, smacking thousand-pound lips with four whopping tongues. Yum yum. The creature pulled itself toward shore.

"Smart ass is two words," Jay said. "As in the expression nobody loves a smart ass."

"A smartass," said Monica. "You pronounced it yourself. Ha!"

"Negative."

"Positive."

"No. No."

"Churl fink," Monica said, steaming from the ears.

Jay smiled knowingly as Monica came to another moment of

truth. He sat nodding his head left to right while she counted up her points for smartass and he saw she was consumed with guilt. He sprang.

"Did you think my performance in Beowulf was solid class-A caliber?" he said.

Monica shivered, wet her lips twice and told him.

"You were like walking constipation."

Jay swallowed dry foam. Tears welled in his eyes. He went for a swig of Beefeater.

"You asked me," Monica said. "Who asked you to ask me?"

When Jay came back to the Scrabble arena, the tears had dried to an opalescent wax. Monica thought he looked sexy that way, with the eyes of a stuffed moose in a men's bar. She noticed him fastening his wax eyes to a spot on her neck that showed a thin crease and tried not to but couldn't help pulling at the collar of her dress.

A few hundred yards away, still submerged, the creature experienced a sensation of itching in what could be called its nose. It arched, making an island, then rolled, making a wave, then sneezed, bubbling a billion gallons of brine. Inland, one of the studio guards asked the other if he heard a strange sound. The other, absorbed in a magazine, had heard nothing.

The sneeze, a megaton of mucus, refreshed the creature and left it more awake and hungrier. Onward it went, flowing forward in slimy progress. The creature thought vaguely about its mate somewhere in the Red Sea. The thoughts waved like theater curtains, rippling through its head. The creature had not made love in a decade, back in the Strait of Magellan. Its scales practically glowed as memory flared and faded. It felt a bit horny.

The creature's instinct interrupted its reverie. "Eat first," the instinct commanded. So the creature sniffed for and found tantalizing promise of gratification. It came faintly from the abbey, borne on the water-whipping wind. It was Monica's perfume the creature smelled, mingled with Jay's mortification. Mmmmmm. Very tasty. Very juicy.

Fifty miles inland, Harold Bipley, the producer-director of *Beowulf*, sat beaming behind a massive desk with legs carved like tree roots. Into his office came Harriet Troom on plump legs of her own.

"Pineapple," she said.

"Melon, baby," he said. "Sit down. Rest yourself."

Thirty years before, a famous philosopher had gasped and died between the pudgy legs which Harriet Troom crossed neatly. He had just completed his worst book. Her legs were famous in intellectual circles just as her column was beloved by millions of readers on many sides of the Atlantic.

Harriet Troom was big on both ends of the IQ spectrum. Her heart held many secrets involving the living and the departed. Her body had shared heat with a variety of types ranging from old child stars to the famous philosopher. The residue of all that experience gave her terrific poise. Harold Bipley was impressed. But that very morning he had had a warning from his doctor. He went to the doctor because his arms felt tired, like heavy salamis. The doctor took Harold off sex and cuff links. Harold liked both. Without sex he felt restless and sleepless. Without big cuff links he felt as if his arms would fly out of the floppy sleeves of his silk shirt and hit a total stranger.

"There better be a story," Harriet was saying. "This is my bridge night and I gave it up for you."

"There is a story," Harold said. "As God is my witness."

"Continue."

"Word follows word, darling. Word follows word. You know about Monnie and Jay in seclusion?"

"Of course."

"That's where they are right now. In seclusion."

"So?"

"In a fat old church house by the water. Desolate. Bare. Empty."

"And?"

"Nobody around. Death to intruders. Get the picture?"

"Sure."

"So everybody is thinking of what's going on *inside* that seclusion, is that accurate?"

"Proceed."

"So one person emerges from the horizon to tell them. You."

"Ah."

"And it's spontaneous, Harriet. Not even Monnie and Jay have inklings. You go out there with a camera and a pad. Top secret. Peep a little. Bust in on them. Do what you want. It's all yours."

"I like it. I buy it."

"I was so sure you would," Harold said, "I called Hertz. My Rolls is waiting outside."

"I go alone."

"Any way you wish it is the way it will be."

"Where?"

"I happen to have a map."

"When?"

"Better soon. You know what a honey bucket Monnie can be. And Jay has no concentration either. How long will they last without electricity?"

"Tonight."

"It does me good to hear you say that, Harriet. Your readers are a hundred percent lucky to have somebody like you."

Harriet Troom took the map and went for the car. Harold Bipley watched her behind sway while she walked. His son was a Navy pilot who landed on aircraft carriers. He felt sorry for the boy. A moving target is nice and challenging. But difficult.

At the moment when Harriet Troom aimed the Rolls down the highway toward land's end, the creature reached land's beginning.

Before assaulting the beach it gathered its parts together. There was a helter-skelter quality to such size. Pincers, legs, feelers, arms, buttocks, ears, etc., had a way of wandering off. The creature had a natural sense of order, so from time to time it paused to take inventory and consolidate into a comprehensible lump.

It piled itself half in and half out of the surf. Because of the foggy dark the mountain it made was invisible. Now the creature, which was extremely light-sensitive, felt a sting in a secondary eye. The eye detected a pin dot of light from a chink in the abbey wall. At the same moment a hectic spasm of wind wafted a ripe scent of the abbey's human visitors. The creature perked.

At once the entire scene seemed familiar. Of course. Years before the creature had visited that very beach and enjoyed a supper of Dominican Fathers. Bingle, bong. There was the bell. The creature's primitive head remembered the bell which it had nibbled for dessert. Brassy and tart. It jiggled for a year afterward. The creature grinned, or tried to grin. One gray-green mass separated from another and exposed a slit of flecked orange mush. For the creature, that was a big, broad smile.

Inside the abbey Monica was feeling the empty triumph of the conqueror. She had won the Scrabble game by hook and crook. As she totalled her points she cried.

Jay was still in pain from her dirty remark about his talent. She felt sorry for him and for herself. Victory in the game calmed her. She was now free to be nice. Jay needed some nice. He looked older by firelight.

"Darling," Monica said, "forgive me. There's always room for improvement. And it's not easy for me either with every erectable male person in the whole wide world wanting to have genital connection with me. Sometimes at night I can feel my fans dreaming so hard I practically drown in seminal fluid."

"Don't I have that too?" Jay said. "The women plus the queers."

"Cheer up," Monica said. "It's so clammy and dismal out.

We've got hours to kill and I'm not sleepy. I'm not the least bit
sleepy. Tell me a story. Tell me how it was when you first
saw me."

"No."

"Please."

"Stop tonguing your upper lip."

"I will."

"I first saw you in your first flick, *Beloved Runt,* and my
breathing clamped. I thought at last the Lord hath made a broad
sufficient unto me."

"Fabulous."

"And I thought, I've got to have her. So I met you and had
you."

"What a way to tell it," Monica said. "How you hate me. You
left out the entire love-play sequence."

"You came at me so quickly I had no time for love play."

"I came at you? Jay, I was a star while you were doing impro-
visations in the Village."

"I did not say you had no distance on you when we met."

"I was discovered at fifteen."

"I'll bet you were."

"It was never like that. Never."

"Baby, you saw more ceiling before twenty than Michelangelo
in a life of decorating."

"You are a filthy mouth. A sore loser. And don't ask me to
calm you down when the going gets rough. Whisper never talked
like you talk."

"Whisper Jones weighed fifty pounds when you married him
and thirty-four ounces at the divorce."

"Annulment."

"All he wanted was custody of the oatmeal. You broke that
boy's spirit."

"And Sherril? Didn't her pubic hair fall out from nerves?"

"How do you know that?"

"Never mind. It was all over town. Her follicles shriveled from mental cruelty. Hell, it must have been mental."

"What does that mean?"

"You break the code. Big virility symbol."

"Listen, Monica, face the fact that your entire reason for being is to transport your mammaries to and from the studio. My work at least has a chance of contributing something, some little thing to the pool of artistic achievement. The best you can hope for is a medal in the tit olympics. And they're getting saggy, if you want to know."

Monica inhaled and held her breath. Her face turned red. Jay watched her take in still more air. And more. She did very well.

"If you burst it's on your own head," he said.

Monica let the air gush out.

"Saggy?" she said.

She looked for something to break but there was nothing, only her hand mirror, so she threw a can of vegetable soup, which went rolling around the stone floor.

Jay fell to his hands and knees and roared. Monica threw another can, string beans this time, and he scampered away. He knew that she would soon begin to play zoo, being a cat or some kind of rhino, and that the argument would end up in jungly love. They had played zoo five times in six days and he was bored with it, but there was nothing better to do. The stone chilled his kneecaps.

A log fell into the fire and sent up a shower of ash and sparks. The shadows leaped too, filling half the room with Jay and Monica, dolls cut from black velvet.

Outside, the creature made a sound like *goorumbumbum* for no particular reason. It was on land, sloshing along. The air felt funny after years of water, amphibious or not. The switch from gills made the creature heady, a little drunk. It waved a score of flippers and swooshed a hairy tail. The wind confirmed that fresh meat was imminent.

The creature was sure of its prey. It began to think selectively, like a housewife at a butcher's shop, trying to remember the Dominicans and what part of them was most succulent. Bonk. Its vanguard antennae touched something. The abbey gate. The creature had no time to knock. It secreted chartreuse juice, dissolved the rusty metal and squished toward the house.

"Sleep in your own bag," Monica said to Jay.

She was wriggled inside the sack, all the way in, and curled up sniffing her own perfume. Jay was pacing back and forth hitting his fist into an open palm.

"Once I stepped on a child star," Jay said, "and she didn't scream or yell or howl like other kids. You know what she did? She said 'Hi, there.' "

"I'm sleeping," Monica said.

"And the awful thing is, Monica, that child star could have been you. It's what you would say. 'Hi, there.' Oh Christ Almighty."

Monica's head came out of the bag.

"Try it," she said. "Try stepping on me."

"I am speaking symbolically," Jay said, "so I don't expect you to comprehend. Go back in the bag."

"Hi, there," Monica said. "You think you're so damn superior. Didn't Mr. Bipley tell me how you were latching on to my star?"

"Huh?"

"How did he put it? He's marrying you for your light. He is a planet, a lousy planet, not himself a source of heat and smoke. That's what he told me. Hi, there."

"Bipley told you that? Well, stop the presses. He told me the same thing. He said Jay, let's face up buddy baby, if He hadn't rested on the seventh day maybe things in the world would be rosier, but He rested so we're stuck with our kismet and must own to basic truth. . . . Monnie, which is what he calls you, is a great shape but an empty bottle and you will empty yourself trying to fill her. Beware, Jay, she needs your inner illuminations."

"Bipley told you that?"

"Monnie is a vampire who lives on reflections, he said. Reflections from mirrors, from eyes, from puddles, from hub caps, from sunglasses. Boy, was he a hundred percent accurate. Zowie."

Monica began twisting inside the bag.

"Finished," she said. "It's done. You are out of my life. You are dead and buried. You are garbage. I'm going home right now, you miserable pig bastard, and in a year from now nobody will remember you except like they remember a stain on the toilet bowl."

"That's great imagery coming from a girl," Jay said. "Go wet your lips."

"Don't worry yourself about my lips," Monica said, jumping out of the bag. "Worry about acting lessons."

"You membrane," Jay said. "You no talent. You physical bum."

"Listen to limpy," Monica said.

The creature wrapped itself cozily around the abbey like a moist rag. It started on the East Wing, then gooed over the North, slithered part of itself to the West and met its tail with its nose on the South. The moment of confrontation, front to rear, was rare for the creature, and for an instant it fell under the impression that it had encountered a friend. It would have tipped its hat if it had a hat, but it had no hat so it snorted recognition. Its rear end gave no sign, except a faint pulsation, so the creature bit it in primitive rage. A bubble of pain ran through its nervous system along internal cords like seaweed and reached its medulla oblongata with a clonk. The creature wailed. A teardrop formed and gurgled out of a red eye.

"Both parties suffer in divorce," Jay was saying when the wail sounded.

"If you're dreaming dreams about community property," Monica said, "over my dead body. Because I've got you under your own skin. Don't think she didn't tell me."

"What tell you? Who?"

"What tell me who? Bessie."

Jason froze.

"My God," Monica said. "The fattest cleaning woman in human history and you married to me. You had to do it with Bessie the fat cleaning woman. You are some kind of pervert, if you ask my jury."

"So she told you, did she?" Jay said. "I'm glad. And maybe you will understand about how it was with the rain falling and me alone there in the house and this woman—*woman*, Monica, *woman*, not girl. Obese, yes. Older, yes. But a *woman*. A *woman*, Monica."

"A fat cleaning woman."

"It was the best and purest moment of my life," Jay said.

"Yeah," Monica said. "I had to give her the rest of the week off. And the worst is not the threat of blackmail, no. The worst is, she was disappointed. She was crushed. A movie buff left dead with no more dreams even from you."

"Muskless person."

"I have more musk in my little finger," Monica said.

"The deposit-bottle boy told me," Jay said.

Monica twitched and quivered.

"What deposit-bottle boy?"

"That deposit-bottle boy. The centerfold from the Scout Handbook. Be prepared. Oh, lordy. It was all over the supermarket."

"I admit it," Monica said. "At least I felt youth and strength surging white heat through my loins."

"Youth and strength? From that senile midget? Youth and strength? They only sent him out after the six-ounce empties, the two-centers."

"He was so grateful. So damned grateful he cried. And you know what? I'm glad they know in the market. I'm glad because as long as that boy goes around on his bike it's like written on a wall you were not man enough to satisfy me. It's a bug on your plate."

"It cost me a hundred dollars to keep him from selling descriptions to the magazines. That fink wrote a piece called 'Acne Valentino.' "

"You stopped him?"

"For you, honey. It was a *knock*."

"Hoooooo."

"He complained you didn't tip him."

"Hoooooo."

Curled around the abbey the creature cuddled its potential goodies. The rump-nip was like an overture to satisfaction. Its gastric mechanism stormed. The creature fed by absorption. It could have absorbed the building, but stone lay lumpy in its gut. It sensed the abbey as a shell with the nourishment deep inside. This kind of feasting came natural to a sea beast. The point was to get the inside out.

The creature, cautious, extended a tentative tentacle through a window. A fuzzy purple snake, it squirmed to the floor and along the ground.

"What's fuzzy purple and squirms along the ground?" Jay said.

"No elephant jokes," Monica said.

She was packed, dressed, coated. She threw a kiss at Jay and went to the door.

"Monica," Jay said.

She opened the door and walked through it squoosh into the creature's underbelly. Monica recoiled into the room. Backward she came and tripped over the fuzzy purple tentacle.

"There's something damn strange going on here," Jay said.

The tentacle was exploring Monica. She watched this happen, then leaped to her feet. She wanted to scream but could not muster sufficient wind.

"It has suction cups," Jay said.

"I deplore suction cups," Monica said in a daze.

Then she let out a bellow that sent vibrations up and down the creature's epiglottis.

"Help, help," Monica shouted.

"I'm here, darling," Jay said.

The creature sent two or three more tentacles into the room. They played tag with Jay and Monica. One of them had an eye at its end, one a lobster claw and one a nostril. All were active.

"Watch out for the squiggly devils," Jay shouted.

"My earring," Monica said.

A deft movement of the second tentacle had snatched an earring off Monica's lobe. It vanished in a bubble of acid. The earring pleased the creature as an oysterette might please a guest at an informal dinner. It wanted more. The tentacle gyrated gluttonously.

"My ear," Monica said.

"Throw it the other earring," Jay said.

Monica hurled the second earring onto the floor. It was caught and consumed.

The tentacle with the eye came over and gawked at Jay. He patted it. It withdrew, blinking.

Jay's hand was covered with goosh.

"It's not plastic," Jay said. "I don't think this is a gag. Monica, this isn't 'Candid Camera.'"

Jay quickly lost his composure.

"Do something," Monica said. "It's trying to eat us."

The pincer lunged at Jay's shoe. It got a lace, no more. The nostril sniffed at Monica's discarded luggage. The eye kept its distance but changed expression. It seemed less passive and more malevolent.

Jay and Monica huddled in the center of the abbey's great hall. Their move was strategic. The creature had limitations and one of them was the length of its tentacles. It could not reach them.

But it also had the capacity to divert growth-energy into any special part, and its growth was consistent and impressive. With solid will power it shifted its biology and the tentacles began to add inches.

Also, to curb its impatience, the creature forced itself as close into the room as was possible. It seeped in bulges through the windows and the open door. A flap of it squeezed through a crack in the wall. An appendage came down the chimney like Santa Claus and blobbed into the fireplace. Its dampness hissed out the flames. The abbey was pitch pitch black except for the tentacle eye, which had a shoddy luminescence.

After a short silence in which Jay and Monica stood smelling the creature's fabulous presence, Jay stroked Monica's hair.

"We are definitely going to be consumed," Jay said. "Unless this is some Oedipal dream."

"Why? Why?" Monica said. "So full of hope. So vibrant and so dynamic. At the beginning of her career."

"*Her* career?"

"Our. Our careers. Don't nitpick. Not now."

"A few minutes ago we hated each other," Jay said.

"E pluribus unum," Monica said. "Qué será será."

"Now we are lovers again. Confessed-out lovers. I feel reborn."

"I too."

"Yet we can't even carve a heart on the floor," Jay said. "We can't even leave a note."

"It sounds hungry," Monica said. "You can sense its ravenous hunger."

The creature's stomachs had begun to rumble.

"It wants food," Monica said. "You could take bets on that."

"Oh, it's a people eater all right."

"One wonders how much food is food for something like that," Monica said.

"Whole cities."

"Not if it were snack hungry. Not if it were hot for a nosh."

"I don't think so."

"Sometimes a potato chip is what a person wants more than a steak."

"Not in this case."

"You don't know."

"Not for certain."

"Then why should we both die if maybe a piece of just one of us would do the whole trick?"

"I get your thinking," Jay said. "It's pretty creative."

"In lifeboats they eat each other rather than all starve. It makes sense, honey."

"I can't let you do it," Jay said.

"Me do what?"

The creature had already added six inches to its tentacles. A foot or so more and it would reach vitamins. It huffed and puffed.

"Who then?" Jay said. "Certainly not me. In lifeboats the decisions are made by last-minute logic. The survivor is the most important, the one who has the most reason to survive."

"So? The cleaning woman is pregnant?"

"Frankly, sweet, I was thinking along artistic lines."

"Artistic lines?"

The house shook as a flutter ran through the creature. It was a flutter of confusion, the confusion of appetites again. Now that its eye and nostril were nearer to Monica it experienced an unexpected urge to replace the pincer tentacle with more refined anatomy. It felt a surge of love.

Jay and Monica noticed the flutter and instantly understood from their own personal experiences.

"It's a female," Jay said.

"Not in a million Sundays," Monica said.

"So what's the difference? Those things carry you into the sea to a fate worse than death."

"It's better than being swallowed."

"You would think so."

Monica was already smiling in the dark. The eye turned away. The nostril tentacle advanced and Monica kissed it.

"Stop that," Jay said. "Don't act like a whore."

Jay pulled Monica back and the pincer took a crack at him.

"It's me," Monica said. "I knew it."

Jay acknowledged the attraction. He felt a surge of jealousy and envy. So did the creature, which squeezed harder at its growth cells. It had determined to eat Jay and spare Monica so that it could carry her into caverns of green to a fate worse than death.

"That's no kind of relationship," Jay was saying.

Monica wet her lips for good luck. The pincer was now a fraction of distance from Jay.

"Goodbye, dearest," Monica said.

"Seriously, what did you think of my job in the film?" Jay said.

Monica chose the course of honesty and said nothing.

Jay bit the creature. He was hysterical with rejection. He took a chunk out of the nearest tentacle.

"Like sardines," he said.

The creature took a piece of Jay's index finger. Simultaneously, it got sick.

"Everybody is a critic," Monica said.

"What's with this cruddy beast?" Jay said, licking his fingertip.

Monica hardly noticed that the nostril tentacle was wrapped around her lovely waist. She only saw the creature withdrawing from Jay and could detect that it turned a wee bit greener by the luminous eye.

"It doesn't like the taste of you," she said.

"Come back here," Jay yelled, and took another bite.

The creature was completely intimidated. The fingertip caused chronic indigestion. It wanted to get back to the cool ocean.

"The hell with you," Jay screamed.

"T.S.," Monica said, being drawn by the tentacle. The creature felt icky but still very horny.

"The best to you," Jay said. "I hope you'll be very happy together. You deserve each other."

"We have similar tastes," Monica said. Then she realized that she was in deep trouble. Flattering as it was, she did not want to go into an unknown world, especially one without mass media. And she could not even trust that Jay would tell the story without distortion.

The creature pulled Monica up and through a window. It carried her like a suitcase as it scuttled toward the water. Jay ran after it, taking nips.

"Get me down," Monica said. "Please, Jay. We work well together."

The creature hesitated. A prehistoric memory waved curtains in its brain once more. It recalled being caught by its mate in the company of a German lady way way back. The memory was unpleasant, full of flailing. It loosened its hold on Monica, but not entirely.

"It's feeling guilty," Monica said with perfect intuition. "It's letting me go."

"Talk about summer romances," Jay said. "Wait when Variety gets this poop."

"You wouldn't. Not even you would."

"Hi, there," Jay said.

"Take me," Monica was screaming. The creature was trying to shake her loose, but she held on with long fingers.

"Oh, look there," Jay said.

Harriet Troom, camera ready, came rushing down to the beach in Harold Bipley's Rolls.

"It wouldn't eat him," Monica was saying.

"It wouldn't have relations with her," Jay was yelling.

Harriet Troom, clicking flash pictures with her non-driving hand, pulled the Rolls as close as she could. The creature, terrified, was half in the sea, still whirling Monica around like a propeller. The car with its lantern headlights and the popping flash and the white-lit face of Harriet Troom grinning widely under glass was too much for it. It resorted to a kind of flying apart which creatures of its type could manage. It turned itself into a broken jigsaw of parts, then fused together.

In the splash and roar, Monica was dislodged. Harriet Troom, driving too close, got incorporated. The lights of the Rolls and the popping flash could be seen through the creature's crinkly hide as it vanished under the waves.

Jay and Monica stood on the shore. Neither spoke. Both were committed to eternal secrecy by events that interacted like penalties which nullify one another in football games. They waited there until high tide rinsed the sand and washed away the tire tracks and creature marks.

Back in the abbey they gathered their belongings.

"We shouldn't leave until morning," Monica said.

"No," Jay said. "And we have hours before dawn sheds its rosy glow on all concerned."

"I have a pencil," Monica said.

With Monica's eyebrow pencil, by the light of some stars, they wrote Harriet Troom's next column. They could keep filing columns until she was missed or something came up on a beach somewhere.

Later they crawled into Jay's sleeping bag.

Up a way, the guards were fast asleep.

Back in the studio, Harold Bipley dictated a press release into a tape recorder. It told how Jason Briar and Monica Ploy were purged and purified through their ordeal of isolation and seclusion.

"Like an atomic-age Adam and Eve," he said to the microphone, "two million-dollar talents came back to the world today with new maturity and a solid sense of direction." Then he said, "Hold for release." Then he thought soft thoughts about his two favorites and how things were going for them out there. Spiritually, he was right with them in the bag.

A MUSICAL EDUCATION

HARRY CRAFT'S MUSICAL CAREER BEGAN WHEN A MAN FROM THE Witzheimer School came to visit his parents. Harry was nine, a bright boy. His mother and father resolved to give him every advantage.

The visit of the man from Witzheimer came at approximately the same time that Japanese pilots were rehearsing the bombing of Pearl Harbor. When he came, Harry Craft was busy playing with lead soldiers in his room. Drums from the future war had already reached his ears. He was obsessed with his tiny army.

The man from the Witzheimer School, a good strategist in his own right, came with a plan. The plan allowed for the purchase of a musical instrument and a beginner course of lessons, all on installments. It was a plan which had been accepted by three of Harry Craft's cousins. Over the river, in Brooklyn, Cousin Irwin was blowing notes on a trumpet. North, in the Bronx, Cousin Marvin was squeezing an accordion. Through the long tunnel, in Queens, Cousin Sharon could manage a spirited "Humoresque" on a violin.

While he played in his room, Harry Craft's parents accepted the plan for their son. Harry's father shook hands with the representative of culture. Harry's mother was so excited her cheeks glowed. Harry was called into the living room.

"Harry, you are going to play a musical instrument," his father said.

"It's a wonderful opportunity," said the man from Witzheimer. "You are a very lucky young man."

"Are you excited?" said Mrs. Craft.

Yes, Harry was. It seemed like a good idea for him to learn an instrument. But which instrument?

"What instrument?" Harry said.

"The instrument of your choice," said Harry's father.

Harry was surprised. He had expected to be assigned to an instrument. Instead he was being allowed the dignity of decision. His parents were pleased about this. It was important for them not to force.

"What instrument do you like best?" said the Witzheimer man.

There was a deep silence in the room. Harry felt frightened without knowing exactly why.

"Tell us," his father said, "of all the instruments, what is the one instrument you like best?"

Harry thought of all the instruments. He did not know too many. Or, if he did, he could not think of them on the spur of the moment. But there was the empty space in the room again.

"The guitar," he said.

"The guitar?" his mother said. "Are you sure?"

"Yes."

"Not the piano, accordion, trumpet, violin . . . ?"

"The guitar."

"Not unusual," said the man from Witzheimer. "The guitar is a fine choice."

"Are you sure, Harry?" said his mother.

"Yes," Harry said.

"Let it be," said Mr. Craft. "I never expected that to come out of him."

"You never know with children," said the Witzheimer man. "The fact is we have an excellent course in the guitar. It's a wonderful instrument. I sell hundreds."

"Hundreds?" said Harry's father. "Hundreds of guitars?"

"Can I play it?" Harry said.

"Sure," his father said. "If it's what you want."

Arrangements were completed and the man from Witzheimer went away. Harry Craft went back to his game of soldiers. His parents laughed in the living room. Harry heard his father say, "Our kid has his own mind."

That night in bed Harry Craft thought about the guitar. If his parents were surprised that he had selected it to be his own instrument, he was more surprised. He had never really thought of the guitar before. He had seen guitars in Western movies and he had heard them twanging on the radio. Now, in the dark, he tried to remember their sound. He couldn't.

He could remember Gene Autry and Roy Rogers playing them, singing alone to the desert or to a girl on the steps of a box-shaped house made out of white mud with poles sticking from the roof. Harry disliked these scenes when action was frozen for romance. Yet he himself had chosen the guitar. He wondered why. Now his musical destiny was determined. It happened so quickly.

Snuggling the pillow, Harry thought about music. He had watched music being made at his aunt's summer hotel. The band there was a piano, a saxophone, a trumpet and a drum. Why had he chosen none of those instruments? Or the instruments he knew from the band that paraded every Sunday when Holy Redeemer Church marched its might around the block? No, he had picked the guitar, an instrument of the celluloid prairie, a lonely creature of moon and sand.

Things considered, the guitar was not a bad choice. The drum was not music but boom boom boom. The saxophone looked like a hunchback and sounded too bloo bloo bloo. The trumpet was loud, blah blah blah. Harry had hated the accordion since he saw a child star named Sunshine Unger play one during a benefit for Palestine. While she played she bent over backward and picked up a handkerchief with her teeth. The piano was too much to do and the violin was for girls.

In and out of sleep's mouth, Harry thought next about the record player in the hall closet. This machine, an Aeolian Vocalian, had been broken before he was born. The metal arm with the needle was snapped off its mounting. There was one record in the cabinet, a homemade record of "April Showers" sung by a family friend named Louie at a party. Harry's parents talked about the night Louie made his famous record and about having the Aeolian Vocalian fixed. Once Harry wound the machine and held the needle over the record, but all he could get was a ghostly urrr urrr.

A week later a guitar was delivered to the Craft apartment. One day earlier a letter had arrived from the Witzheimer School containing a carbon copy of the contract Harry's father had signed, a book of twenty-five tickets, each good for a lesson, and a certificate for Harry showing that he was officially enrolled.

The guitar was in a black cardboard case with bumps to simulate leather. The case was lined with fuzzy purple cloth. And there, inside, lay the guitar. It was a small guitar suited to Harry's size. It was made of brown polished wood for the body, a black stem and tuning handles, six strings running from the base of the stem to a chromium mount, and had a metal plate near the top that said Radiola.

Harry was given the guitar when he returned home from school. He knew it was coming, especially after the certificate, but not so soon. He carried the case to his room. His mother said, "You should see yourself carrying that," so Harry looked in the bathroom mirror.

He thought he looked good carrying his guitar.

In his room, Harry took the guitar out of its case and tested it. The silver strings made plinky music, the brown heavy strings made deep hums. He discovered that if he tapped the wood of the body it sounded like a drum. If he hit his nails on a certain place where the strings ended, then the sound was Chinese. When his father came home, Harry learned that if one hand plunked the strings while the other moved up and down the stem the guitar made up and down sounds like Hawaiian movies. There was a lot to learn about the guitar.

Harry was told that his lessons were scheduled to start on Saturday morning. He accepted this willingly. Everything was falling into place—the visit of the man from Witzheimer, the book of tickets, the certificate, the instrument itself and now the lessons.

Afer supper Harry went to his room to do homework. The guitar was there in its case. Somehow its presence changed the entire household. Between history and arithmetic Harry picked up the guitar and strummed its strings. When he looked up he saw his mother and father standing at the door of his room smiling.

Between Tuesday and Saturday the guitar absorbed into Harry's life. At first he was startled to see it still in his room. After a while his encounters with it became more routine. Twice he dreamed about the guitar being a mummy buried alive. Once he got out of bed and opened the case to look.

As the week went on Harry saw his parents grow more and more involved in the prospect of his music lessons. Harry heard conversations that displayed their great pleasure in the whole affair.

"It's a marvelous instrument."

"Will he be able to enjoy it when he gets older? That's when he'll thank us."

"He can't keep his hands off it. I'm amazed. I thought it would be like pulling teeth."

One evening Harry's Aunt Minette came for dinner. She was shown the new guitar.

"You never should have let him have it," she said. "You should have insisted on a more practical instrument."

Harry winced when she said it. He suspected that she was right. For though he toyed with the instrument nearly every night, he and the guitar were not yet friends. Having the guitar was like having a pet you do not love and who does not love you. Neither friends nor enemies. The guitar was there, that's all.

"You don't shove music down a boy's throat," said Mr. Craft.

"What does he know yet?"

"He knows what he wants. He knows what he likes."

"Harry has always wanted to play the guitar," his mother said.

Harry, sitting there while they talked about him as if he were made of stone, sensed his parents' deep conviction. They seemed to insist that he and his guitar were fused together.

When his aunt went home Harry walked around the apartment banging the guitar's strings and singing anything that came into his head. His mother beamed. His father carried him to bed, guitar and all.

Later in the night Harry was awakened by his father again. This time Mr. Craft was tucking him in. He felt the blankets being pulled around him. It was very late. The house was completely quiet. His father went to his own bedroom. Harry heard him clumping in slippers. Then his mother spoke. Harry was sure she was speaking about what his aunt had said. He heard his father laugh.

Saturday was a bright September day. It was still warm in the city, Indian summer. Harry Craft rode uptown on the subway with his mother beside him. He wore a new outfit—a brown sports jacket, brown pants, a white shirt and red tie, brown shoes and socks. His mother combed his hair while the train rushed them to Fifty-seventh Street where the Witzheimer School was located. Harry carried his guitar. He noticed people looking at him, wondering if he could ride a horse and rope a steer, if he was a ranch-bred boy just visiting the city on vacation.

When Harry and his mother reached the Witzheimer School, Harry saw that Witzheimer was a store. He had imagined something much different, but he could not recall exactly what. In any case, Witzheimer had a store downstairs that sold musical instruments. Its wide windows were filled with every kind of playable device, from little drums to great, glossy pianos.

Inside, the store stretched endlessly. Counter after counter displayed the tools of music. There were more instruments, books, song sheets, music boxes, recordings. Harry had not realized that music involved so much.

He went with his mother to the Information Desk.

"Harry Craft," his mother said to the clerk. "He has a lesson at ten. His first."

"Craft, Harry. Beginner guitar. Here it is," the clerk said, pulling a three-by-five card out of a green metal box. "Señor Erranda, Room 304. The elevator is at the rear to the right."

On the way to the elevator, Harry wondered what would have happened if there was no record of him or his lesson. He, his mother and the guitar would have turned away.

Riding up, Harry noticed that the Witzheimer School had a certain smell to it. The smell was like the smell of pianos, a shellac smell. He sneezed twice and blew his nose into a clean handkerchief.

On the third floor, Harry and his mother were told to take chairs in the waiting room. It was not yet lesson time. The practice was for teachers to greet their students at the reception area. They sat. Harry heard musical sounds coming from rooms along the hall. Across from him sat a teen-age girl holding a flute. Harry's mother smoothed her hand over his hair. He pushed the hand away.

At ten o'clock a small brownish man came to fetch Harry. He was smiling and bowed slightly to Mrs. Craft. While he spoke, Harry noticed how amazingly skinny he was.

"I am Erranda," he said. "It will be my pleasure to teach your son."

"How do you do," said Mrs. Craft. "Harry . . ."

"Hello," Harry said.

"Let us shake hands," said Señor Erranda.

Harry shook a hand the color of a shopping bag and just as weightless.

"Do you have the card and book?"

"Yes. I'm sorry."

Harry's mother gave Señor Erranda the three-by-five card and the book of tickets which had come in the mail.

"Thank you. I keep the card and ticket number one."

Señor Erranda tore ticket number one from the book and handed it back.

"Now, Mr. Harry," he said, "take your guitar and come with me to my studio."

Harry took the guitar and stood up.

"Pay attention," his mother said. The flute girl was staring at Harry's guitar case.

Harry followed Señor Erranda. Once he looked back. His mother was watching him go.

Señor Erranda's studio was far from the waiting area. Finding the room was not easy. The route required four turns: two lefts, two rights.

While Harry walked this maze, lugging his instrument, he passed through fragments of broken music: scales, bits and pieces of songs, just noises. There were voices too, some angry.

The walk was demoralizing. Harry wondered, trotting after Señor Erranda, if this time would be deducted from his hour. Then there was the getting back. He looked for signs which would help him find his way. Suppose Señor Erranda did not plan to deliver him?

Finally there was a diagonal corridor which split off the main hall. Down that corridor, past a door marked MEN and another marked EXIT, there was a door with a nameplate: J. ERRANDA.

Señor Erranda dug into his pocket. He came out with a key, the kind of key they used on doors in the country. The key was tied to a cardboard circle with the initials J.E. in thick brush letters. The key opened Señor Erranda's studio and in went Harry and his teacher.

Harry examined the scene of his musical initiation. A ceiling light covered by a pot-shaped globe hung down into the room's center. The room itself was tiny. There were two chairs side by side. Between them a music stand of black metal stood waiting. There was a cabinet against the far wall, but it seemed empty. An adjoining space of wall was broken by a half-sized window with the glass painted over in yellow ivory, the color of the place.

The most impressive piece of furniture was a massive guitar sitting propped on one of the chairs. It was a marvelous thing, twice the size of Harry's own, huge and curvy, polished so bright the light bounced off it in splinters. Its stem and tuning pins were pure white and in the section below the hole rhinestone initials blazed J.E. Señor Erranda picked it up in one hand.

"This is Señorita Eleanor," he said. "Miss Eleanor, meet Mr. Harry."

Harry laughed. Señor Erranda did not.

"It is named for my sister Eleanor, now dead, rest her soul in eternal paradise. Now, kid, tell me what you know about music, what you feel about music. Why are you here in this room today?"

Harry had nothing to say. He knew nothing about music beyond what it was. He had no special feelings one way or the other. He was still not sure he was in the room today, much less why. Señor Erranda accepted his silence with a shrug.

"No tongue?" he said. "Let it alone, then. But hurry up and take out the instrument. Give her some air. Let her breathe. Sit down."

Harry took out his guitar. It seemed to have shrunk.

"Do you know the strings are made to play?"

"Yes."

"Ah, yes. Good. Play."

"What?"

"Just play."

Harry hit the strings. The six metal threads vibrated feebly.

"Stop."

Harry stopped.

"Do you want hands or bloody pulps?"

"Hands."

"Hands. All right. The pick."

Bending into his guitar case, Señor Erranda emerged holding two shapes. They were paper thin and pointed, like elf ear lobes. He gave one to Harry.

"Tortoise," he said. "Watch."

Señor Erranda held the pick between two fingers so that it disappeared except for the point. This he ran over the strings of his own guitar. The result was a terrific sound. Harry jumped.

"Now you."

Harry took his pick and stroked the strings of his Radiola. Its music was thin soup by comparison but better than the response to his fingertips.

"Look there," said Señor Erranda.

"Where?"

"Up there. *There.*"

He pointed to the wall they faced. On the wall was a picture no bigger than a playing card, framed and under glass.

"Go closer."

Harry got up and went closer. He put his face to the picture. It showed four people, one of whom was Señor Erranda. All stood in a crescent facing a microphone that said WJZ. Two of the picture people were girls in long gowns. They leaned forward toward the microphone, mouths open, full of song. The two men wore frilly shirts and tight black pants. One carried a pair of maracas. Señor Erranda, who looked even thinner next to other human beings, held his guitar. His skin glistened like the wood of his instrument.

"That, Mr. Harry, is from the network radio."

"Oh."

"Oh. Oh. That is where I played. That is where I belong. That is where I will play again when this stinking depression is finished. Coast to coast, Mr. Harry. Do you know what they pay for coast to coast?"

Then, without warning, Señor Erranda began to play. He closed his eyes and hit the huge guitar. Harry immediately knew two things. First, he knew why Señor Erranda's studio was at the end of a special hall. Nearer to the rest of things his music would shake the whole school. Second, Harry knew that something was wrong. Señor Erranda was playing Spanishy music, rumba music, music from movies where girls wore fruit on their heads. Harry's heart sank. He knew this music from his aunt's hotel and he hated it, every note. Señor Erranda's hands leaped over the guitar. His fingers bent, spread, pressed, withdrew, beat the wood. He wrestled the instrument as if it were a captive cat. He played furiously. Harry thought of arithmetic—when the teacher hurled numbers at the class and then called on somebody to give a quick total. The music flew at him.

Harry could not decide to sit or remain standing. Señor Erranda gave no direction. He was in another world. He grinned to himself. His lips moved, but only air came out. There was sweat over his top lip and a rivulet on his cheek.

Harry sat. Señor Erranda continued to play. He was making romantic sounds, slow twangs, quick twangs, hard twangs, tap taps on the wood. His foot kept time.

No question about it, it was the music of Harry's aunt's hotel. Harry could practically see his Uncle Abe wiggling across the casino floor, twirling a woman whose husband was working in the hot city. This music had nothing to do with howling coyotes or dust storms. It had nothing to do with Harry Craft.

Señor Erranda was in a big sweat now. Harry saw that he had a very little head. His head was an in-between size, like a baby beach ball. His feet were imp feet. He was like a skeleton all over. One blue vein jiggled in his forehead while he played. Harry waited.

After a few more minutes Señor Erranda began a clucking sound with his mouth. The teacher took a deep breath and the playing ended.

"How's that?" he said.

"Nice."

"Nice. Nice coast to coast. Nice."

Harry squirmed in his chair.

"Stop fidgeting. Let's get going. Time flies away."

Señor Erranda pulled a book out of his guitar case.

"Your mother must buy this book for you. *Nick Armada Guides You.*"

He gave Harry the book. On the cover was a man in a tuxedo holding a guitar even bigger than Señor Erranda's and plugged into an electric socket.

"I write down the name. Flip the pages."

Harry flipped through the pages.

"You will play all that before they can say Jack Robinson. Today is only the first time. We go slowly."

Señor Erranda explained notes.

"E-G-B-D-F. Every Good Boy Does Fine. F-A-C-E. Face, like your kisser, eh?"

Harry got a pat on the cheek.

"Easy to remember? Every Good Boy Does Fine. Face. Good?"

"I think so."

"Our time is up. Next week we go deeper and deeper. Practice, practice, practice. We got about three minutes," said Señor Erranda. "I play for you."

"But . . . ?"

"Oh, yes. The gold stars."

From his guitar case Señor Erranda produced a booklet and a box. He gave Harry the booklet. On the cover was a picture of a boy and a girl about his own age and the words MERIT AWARD. MY BOOK. Inside, the pages were broken into squares by thick lines. Each square was numbered. Señor Erranda took a gold star with a glued back from the box. He wet it with his tongue, then slapped it into square number one.

"Congratulations on the first star," he said. "When you do your homework you get each week a star. Fill the book and you get the Merit Award. Where it says 'My Book' you write in your own name. Get the idea?"

"Thanks," Harry said, accepting the booklet. The square with the first star was wet from too much spit.

"I keep the stars, eh?" Señor Erranda said. "Like God."

He put the box of stars back in his case.

"Now some music to see what you will do with practice, practice, practice."

Harry swallowed. The music came at him again, loading the room. Señor Erranda's fingers were so skinny to produce so much music. Harry wondered what his arm was like under the jacket sleeve. Probably a naked bone. This was a happier song than the last. Señor Erranda sang to himself in a mixture of English and Spanish. He made several moaning sounds and the same clucking noise as before. By the time his hour was over, Harry had a headache and his stomach hurt.

Harry packed up his guitar and put the pick, which was Señor Erranda's gift, into his shirt pocket. He took the star booklet too. Señor Erranda led him back through the hall. Harry's mother stood up when she saw them.

"You have a fine boy," said Señor Erranda. "He earned his first gold star today. He will do fine with practice, practice. Every good boy does fine, eh? I must ask you to buy him a special book. They sell it downstairs."

"Thank you very much," said Harry's mother.

"My great pleasure. See you next week, God willing."

Harry felt dizzy on the elevator. He waited downstairs while his mother bought the book.

For reward, Harry's mother took him to Nedick's. He had a frank and an orange drink. Then they rode home. The subway downtown was crowded. Harry and his mother stood all the way to Fourteenth Street. With the chewed frank and sweet orange drink inside him, Harry felt much better. But the shock of the lesson was still with him. Once, when the train waited between stations, its motor made a whining sound and Harry imagined a weightless hand strumming the tracks.

At Fourteenth Street the crosstown bus was even more crowded. Harry had to stand his guitar up and down. People kept bumping the case. It was like having a young brother leaning against him.

Harry wanted to tell his mother about the kind of music they were teaching him. He wanted to tell her about the picture of Señor Erranda on the radio. He wanted to tell her he had done nothing in the lesson but listen to himself playing from the future and how he had not earned the wet gold star. He wanted to tell her and he didn't want to tell her. In any case, he didn't tell her.

At home, as Harry expected, his mother had him display the star to his father. Harry noticed that Señor Erranda's saliva had dried and except that the star was not centered in its square, it looked nice on the page. Harry's father said nothing in particular, but he was pleased.

Harry took the guitar to his room and put it on the bed. He got out his soldiers, divided them into two armies, assigned an army to his left hand and his right, and let them make war.

At the end of that Saturday, when his father brought home Sunday's papers, Harry took the comic section. He lay down in the living room, stretched on the rug, and began to read them back to front. The best comics came in the first pages. Harry saved them for last.

"A little practice?" his mother said.

Harry looked up from the funnies.

"Did you know that 'Home on the Range' is President Roosevelt's favorite song?" his father said.

Harry got up, found the Nick Armada book, and plopped down again.

"He was assigned the book," his mother said.

"Fine," said his father.

Harry went through the book page by page. On its cover was the picture of Nick Armada in his strange suit. This was no cowboy. Harry did not like his face. He looked nauseous. Harry traced the cord from Nick Armada's plug-in guitar. It ran across his leg, down to the floor and into a wall socket. Harry wondered if the guitar lit up.

The rest of the book had few pictures. There were some of Nick Armada's hands, showing finger positions, and some text on how to make the various notes happen. The rest of the book was made up of things to play. The easy songs were first. "Twinkle, Twinkle," "Little Bo-Peep," baby songs. Then the songs got more complicated. The first pages were filled with simple-looking balloon heads on separate sticks. Later, the fat black heads came in crowds, then bigger crowds. Finally, the pages were jammed with dots, lines, dots pierced by lines, dots with flags, bridges, curves— the last pages looked hopelessly complicated. These pages were the sounds that Señor Erranda had made, thick, big, vibrating jumbles. Harry could hear them just by looking.

Harry wondered, as he had at the start of every school term, if he would ever absorb so much knowledge. He went back to the beginning of the book. The early pages seemed so comfortable. E-G-B-D-F. F-A-C-E.

His father was reading the news section of the paper. His mother was sewing a shirt. He held the book for a few minutes more, then put it down and took the comics to his bedroom.

"Practice makes perfect," his mother said when she tucked him in. Harry wiggled under the cover.

"Sweet dreams," his mother said, bending to turn off the lamp.
"You too, Ma."

The last thing Harry saw as the light died was his guitar case
leaning against a wall. In the flash between light and dark he
wished he could get up and break the guitar into garbage. He
wanted to jump up and down on the shiny wood, rip the strings
and tear off the chrome plate. He fancied the guitar's protest in
clucking moans.

"Good night, little musician," his father said from the living
room.

During the next week Harry Craft spent many hours with Nick
Armada's guide. He did not know exactly what to do with the
book, but he held it, thumbed it, concentrated on the first pages,
even picked some notes out on the guitar.

"I had my doubts," he heard his mother say on the telephone,
"about Harry's concentration, but no more. He takes to it like a
duck to the water."

From time to time Harry thought about complaining. He
wanted to complain. Complain about what? The Witzheimer
School taught thousands of guitarists every year. Señor Erranda
always had another student before and after Harry. Besides, he
had sent his music from the Atlantic to the Pacific on network
radio and would again. Complain about what? If this was the way
to President Roosevelt's favorite song, this was the way. Complain to who? Harry's parents were very satisfied. The Witzheimer
School was blameless. Harry himself recognized a growing hunger
for more gold stars, a whole bookful. He had chosen the guitar
by his own declaration, in front of three witnesses. If the guitar
now demanded a certain obedience, it seemed fair. Complain
about what, to who?

Harry complained, mildly, to the guitar. When he held it, he
held it too hard. He hit the strings instead of stroking them. He
tapped the wood with his nails. But Harry was not too rough on

the instrument. The very newness of it was inviolate. It could not be hurt. It would not be maimed. The wood, chrome and steel glistened. Even the case was tough. And Harry did not want it to be blemished.

Because they were late, Harry and his mother took a taxi to the Witzheimer School for his second lesson. His mother was anxious on the trip. She did not want to offend Señor Erranda.

"You tell him we were delayed by an emergency," she said. Harry suspected that she was afraid of the teacher.

When the cab pulled up in front of the school Harry was also afraid. Five minutes of his hour were gone. His mother got tangled in her purse and it was another five minutes before they were riding the elevator up.

Señor Erranda came quickly to the waiting area.

"Señor Erranda, please excuse our lateness," said Mrs. Craft. "I received an important call just as we were leaving the house. You know how that always happens. And the traffic was terrible."

"Of course," the teacher said. "No matter."

"We like to come on time."

"I fully understand."

Following Señor Erranda down the corridor, Harry knew he did not really understand. If he did, he was not ready to forgive. Harry could tell this by his walk. His tiny feet went too fast. Inside the studio he said, "You have lost twelve minutes. These minutes are lost forever. Do not think I will make them up to you. After lessons I rest for ten minutes before the next pupil. He is an excellent student. I must have those minutes for my fingers to come back to give him my best. Sit down. Take out the guitar. What is her name?"

"Her name?"

"What name did you give the instrument?"

"You didn't tell me to give it a name."

"Tell you? I didn't tell you? You are a funny kid."

Señor Erranda made a fist with one hand and punched it into the palm of the other.

"The first thing I did with my first guitar was to give her a name. The first thing. And it was no guitar like yours. It was a piece of junk. But the first thing I did was to name her. I even baptized her. With water from the sink. What is the name of your mother?"

"Mrs. Irene Craft."

"Irene. Let it be. To you kids today everything comes easy like ice cream. Sit straight. Look proud. Did you practice?"

"I looked at the book."

"That's what you did?"

"E-G-B-D-F. F-A-C-E. That's what you gave me."

"Gave you? Nothing but what I gave you?"

"No."

"Someday I will tell you about my first night with the guitar. My first night."

Harry felt a flush of guilt. He was late by twelve minutes. He had not named his guitar after his mother or anybody else. No magic happened on his first night alone with his guitar.

Señor Erranda was stroking the long curves of his own instrument.

"We've got to get moving," he said. "All talk and no work."

Then Señor Erranda played for four minutes. Harry's stomach tightened and his eyes burned. He wanted to cry.

His teacher came up from the barrage of music like a swimmer popping out of a pool. He stopped in the middle of a note.

"This damn lousy city makes my joints stiff. And all winter is still left. Shit, kid, in South America it is now spring. Do they teach you that?"

Señor Erranda took Harry's hands in his own. He turned them palms up, then over. He bent the fingers.

"Playing with little fat hands is like walking on little fat legs. Oh my God."

Harry wished that the weekend were over and that he was back in regular school. He thought of school, where he was doing very well. Everybody liked him in school. Harry looked up at the painted window.

"But we make the best with what we have," said Señor Erranda, breathing through his mouth.

They worked on scales. Señor Erranda explained finger positions. He moved Harry's fingers around to where they belonged, manipulating them like pipe cleaners. He showed Harry proper posture in the chair and the pages in the Nick Armada book that would be his homework.

"Behind," Señor Erranda said. "You are falling behind. It is absolutely necessary that you devote yourself. And thin down your digits, kid. Make them into spider legs."

Señor Erranda made a spider out of one of his hands and walked it around his guitar. He played the first song in the book slowly, picking out the tune note by note, sniffing it. Then he took the simple song and blew it up into a massive balloon. He improvised. He stood and went swaying around the studio. His eyes snapped shut as they did when his hands went to work. The ceiling light reflected sharply against the rhinestone initials of the grand guitar. Even Señor Erranda was bathed in light. It glowed in his hair, from his face, the silky material of his suit, from his black, shined shoes without laces. He banged the guitar twice and halted his recital.

"No golden star today, kid."

He said it while his last note vibrated and evaporated, a bubble of sound. Water gushed in Harry's eyes.

"Twelve minutes late, a slow learner, no, no star."

"I did my lesson," Harry said. His voice sounded wet. Señor Erranda looked down at him as if he were a dwarf.

"Hoo, oh, ah, this Mr. Harry likes stars. He wants more stars." Floom. He struck a chord.

"Why not," Señor Erranda said. "Stars are nice, beautiful nice stars. All right. I have a heart in my chest. I will give you a star for your book. But I do it against my judgment."

Harry did not want to give him the Merit Award booklet, but he did. Señor Erranda wet a star and shoved it onto the page. It landed far off the center of its square, and like the first, it was soaking.

"Time is up. Can you find your way back? Or must I take you?"

"I know the way."

Harry went, carrying his instrument. When he was past the first turn in the hall he stopped, put down the guitar and took out the booklet. He tried to move the second star closer to the middle of the proper square. One point had already dried. It began to rip. He left the star alone.

At dinner Harry told his mother that he named his guitar Irene. She kissed him on the cheek. His father came into his room later, where Harry was playing with his soldiers, and gave him a dollar bill which Harry folded and dropped into his bank.

Two things happened in the week between Harry's second and third lessons. First, his teacher in public school asked all children who played musical instruments to bring them to class "except for those who play the piano."

The next morning a host of instruments appeared and among them was Harry's guitar. Harry was not sure why he'd brought it. He wasn't required to, he couldn't play anything yet, not even the first song. When each student played something Harry stood in his turn and told his classmates and Miss Steengraf that he was only as far as two lessons.

"Well, in no time you'll be playing and singing like a little bird," Miss Steengraf said and began to applaud. The class applauded with her. Harry burned.

The second thing that happened was more private. It happened at home.

On Sunday night Harry's mother reminded him to practice.

Harry went to get the guitar. He found his lesson book, took the pick and hit the strings. He just hit the strings with one hand while the other hand wandered over the guitar's stem. He played nothing, just noise. His parents were drinking coffee in the kitchen. They could hear him but nothing was said.

Harry wondered why his parents were being so indulgent. They trusted him. "You're not the kind of kid who needs somebody looking over his shoulder," his father said.

On Monday night Harry repeated his concert of nothing. And nothing was said against him. He did this again on Tuesday, on Wednesday and Thursday. He just hit the notes harder and louder for exactly an hour each night.

On Friday he practiced seriously. This was because he remembered Saturday. He played the lesson Señor Erranda had marked. He bent and unbent his fingers. It was too late. The week was done. Harry felt sick. He knew there would be no star. He knew there should be no star because he was a cheater. What did his parents know about music? Señor Erranda would know, would smell the wasted hours, would punish him and expose him.

On Saturday morning Harry got his third star.

Harry and his mother went early to Witzheimer. Señor Erranda met them at ten. He walked slowly with Harry to the studio. In the studio they got right down to business.

"Play for me, sonny."

Harry played lesson number one. Everything went wrong. He played it again, worse than before. Harry turned red. He waited for lightning. He got a pat on the cheek. He also got a star five minutes after the lesson began. Señor Erranda pasted it in the exact center of its square.

"Look, Mr. Harry," Señor Erranda said. "I am not well today. I feel bad. I am tired and constipated. My own kid your age has the mumps. He kept me up all night. I am dead tired and sick myself. You understand?"

Harry nodded.

"I got to get some rest. You play a little. I'll listen. Between you and me we have an understanding today. Right, kid?"

"Yes."

"Very good. Now go and play. I will sit here listening with my eyes closed."

Harry repeated his tune. When he finished Señor Erranda was sleeping. He kept playing until his hand hurt. Señor Erranda was snoring. Harry put down his guitar and looked in the star booklet. With three stars his collection was growing impressive.

When Señor Erranda woke, Harry was examining the radio picture.

"What time is it? My God."

The lesson was over.

"Sonny," Señor Erranda said as Harry opened the studio door, "between us, here is a special star." He gave Harry a fourth star. In the hall, Harry pasted it into the booklet. Four stars in three weeks. Harry wondered how he could explain that. He pasted the star perfectly in place. While he was doing this Señor Erranda came after him.

"Go on to the next song," he said. "Read it in the book. My wife was sick all night. You know how it is?"

"Yes," Harry said.

"Good kid. Nice work."

Then Señor Erranda went back inside his studio and Harry went to his mother.

Harry was not asked about his gold star collection so he did not mention his bonanza. He looked at his stars many times during the week.

Each time he looked he felt good. As in the week before, Harry practiced nothings. The first night he tried using the Nick Armada book. But he went back to playing nothings, a long line of random sounds. Harry did this for precisely one hour each night. He timed himself with a Big Ben alarm. He stayed in his room for one hour and pulled on the strings.

This time even Friday was no different. And when he went to bed on Friday night he was eager for the time of his lesson to come. He thought about Señor Erranda sleeping someplace or playing his big guitar while his wife and child watched. Harry imagined the child as a doll with lips as thin as scissor blades and a body like a pencil. Harry was impatient to see Señor Erranda. He wanted to fall asleep quickly so that he could wake into Saturday.

The next morning it was easy to see that Señor Erranda was back to himself. The teacher walked crisply along the hallway. Following, Harry turned to wave at his mother. She waved back. Señor Erranda was five steps ahead of him. Harry ran to catch up.

When Señor Erranda sat him down and said, "Mr. Harry, what did you learn this week?" Harry laughed.

Señor Erranda laughed too.

"Good," he said. "What I guessed. Lazy fat fingers, you want candy?"

"Yes."

Señor Erranda took a pound box of chocolates from inside his guitar case. There were some candies missing from the box, but most were still there. Harry looked for a nut.

"More?"

"Yes."

Harry looked next for a cream. He chose something chewy instead.

"You feel good today, kid. I can tell. You like this Witzheimer School, don't you? You like your teacher here?"

"Yes, I like it here," Harry said.

"We have a system. Every fourth week is the time for a progress report to the mother. You see? Today our lesson will last fifty minutes. The last ten minutes is for this progress report."

"All right," Harry said. "My mother is here."

"I know that," Señor Erranda said. "Didn't I just see her?"

They both laughed again.

"Now we will make some progress for the report. We will play together, a duet. Turn your book to page nine. Get ready for action, kid."

Harry fixed the guitar on his lap and set his fingers for the first note.

"Now, one and two and . . ."

Harry hit the strings. He tried to move his fingers to the right places, but mostly he just hit the strings as he did at home. Señor Erranda played the tune, hummed it, boomed it into the room.

Later, Harry had another candy. Señor Erranda turned the book to another page. He played alone while he explained the new lesson.

Harry listened and tried to follow him. He listened but not too hard. He had noticed a crack in the ceiling leading from the light all the way down the far wall. They played together once more.

When fifty minutes were used, Señor Erranda told Harry to put away his guitar.

"Are your mamma and daddy happy with your progress here?"

"I think so. Yes."

"Are they pleased? Does your mama like me?"

"She seems to. She never said."

"OK, kid. That's fine. Now we go and talk to her."

"I brought my stars," Harry said. He held out the Merit Award booklet.

Señor Erranda found his box of stars, wet one and pasted it to Harry's forehead. Harry peeled it off, put it in the book and smoothed it down.

"Harry is coming along very nicely," Señor Erranda said to Mrs. Craft.

"I'm so glad to hear that. He's working every night."

"Practice, practice," Señor Erranda said. "Harry, you like it here? You like your hard old teacher?"

Harry giggled.

"Mr. Craft will be very pleased," Harry's mother said.

"Progressing nicely," Señor Erranda said, writing the words on the white three-by-five card marked *Craft, Harry.* He dated the entry. "Will you sign this please?"

"Yes, certainly." Harry's mother wrote "(Mrs.) Irene Craft."

On the way home Harry felt good.

"You know I'm proud of you," his mother said.

"I know," Harry said.

That night the family went to the movies. Harry got another dollar for his bank.

"You'll be richer than the old man if this keeps up," his father said.

"Harry is saving for college," said his mother.

Harry wondered how much he had in his bank. It was the kind you had to smash to open.

The next week passed without incident. Harry did his schoolwork, played with his friends and alone with his soldiers. He practiced each night in his manner. On Saturday he woke to a blizzard. His mother had a head cold. He missed the lesson.

"Don't worry yourself," Harry's father said. "I'm sure the school will make it up."

Harry's routine went on. He kept the guitar outside its case now. He picked it up many times during the day to play just for fun. On their sixth Saturday he and Señor Erranda played side by side again. Toward the end of the hour his teacher played the song he had been playing when his picture was snapped. Harry did not like the song. It sounded like all the others. Yet the fact that it had been heard coast to coast gave it special flavor.

By the end of the tenth week, Harry had fourteen gold stars.

They spread over three pages. Señor Erranda informed him that twenty-five stars could be traded for a diploma of merit. If Harry should choose to take the advanced course, the possibility of stars was infinite. Harry talked to his parents about the advanced course.

"We'll see," said his father. "We'll cross that bridge when we come to it." The way his father spoke gave Harry every encouragement.

On the eleventh week, Harry did not go to Witzheimer. He woke up not wanting to go. He said he had a headache. Later, he wondered why he had done it. He just did not want to go to the school. Losing another star saddened him. But there was hope of earning it back. Next week was a progress report.

On the twelfth week it was Señor Erranda who was absent. The school tried to telephone, but Harry and his mother had already left. When they arrived at Witzheimer a substitute teacher was waiting.

Harry refused to take his lesson.

"He's so attached to Señor Erranda," his mother explained to the substitute. "I think we'll let this week pass by."

She took him home.

The next day, Sunday, Harry's older cousin, Irwin, came with his mother and father for a visit. They came in the early evening. This meant Harry would miss certain radio programs he liked. After dinner, Harry's Aunt Julia, Uncle Reuben, Cousin Irwin, mother and father sat at the kitchen table just talking.

Harry went to his bedroom and took up the guitar. He set his clock for an hour, then he played.

Cousin Irwin walked into the room. Irwin, who was sixteen, also studied at Witzheimer. He was taking Advanced Trumpet and already had formed a band to play in the mountains.

"What are you doing, Harry?" Irwin said.

"Practicing."

"Don't crap me," Irwin said.

Harry kept playing.

"That's not practicing."

Harry played harder. His stomach began to hurt.

"You're really full of crap," Irwin said. Then Irwin went out of the room.

From the kitchen, Harry heard his father say, "What? Don't be stupid."

"He's not playing anything. He's fooling around."

"That's ridiculous. It's not a trumpet."

"If Irwin says, he knows."

"He knows nothing."

"He's crapping around."

"Irwin."

"Fooling around."

"Is it your business?"

Harry closed his door. He got into pajamas. Then he played until the alarm rang and got into bed.

Before his relatives left, Harry's mother came to his room and opened the door.

"He fell asleep with the light," she said.

"What a kid," said his Uncle Reuben.

Harry heard them leave. He heard Irwin say goodnight. He waited for something to happen.

Harry's parents had another cup of coffee. He heard them talking from the kitchen.

"Irwin is a pimple farm," his father said. "I never saw such a case of acne."

"That's disgusting," his mother said. "Boys have that problem."

"They should put zinc ointment on him," his father said.

"I'm sure they do. They had him to a specialist."

Harry's father went to bed. His mother washed dishes. Finally, she went to bed too.

On the day Harry got his fifteenth star it was cold. On the day he got his sixteenth the temperature was near zero.

"This city stinks like a frozen hole," Señor Erranda said on the fifteenth week of lessons and the week of the seventeenth star. "My fingers are like rods. Where I grew up it is hot as fire now. Here I got to melt my hands in water. This damn building stinks too. It's frying or it's freezing. God damn this place. This is no work for an artist, kid. Take my word, you would be surprised how many stinkpots make money right now on the radio. They know somebody. You must know somebody. Like Nick Armada. He must be sitting now in Miami Beach. Why not? I would too. You would too."

The studio seemed gray, as if the light bulb were losing power along with the sun. Even the J.E. on Señor Erranda's guitar looked faded. Señor Erranda himself had a pale face with a yellow feeling. Harry noticed a stain on his shirt.

"Someday," Señor Erranda said. "Someday, watch out. It's my turn, kid."

They played. It was for the last time. Harry got his last star.

The next day, Japanese planes bombed Pearl Harbor.

Harry heard the news on the radio. He ran screaming to his parents.

The radio stayed on all day. Harry heard reports of burning ships and dead sailors. The music of war was already on the air.

Later in the afternoon of December 7th, Harry got out all his soldiers. He fought a tremendous war. None of the soldiers were Japanese, but half were selected as the enemy.

Among the soldiers, one was made of cast iron. He had come to Harry from somewhere and wore the uniform of World War I. He was an ugly soldier but easily the strongest. He became the leader of the Americans.

Half through the game Harry began to break enemies with the iron soldier. He did this by crashing lead soldiers against him. He broke twenty soldiers that way. In the evening, he put all his soldiers into a shoe box.

Then Harry took his guitar and played "Home on the Range," "God Bless America" and "Over There." That is, he banged on the guitar while he sang the songs. Then he put his guitar into its case and the case in his closet.

Harry stayed up late that night. He listened to the radio with his family. The radio warned of air raids and reminded them to be alert. When Harry went to bed he listened for sirens.

Listening, he fell asleep. Harry dreamed of Señor Erranda. Señor Erranda was in the Army. A Jap blew his arms off with a machine gun. Bleeding, Señor Erranda cried. He lay on the floor of a room and cried. Harry wanted to go and kiss his torn arms.

Harry woke up crying.

There were no sirens. Harry sat up in bed. He was afraid that his parents were dead. He got up and went to the toilet. He purposely made noise. He flushed the bowl twice. He banged the bathroom door. Three times he banged the door so that its knob hit the tiles of the wall. Still there was no other sound in the house.

Harry stood outside his parents' room. He had never felt the darkness so deeply. He went into their bedroom without knocking. He saw his mother and father asleep in their big bed. He wondered if they were breathing.

"Ma," he said.

Mrs. Craft sat up immediately.

"Are you all right?"

Mr. Craft moaned and began to grind his teeth.

"I'm all right. I just went to pee."

"Go to sleep, Harry. Tomorrow is a school day."

Harry went back to his room. The real war had begun. He wondered if planes were coming. He waited for motors and the sound of sirens. It was an exciting night.

THE VOYAGE OF THE PEANUT

"**E**VERY MAN WISHES TO MAKE HIS MILLION AND FIND HIMSELF a friendly belly where to rest his head." This is what my Uncle Feig told me on the night I went out in the world. He squeezed this wisdom out of himself by a major effort of will. He had to give me something to take along for my flag, and it certainly wasn't going to be convertible currency. So he sat me across from him at the kitchen table and put his head between his hands and pressed. It was like watching an apple commit suicide in the juicer.

Uncle Feig had powerful arms from his days in construction, and his habit of putting the vise on his brain made me nervous. It was his way of thinking. The night of my departure from the homestead he was squeezing especially hard, and I sat there in a sweat ready to dodge his eyeballs in case they blew. After his thought came, he relaxed and smiled. He was pleased with himself and why not? He knew he had said something really big that I could carry in my pocket.

Then Uncle Feig took an egg out of the fridge and said, "Murray, try to bust this by shoving from both ends." I tried until my face was red and Uncle Feig laughed and slapped the table.

"I can't break the egg," I said.

"It goes to show you," he said. "Nature is nature. It's got a way of balancing things out. If a lousy egg can take a beating, you can take a beating. If a stupid eagle makes it to Miami for the cold months, you got no worries. You're a nice-looking boy."

It was getting near time for my bus so I thanked him. "Forget it," he said. "And keep me in touch. If something good happens send me a postal, and if something bad, a Western Union. Remember, you got relations. My final advice to you is don't be a noodge and don't get impatient. When you're ready for it, it comes to you. The road opens up."

I put on my jacket and picked up my bag.

"Goodbye," I said. "You'll hear from me."

"I was your mother and your father the way things worked out," Uncle Feig said. "Make me proud parents."

"I'll try my best," I said. I was beginning to feel weepy and I didn't want to cry. It wasn't so much that I was embarrassed but I was afraid to scare myself. After all, my room was still there inside, it was a pretty good life, and I wasn't in bad with the cops. Nobody was whipping me to go.

Uncle Feig came over and kissed me on the cheek. He hadn't done that for years. His beard was like wet Brillo and he rubbed it against my face.

"Are you sure about this trip, kid?" he said.

"Oh, yeah, yeah."

"Go and sow your oats. Get them out of your system."

Then Uncle Feig handed me a box. I opened the box and in it was a pigskin wallet. I flipped the wallet and found a ten-dollar bill and a picture of Uncle Feig under the celluloid. It was an old picture of a much younger man but you could see it was my uncle.

"Smell it," Uncle Feig said.

I smelled the pigskin. Its newness came through in a sweetish, good smell that is proof of the genuine article.

"That's terrific," I said. "I really appreciate it."

"Nothing," Uncle Feig said. "Have fun, kid."

"Take care of yourself," I said.

"I'll take care," Uncle Feig said. "You take care."

"So long," I said.

I caught my bus.

I found a seat by the window and settled in. The glass was

mistish from rain, so I made a porthole with my hand. Under the hole I wrote my name, Murray Welkin, and the date. Don't ask me why. I knew it wouldn't last, like the carving on a tree, but it gave me pleasure. I suppose I wanted to mark that night one way or another and there were no walls handy to scrawl on.

When the bus lights went out and the driver hit the gas, the motor roared like a bull in heat. I nearly jumped out of my skin. I was very excited. I felt the vibrations of the bus zoom through me. I was so charged up I could have been plugged in a socket. We moved out of the station and through the town. I grew up in that town and knew every store and face, practically, but that night the street looked different.

The bus went through the Tenderloin and turned on the highway. It shook free of the last houses and picked up speed when the road widened. I was sailing, pointed due west.

West was my chosen direction and with a reason.

I wanted to be in the movies. That is something I never told anybody. Take it or leave it, that's how I felt. My ticket was good until Los Angeles and that seemed a damn fine start.

I put my head back against the seat and looked out my porthole. All I could see were lights and some lumpy black shadows. I felt pretty jazzy, as you can easily comprehend. I was eighteen years, four months old. I was finished with high school. I was relaxing on a Greyhound over a set of fat whirling wheels that chewed up a mile a minute for me. I had a goal.

If there was a single thing in the world that bothered me, besides leaving Uncle Feig alone back home, it was one correctable situation. I was still a virgin. Not that I was sick or incapacitated. It's mostly that I was a busy kid with outside interests.

That night on the bus I thought things over and I realized I had plenty time. And I was even glad because I felt saved up. I had figured that my unique condition in the sexual area had some value. I didn't feel exactly boasty about being what they called unspoiled, but I wasn't too sorry. Everything was happening to

me for the first time, so why not that too? Besides, I wanted her
to be a movie star. That's right, a movie star. Which movie star
I wasn't particular about, and why a movie star I can't tell you,
but I wanted the initial experience to be with a movie star. Is
that unreasonable? That's the way I was. I had my own ideas
about things.

You notice I didn't tell the name of the town I left from, and
that was on purpose. I did it to protect the innocent. So when I
say now that a day later the bus pulled into Los Angeles, you'll
have to take my word. Also take my word when I say that the first
place I tried for a job I hit it lucky.

I was in a luncheonette near the terminal eating some sunny-
side ups when I noticed the counterman watching me. I eat my
bull's-eyes in a slightly peculiar way. First I eat the whites until
the yellows are isolated. Then I maneuver the yolks onto my fork
and slide them into the cave still whole. It's a game I play with
myself. This counterman got a big kick out of it. It broke him up.

"How come you do that?" he said.

"It's a habit," I said.

"I got the same habit," he said. "With me, if a yellow breaks
I'm in a lousy mood. You got that?"

"Not exactly," I said.

"It ruins me," he said. "I can't stand it. You know, it's psychological."

"Yeah?"

"No question about it," he said. "It's a proven fact. My sister
in college gave me the poop."

"Imagine that," I said.

"Everything has a meaning," he said. "Do you dunk?"

"I can take it or leave it," I said.

"Dunking has a meaning too," he said.

"What does it mean?" I said.

"It means you're a slob," he said, and he started to laugh.

The result of all this was he told me about a job. He didn't have too many details but he wrote out the name of a man to see who managed a place called Goobertown. I thanked him and left him a quarter tip.

It was still early and I felt seedy from the trip, so my first official act was to find a pad. Normally I would have gone to a hotel because I am not a shy type, but I chose the YMCA because they had a swimming pool. I thought a little splashing around would be just the thing after twenty-four cramped-up hours. Can you blame me?

There is a Y on Turk Street that sold me a room with privileges for three dollar bills. My room was small but it was enough to make do. I put my trunk on the floor, hid my money in the Gideon Bible under Solomon, and went down to the gym. They gave me a locker and a towel and a card to fill out saying that if I drowned or dropped dead they were not responsible.

I stripped and showered, then walked through a puddle of chlorine until my toes were sterilized, then out to the swimming room. For some reason everybody at the Y swims naked and as it was crowded in the pool, naked men and boys were leaping around or lounging against the walls. The sight of all those bodies under fluorescent lights made me dizzy. It was like being in a monkey house where the fur suddenly dropped off the apes, and I was as bad as the rest. The shapes and sizes of the Los Angeleans had plenty variety, and I admit it gave me some comfort to know that I stacked up well alongside them.

I was in trim condition without loose beef and I pulled myself in and did a neat racing dive into the greenish water. I swam around loosening my muscles, then got out, rubbed dry, dressed and went upstairs. I felt a little tired and it was only eleven-thirty, so I pulled back the blankets, took off my shirt and pants and lay down for a nap.

I remember my dream as if it was painted on the wall. I was

taking a screen test in a big studio full of cameras and lights. There was a band of music playing a New Yorkish song and a girl in a cruddy dress sitting on the steps of a house. They had me decked out in a tux and high hat, complete with cane, and I was walking down the street coming home from some tremendous evening, just slumming along doing a snotty tap dance. The girl saw me and I saw her and we fell in love. We went dancing around together and a chorus came out dressed like pussycats and danced with us. It was a great number. Then it started to dawn and the girl said goodbye because it could never work out. She ran into a tenement and got lost. I went home to my penthouse and tried to shake her but I couldn't get her out of my mind. So I called my Jap and told him to case the street until he came up with her. My Jap was very devoted and would have died twice to keep me comfortable, and he went out and found her hiding behind a wash line. I came tap-dancing over to her place and proposed a quick marriage and she naturally accepted while crying, and we headed for city hall while the neighbors hung out of windows singing this mad song. It was a pleasant dream and I woke up smiling. But I didn't smile for long.

I blinked my eyes a few times to corroborate what I thought they saw and sure enough there was this lady. Y ladies are a very particular kind, picked I suppose for their being extremely safe. She was easily a hundred years old and stood holding a dustpan and a broom. She was standing over my bed making a sound like milk curdling, a kind of chilly inside clucking. I did a quick check to see that I was covered, which I was by my underwear which is the same as shorts.

"What can I do for you, lady?" was the first thing that came to my head so I said it.

"You can't do nothing for me but get dressed and get out," she said. "It's cleanup time."

"OK," I said. "I'm getting up."

"A young man like you sleeping away the best part of the day," she said. "It's a sin and a shame. You should be outside getting sun on your bones."

"Sure," I said. "You're perfectly right."

"There's fortunes to be made in this day and age," she said. "But not by the lazy nor the slothful."

"Certainly," I said. "If you'll excuse me . . ."

"Myself, I would seek out uranium in the bowels of the earth or enter the real estate field," she said. "There's wealth in owning property."

"Yes, ma'am," I said.

"A young soul should welcome the day with a head full of ambitions," she said, waving the broom. "Out into the world of commerce."

"As a matter of fact," I said, "I've got this appointment with a big oil man."

"Oil is good," she said. "What with the Dow Jones average hitting new highs and Wall Street, pardon the expression, bullish."

"I'm getting dressed," I said. "I'll be out of here . . ."

"See that you do," she said, heading for the door. "There's dust and dirt in this room. It's marked for destruction, and nothing or nobody can stop that. Remember my words."

I remembered.

I dressed like a greased flash in my blue suit, white shirt, red tie and black shoes, combed my hair and got out. I passed the lady in the corridor sitting on a pile of laundry reading the stocks and bonds section of the *Examiner*. Her lips moved when she read and I swear she was saying something about the Erie Railroad that she shouldn't have said.

The elevator hustled me downstairs and I walked out into a glary day. It was muggy and close but the swimming had primed me and, give or take a few aches, I felt very optimistic. I had the address of Goobertown written on a piece of paper, so I asked a pedestrian for directions. He pointed out the rights and lefts and

I found my way without trouble. I have a very good sense of direction and could find my way out of a ball of cobwebs if it were necessary.

Goobertown turned out to be a store with a fancy front of blue marble and chromium that sold nothing but peanuts. The windows were full of peanuts in every living known variety. There were plain roasted peanuts and chocolate-covered peanuts, peanuts and raisins, peanut butter, peanut brittle and peanut you-name-it. Even on the outside there was this peanut smell which was extremely tempting.

I went into the store through an automatic door that worked on an electric eye and saw right away that the inside was even fancier than the outside. There was music and air conditioning and snappy glass counters along the walls. The counter girls wore white uniforms and caps shaped like peanuts and they were nice and clean looking. The floor was marble and the whole place had a bankish feeling, only instead of money everything was peanuts. It was really a setup.

A floorman came over to ask me what I wanted. I told him I heard there was a job around and he walked me back to the manager's office. He knocked on the door and a voice yelled, "Come in," and I went in.

The manager was a short man, thin, wearing a gray striped suit. I did a double take because for a split second he looked like one of his peanuts. He was sitting at a wood desk with a glass top decorated with peanut bookends and a peanut-shaped lamp. I thought it was carrying things too far, and I began to feel crawly.

"Who sent you?" he said, and I told him I was recommended by the counterman.

"Are you interested in show business?" he said.

I was surprised to hear that and I lit up.

"Yes," I said. "As a matter of fact."

"This position involves showmanship," he said. "It's a job with a future. We're looking for a serious-minded fellow who wants to advance with the company. We want a man capable of growing."

"I think I'm capable of growing," I said.

"We want a man who is not afraid of hard work and starting at the bottom."

"I'm very interested," I said.

He was looking me over.

"Stand up," he said.

I stood up.

"Sit down," he said. "How's your health?"

"Fine," I said. "Tiptop."

"Do you like the outdoors?" he said. "We want a man who likes the outdoors."

"I like the outdoors," I said.

The manager pressed a button on his desk and a girl's voice said, "Yes, sir."

"Send in Mr. Humphrey," he said.

"Yes, sir," the voice said.

The manager sat staring at me and I focused on the picture of a farm where a big machine was harvesting a crop of—you guessed it. I suppose it was the company farm. There was a scrapy noise at the door and this man came in who was maybe sixty or sixty-five. He stood slouched over like a buck private in a comedy. The manager stood up.

"Mr. Humphrey," he said, "this young fellow seems promising. I'll leave you alone with him."

The manager picked himself up and walked out of the room.

Mr. Humphrey was giving me the once-over.

"So you're applying for my job," he said.

"Your job? I didn't know it was your job, sir. I wouldn't want to . . ."

"I'm retiring," Mr. Humphrey said. "I'm retiring to Mexico."

"That's nice," I said.

"Fifty years with the company," he said.

"That's a long time," I said.

"And now I must lay down my shells."

"I'm sorry, sir," I said. "But I don't think I heard you."

"I'm laying down my shells," he said in a louder voice. "I'm out of the rat race. It's a young man's game and my days of service are done. I've earned my rest. I'm going into stud, grazing on the plantation, do you get what I mean?"

"I think so," I said.

"You *might* be my successor," he said.

"Yes, sir."

"The king is dead, long live the king."

"Yes, sir."

"Don't think I'm not looking forward to my leisure," said Mr. Humphrey. "Oh, I love the business. But I have my hobbies too. I've prepared for old age. Make sure that when your time comes to pass your shells on to someone new you'll have other interests," he said.

"Yes, sir."

"I think you'll do," he said. "You have the right cut. I like your style."

"Thank you," I said.

Mr. Humphrey went out of the room and came back with the manager, who was beaming.

"Congratulations," the manager said. "You're on the Goobertown team now, lad. Mr. Humphrey has given you the green light. It's up to you now."

"That's wonderful," I said.

"Let's get him out in the field," the manager said to Mr. Humphrey. "The sooner the better. He's got to prove himself."

"Right," Mr. Humphrey said.

"You'll start at forty-five dollars a week," the manager said. "We'll be watching you. Our eye is always open for executive talent. Now go with Mr. Humphrey, and good luck."

He shook my hand. I followed Mr. Humphrey out of the office, into another room.

"Excuse me if I get emotional," Mr. Humphrey said. "But this is a solemn occasion."

"Sure," I said.

He went over to a big black box lying on the floor.

"Open it," he said.

I opened it.

"Take them out," he said.

I bent into the box and took out a pair of black pants, and two giant half-shells.

"Wait a minute," I said. "What is this?"

"Your uniform," Mr. Humphrey said. "Wear it proudly."

"My uniform?" I said.

"Yes," he said. "Now hang your suit up there and let's try it on for size."

"Am I going to be a peanut?" I said. "Is that what the job is?"

"Naturally," Mr. Humphrey said. "You will represent Goobertown on the streets of Los Angeles."

I did some quick thinking. I weighed the angles. It was a job and I needed a job. I could hit the studios on Saturdays. Besides, plenty of stars were discovered walking around the streets.

"Haste," Mr. Humphrey said. "It takes time at first, but in a few months you'll be able to snap them on in a jiffy."

"All right," I said. "But give me a hand."

He helped me strap on the shells. I felt like I was locked inside a drainpipe. There was a little eye hole and a breathing slot near my mouth. Mr. Humphrey put two black sleeves over my arms and white gloves on my hands.

"You look fine," he said. "I'm proud of you."

"Put me in front of a mirror," I said.

"Vanity, vanity," Mr. Humphrey said. "I know just how you feel."

He led me to a mirror. I couldn't believe what I saw. I was a peanut, a human peanut. Mr. Humphrey was excited. He took me into the store. The customers did a double take and the counter girls giggled. I figured what the hell and bowed at a fat blonde holding a bag in her hand. She roared. The manager came over.

"A fine start," he said. "Now wander. Keep moving. Get yourself seen. Be back here at six and don't stop to dally."

"Yes, sir," I said. And I thanked Mr. Humphrey.

I walked outside, and you can understand how I attracted some attention. The first block was the hardest, and watching the traffic lights, but after that I began to enjoy myself. It was hot inside my shell and I was worried about possibly sneezing and blasting my brains out, but, otherwise, a breeze blew in through my armholes and cross-ventilated with the breathing slot, and that made life bearable. I took a slow walk around town looking at the buildings and ogling the crowds. Every once in a while I waved to a kid. And while I went I was thinking to myself, "Things are looking up, Murray. Here you are in town a few hours and already employed." I knew that Uncle Feig would be proud of me and that made me feel good.

Time passes fast in the peanut business. The day shot by. People stopped to trade cracks with me and I even developed a routine. I told them there were plenty nuts where I came from, and said, "What's your excuse?" It went over big. It must have been three-thirtyish when I noticed the car.

I have seen cars and cars in my lifetime before and since but never anything like the job that was cruising alongside me. It was long and low, painted olive green, loaded with chromium and souped up. On the radiator was the figure of a jungle-type girl with her hands stretched out galloping along on top of a panther. A chauffeur handled the wheel and you could see that he was happy with his machine. A saintish look kept him smiling slightly, and he had a dreaming expression on his face. The back of the car was curtained off, but I saw from my shell that the curtains were separated. Somebody was peeking outside.

At first I thought it was a coincidence that the car crawled along next to me. But after a while I got suspicious so I crossed the street and turned a corner. The car turned too and kept crawling. It made me a little nervous and I was beginning to wonder, when out of the blue a little kid off the sidewalk ran up to me and threw an arm lock around my haunches. She wouldn't let go. She had never seen anything like me before and I suppose she wanted to eat me on the spot.

Her mother tried to drag her away but she carried on and screamed. A crowd formed and the kid fell down to my ankles and held on. I was losing my balance. I didn't relish the idea of falling down on the sidewalk because I knew it would be damn near impossible to get up and I would be at the mercy of anything that happened to come along.

The kid sunk her teeth into my ankle and luckily there was a bone, which stopped her. She was yelling, "I love my Uncle Peanut," which was frightening by itself, and she meant it from the heart. Finally they pried her separate, and her mother belted her with a handbag and promised her I would stop around on Christmas.

A cop came over by then and gave me a talking to. He told me to move along, which I was willing to do, and I beat it back onto the avenue at a slow trot. It was hard to make real time because the wind caught my peanut at the corner and nearly tipped me over. By the time I got hold of myself the car was gone and to tell you the truth I forgot about it. I was too busy just sweating and rubbing my bruise.

I was shaking pretty bad. The experience was a mean one. I thought of going back to Goobertown, but I never was a quitter and that forty-five dollars was big time to me. So I looked around for a place to catch my breath.

Now L.A. is a curious town full of peculiar temples. Every few blocks is a churchy-looking building that is not exactly an ordinary church. They have strange names and odd shapes, but all of them are open to the public. I was attracted to one by its four-o'clock whistle. I mean exactly that. At four o'clock this tower on the street gave out a moaning noise like a squeezed owl. My nerves were fraying anyway and that sound threw me. I thought it was an earthquake and that I would be swallowed up. But it was only the tower clock marking time. The building had a big sign in neon that said: HAVEN OF THE JOLLY ATOMS. It also said: ENTER STRANGERS, so I went over and entered.

I had to bend to get myself through the first door and I came up against a second. This one was painted white with gold universy pictures and it had a bronze hand for a knob. I grabbed the hand and gave it a shake. Chimes rang out and the door opened. It was dark inside and my eyes had to adjust. But when they did I saw that I was inside a big boxy room decorated with plastic stars and planets. In the center, hanging from the ceiling, was a ball spinning and little balls whooshing around it. Two spirally columns of flashing lights flanked an altar at the far end. I decided right away that this was not the place for me and I turned to go. But two ladies in white robes came out of someplace and took me by the arms.

"Sister Proton welcomes you," said one.

"Sister Nutron welcomes you," said the other.

"Pleased to meet you," I said. "But I'm on a lunch hour and . . ."

"Enter the kingdom of flux," said Sister Proton.

"Let yourself fragment," said Sister Nutron.

"I came in to rest," I said.

"Of course," said Sister Proton.

"Now rest," said Sister Nutron, sitting me down under the spinning ball.

"There is nothing like disintegration and reintegration," said Sister Proton.

"Nothing," said Sister Nutron.

"You'll be a new man," Sister Proton said, "and for such a reasonable fee."

"Five dollars a treatment," said Sister Nutron. "For the fund."

"Surely you believe in the work of the fund," said Sister Proton.

"Well," I said, "the truth is . . ."

A rainbow of lights began flashing out of the ball and it started to come down over my head. It was suspended by a very thin wire, and whirling that way it looked very ominous.

"Disintegrate, reintegrate," said Sister Nutron.

"Flux is everything," said Sister Proton.

"I don't have five dollars," I said. "This is my first day in L.A. I just started working. . . ."

"You can owe us the five dollars," said Sister Nutron.

"That's nice of you," I said. "But . . ."

A chorus of voices came out of a speaker somewhere and the ball turned yellow. It was about three feet over our heads.

"Now, atomize," said Sister Nutron.

"Fly apart," said Sister Proton.

The ball began to buzz and come down closer and I was worried that it would hit the top of my shell. I probably would have been pulverized if it hadn't been for some quick thinking.

"I owe you five dollars," I yelled. "I owe you ten dollars."

The ball began to lift, the buzzing stopped, the lights went out and Sister Proton and Sister Nutron calmed down.

"Fill in this short form," Sister Nutron said.

I wrote out an IOU giving my name as Sam Humphrey, which was the name of my predecessor, and listing an address that came to my mind.

"Are you refreshed, brother?" said Sister Proton, and I said, "Extremely."

They led me to the door and I ducked outside.

It took me about a half-hour to get over being atomized and by then it was after five. I had walked a long way so I turned back toward Goobertown. I was looking forward to coming out of my shell and doing the town as a civilian again.

About a block from home base I saw the monster car again and things fell into place. The way I figured it, Goobertown sent that car to spy on me, and there was no question but that I would get canned because of the mess on the street. My thinking was very muddy. If I had any sense I would have realized that the car probably cost more than all the company's peanuts end to end, with the fixtures thrown in for good measure.

I ambled into the store like a prince on wheels. I took it slow, with dignity. Inside I looked around and strutted over the marble toward the manager's office. I saw him in back of the place huddled with the chauffeur gesturing and whispering his lousy report. The manager looked serious as hell and shook his head. Then I saw the chauffeur reach into his pocket and pass something to him and things changed. The boss began to smile. He patted the chauffeur on the shoulder and even laughed.

I was practically on them when they saw me coming.

I was ready with a speech of resignation that included mention of my future glorious career, but before I had a chance to deliver even the opening sentence the manager came over to me grinning with his mouth open.

"Hello, lad," he said. "We wondered what happened to you."

"I was out on my beat," I said.

"Yes," the manager said. "You've done very well. I'm hearing good things about you already."

"Yeah?" I said.

"Incidentally," the manager said, "you know this type of work calls for occasional late hours."

"I didn't know," I said.

"Now you know," he said. "And tonight we have a special assignment for you."

"Tonight?" I said. "It's my first night in L.A. and I was looking forward to . . ."

"This is business," the manager said. "Important business."

"Can't I possibly . . ."

"Not possibly," he said. "You work tonight."

"If you say so, sir," I said.

"Good man," he said.

"What do I do?" I said.

"Just go with Mr. Antenna," the manager said. "He'll explain things later."

He pointed to the chauffeur. Mr. Antenna came over and shook hands with me.

"Are we ready?" he said.

"I'm ready," I said.

"The company is watching you," the manager said. "Keep that in mind."

"I will," I said.

I followed Mr. Antenna outside and we walked toward the car.

"Where are we going?" I said. "I haven't had my supper yet."

"Don't complain," Mr. Antenna said. "You should be thanking your lucky stars. You'll get fed."

He opened the car door for me.

"How can I fit in there?" I said. "Get me out of my shell."

"The shell stays," Mr. Antenna said. "The seat bends back. We'll lay you in horizontal."

"I don't know," I said.

"Get in," he said. "It's the best thing that ever happened to you."

I got in somehow and was stretched across two seats. Mr. Antenna got behind the wheel and started the car. We went purring along through the city and I knew from the traffic sounds that we were out of the mash and in suburbia.

"Be a sport," I said. "Where are we going?"

"You're going to heaven," he said.

"Let me in on the secret," I said. "I don't like surprises."

"You'll like this surprise," Mr. Antenna said. "I guarantee you'll like this surprise."

I decided to play it cool. I shut up and waited. Mr. Antenna began singing a popular song. He had the car moving along at a good clip and we must have put twenty miles between us and the town. He was singing along just hitting his stride when he swerved the car into a driveway and we were riding on pebbles.

The car stopped.

"We're home," he said.

He got me out of the car by twisting a little and I saw where I was. We were parked in a forestlike affair in front of a clearing. There was a little lake full of swans to the left and the biggest house I ever saw in my life on the right.

"Now, listen," said Mr. Antenna. "Just accept the fact that you have been selected."

"For what?" I said.

"Just be nice and keep loose," he said. "Come on."

He rang the doorbell and a man came down to let us in.

"Ah," said the man. "Monsieur Peanut."

"In the flesh," the chauffeur said. "He's all yours."

"Follow me, sir," the man said.

I went upstairs. The man stopped by a closed door and knocked with his fingertips.

"Monsieur Peanut est ici," he said in a voice like soft ice cream.

"Eh, bien!" said a voice from inside.

Then the servant, or butler, or whatever he was, went hustling down the corridor and disappeared around a corner.

I was alone. I heard music all of a sudden and I felt like I was back in the temple except this music was stringy, full of violins. I was fidgety in my shell, restless from the suspense.

The door opened and a little girl in black who must have been a maid pointed inside and ran away in the direction of the butler. I went in, shell and all, thinking, "Murray, this day has plenty of doors in it," when I saw her sitting in a golden boat.

No, I am not going to mention names. I have some honor left and I know my responsibilities. But I can tell you I knew who she was because I saw her plenty of times before, and you did too. I said she was sitting in a golden boat but the boat was a bed

with white sheets and cushions and she was sort of nicely draped
out in a gauzy kind of nightgown. I knew who she was all right.
The fact is I dreamed about her a year or so before I started to
shave.

"Hello, Peanut," she said, in what they call a sultry voice.

I was too choked up even to ask for her autograph.

"Sit down, Peanut," she said.

I went over and sat down. I was shivering hard enough to rattle
my shell and I didn't know what was happening. In the movies
she wears things like a middy blouse or a crisp kind of little-girl
dress, but this was confusing and different.

"Relax, Peanut," she said.

She reached over to an ice bucket and pulled out a bottle of
wine. She poured two glasses and held one out for me.

"Much appreciated," I said, "but I either need a straw or to get
out of my uniform."

"Not yet," she said. "Let's wait."

"For what?" I said.

"For the sweet moment when you cast off your shells and stand
before me," she said. "You have no idea how exciting this is."

"No, ma'am," I said.

"You don't know what a drag life can be," she said. "Work,
work, work. Same, same, same. When I saw you today, I wanted
to know you as a woman knows a man. In a moment of discovery."

"You were in the car," I said.

"Yes, my mystery Peanut," she said. "Yes, my unknown quan-
tity."

I was feeling very warm. Her impact was big on me. She was
curvy and warm-looking and her hair was combed out and spill-
ing like a fountain. She began stroking my shell.

"Please stop that," I said.

"Why, Peanut?"

"For personal reasons," I said.

But she cuddled in closer.

"Would you believe that I haven't felt like this for years?" she said. "You do something to me."

"It's probably the uniform," I said.

"You thrill me," she said. "Do I appeal to you?"

"Oh yes," I said. "Oh yes."

"Do you like me for myself?"

"Pardon?" I said.

"Do you love me?" she said.

"Well . . ." I said.

"Do you want to touch me?"

She was curling and uncurling at the same time and breathing in tiny little breaths and I began to get a little dizzy.

"Now," she said. "Emerge!"

"I don't know . . ."

"Now," she said. "Cast off thy shell."

"But . . ."

"Now, Peanut mine," she said. "Reveal yourself!"

"If . . ."

"You're driving me insane," she said. "Come out."

Her lips were on top of my breathing slot and let me tell you I was on fire. I didn't want to do anything I would regret, or take advantage of her, but I am only human and she came at me like a cat. So I started to pry myself out of the shell, the trouble being that I didn't know the combination.

"Peanut, have mercy," she said. "Spring forth!"

"I'm trying to spring forth," I said. "Have patience. Mr. Humphrey didn't tell me how . . ."

"Please, please, please, please, please."

"I think it goes this way," I said. "But I never . . ."

"Help me," she said. "Quench me. Drown me."

"I'll quench you," I said. "But my shell is slightly jammed. Mr. Humphrey . . ."

"Murderer," she yelled. "Seducer! Are you trying to make a fool out of me?"

"Never," I said. "Not in a million years. But the trick . . ."

She gave out with a growling sound that was very tigerish, jumped off the bed and ran to the door, shrieking, "Somebody, get me a nutcracker. For godsakes, get me a nutcracker!"

"Wait a minute . . ." I said. "Just a minute . . ." I was worried.

But she bolted down the hall and I heard footsteps running up and Mr. Antenna and the butler came into the room.

"Stay away from me," I said. "These shells are the property of . . ."

I don't know how they did it, but they did it. I got in a few punches but I wasn't very mobile and they had me on the floor. I came popping out of the shells like a cork on New Year's and they went out of the room. She was standing over me with a terrible smile and I smiled back because what was there to do?

"Delicious Devil," she said. "Bashful Beelzebub. Subtle Satan. Luscious Lucifer."

I didn't even bother to defend myself.

Mr. Antenna drove me to L.A. On the trip to town I sat with my head back on the cushy seat, feeling swallowed and digested. That's the feeling exactly. I was inside the velvety gullet of this high-powered fish and it wasn't the worst sensation.

We went swimming down the river past other fishes with big white eyes. I was enjoying the ride even though I felt slightly dissolved, and the fish thoughts had me feeling really poetic. I'm no Henry Longfellow but occasionally I snap off a rhyme.

We were moving fast and smooth, with me in a 40 percent trance, and Mr. Antenna humming a bumblebee jazz-type noise, working the wheel like he was half dashboard. We whizzed in and out of lanes beating out the other carfish, and life inside my whale was very comfortable.

I must have been just a little bit south of Boobie Village because it seemed like the whole world was submerged and breathing bubbles. What brought me back to dryish land was this Edsel that came at us from the opposite direction. In my condition I could have sworn it was a mackerel, and I'm telling you it smiled at me. I said in this dazy way, "What the hell is that fish grinning about?"

Mr. Antenna stopped humming. He turned around to me and said, "Boy, get hold of yourself." I got hold of myself.

I admit I took my pulse to make sure I was still alive, but I did it shrewdly. I didn't want Mr. Antenna convinced that I was some shlerm from the country who never had an experience before. So I folded my hands politician style until I found the vein. The pulse was not only beating, it was jumping like a Mexican bean, and I think seriously I would have sprung a leak then and there if healthwise I wasn't in tremendous shape. There's plenty to be said for clean living.

Mr. Antenna opened his window and the damp, gray air loosened my brain. The air out there is probably loaded with vitamins because my vital juices started flowing again.

I was feeling better and better. I sat up in the seat like a stuffed cadet. I think if they screwed a bulb in my bellybutton that minute it would have started flashing on and off. I felt like an easy cinch for the Congressional Medal or at least my face on the two-dollar bill. You might say there was a rooster flying around inside me, and I knew that me and the bird were going to stay good friends. It's amazing what certain things can do for a man and a puzzle why they don't run out and tell the kids.

I started to hum with Mr. Antenna and together we managed to handle "Smoke Gets in Your Eyes."

When we got to the Y, Mr. Antenna helped me carry my shells into the lobby and we shook hands.

"Well," he said, "I wish you milk and honey."

"The same to you," I said, "and thanks for the ride."

"Let's not talk too much about this," he said, "if you know what I mean."

He held out a wad of bills packed like an artichoke. "I know what you mean," I said.

I didn't take the cash. Enough is enough. I don't believe in witches but there's only so much a human person can stand. I waved it back at Mr. Antenna like it was a habit with me to leave big tips, and he pocketed the money and left.

I checked the shells with a desk clerk and wrote out a note for Mr. Humphrey resigning my commission and suggesting that he put off Social Security because the country needs men with his savvy what with the Red menace. Then I went up to my room, packed my grip and headed for the road.

They say a word to the wise is sufficient. I was in the City of the Angels for twenty-four hours on my trip, and already I felt cramped. I said to myself, "Murray, L.A. is a nice place to visit, but what else can she give you except smoggy eyeballs? There is a big, sweet, globy world out there which Columbus tells you is round, so why not have a look-see and prove it for yourself?"

I guess I inherit wandering blood from my grandpa, who kept moving until he couldn't read his compass anymore.

So I stood on the concrete wiggling my thumb. The way I saw it, the movies were a corpse anyhow, and that TV was the place to be. I figured someday to give the tube a tussle and maybe to eat off the trees in New York, New York.

I knew Uncle Feig would give me the nod, and I checked to see if his pigskin was still in my jacket with the picture. It was.

There was plenty of moving traffic. The fog lifted and the stars were out thick. A slash of moon came up over the Pacific, and I never saw so much light.

THE LION'S SHARE

MY NAME IS MARTIN STEIN.

I look like a secondhand lion. My face and jaw have a heaviness. My eyes have a prowlish quality. Not an urgent, hungry look, but the look of slow appetite providing for itself. My hair is messy, a fuzzy garden. I walk with a slouch. My body is big. Definitely, I look like a lion, but the kind of lion that is burdened with memories of hard times, penetrating defeats and boring victories. There is practically no spring to me. Do I sound old? I am hardly twenty, still growing. Inwardly, I have a very active life.

I am exuberant, hopeful, full of beginnings and new pride. If anything, I have dangerous tendencies toward ecstasy. The sensations of the new season affect me like a rub with a turkish towel. Hope is my constant companion.

It is nature's accident that my inside does not jibe with my outside. Except when I talk. My voice is deep, clear and mellow. I have a rich, round voice. It penetrates. It stirs up typhoons in the acoustical seas. When I talk I have actually seen houseflies leave cushy perches to buzz in ever-widening circles. Can you imagine what I do to human eardrums, which are tissue thin? Most of my passion expresses itself in my voice. All youth is wrapped in my vocal cords. This I attribute to the fact that my mother believed in the whole man and my father did not fight her. I still have tonsils.

I use my kingly voice whenever possible. Fortunately, or unfortunately, it is my best muscle. I chat with conviction on politics, philosophy, literature, sports, music, art, the drama, love and food. My voice comes echoing from the cave of my mouth like Old Testament music. A dentist once told me my teeth, tongue and palate are a natural mall suited to great orchestras. Believe me, I would invite the philharmonic if I could fit them all in.

To hear and see me simultaneously is confusing. I am badly dubbed. But because of my intrinsic contradictions, everyone on campus knows me. I am a celebrity of no accomplishment. And I am not seasonable. Martin Stein is pointed out whether they are playing football or croquet, during Winter Week or the Strawberry Festival.

Despite my small notoriety, I am shy in new relationships. At fresh meetings, I burn, I die. When you first make my acquaintance, I look at you through squinty lids, giving the impression that your light is so detestable to my brain that I must filter it. Not true. Actually, the chances are I would love you if I could. But I am naturally afraid that you will strip the shell off my soul and find it shivering in dirty underwear.

Why am I this way? Who knows? Maybe it is because my family had money during the Depression. As a child I was removed from the neighborhood's squalor, misery and hunger. From this economic separation I have never fully recovered.

This chronic shyness I feel is, for Martin Stein, the sluggish lion, a thorn in his paw. I need my Androcles with tweezers and warm heart to pluck daily splinters from my pulpy personality. My roommate, Lester Pig, serves that happy function.

Lester Pig's last name is not really Pig, but I call him that. I am justified. He is warm, fat, pink and social. Each night after study period, Lester drives to an eating place called The Palace of Pork for a barbecue. This ritual of his, slightly cannibalistic, plus his general appearance and outlook, gave rise to the name.

"Lester," I say to him, "if you had a slit in your back I would drop in coins."

"Go move your bowels," he answers me, and so we get on.

Lester Pig has done many, many fine things for me, and, indirectly, I for him. He is a born introducer, a man's man. I have local fame and reputation. We use each other, but mostly I use him. He is my go-between, my buffer state. Not only does he help me meet human beings, but he distracts them with sleight of hand while I am adjusting to the catastrophe of coping with a stranger. Thank God for Lester Pig—may he live a thousand years. He is my doorman to life.

Lester Pig builds my ego, a thing of toothpicks and spit. He is always praising me and patting me on the butt. It helps. He forever tells me to dress better, to eat nourishing greens, to sleep more, to send my poems with stamps enclosed to thin magazines, and so forth. I resist him, but it is nice to be regarded by somebody as potentially respectable and successful.

Of course, my grades are straight-A and my baby-fat dribblings are printed in *Thrust*, the literary journal. Wisps of my glory reflect on Lester, or so he believes. He, like the planets, glows by borrowed light. If I have a small triumph, Lester is fluorescent for days. He is proud to know me, which amazes and delights me. And I am proud to know him, which satisfies his needs.

"Martin Stein," Lester Pig once said to me, looking at a grapefruit his father sent from Miami Beach, "the crystal ball shows me things to come. You will be a big-time rhymester writing lyrics for the music of the spheres, and I will go into heavy industry and hack out an empire. With stockholders' approval, one day our talents will merge. Can you imagine? A fusion of poetry and business, gas and grab. We will conquer the world."

Lester Pig is all for merging. Maybe it is because of his essential loneliness. Mergers hold the hope of the world for him. When he reads in the *Wall Street Journal* that Textron came together with Bell Aircraft, he acts as if his cousin got married. He practically sends gifts to the board of directors. And he creams for the girls in the Sunday paper who smile up from the Betrothed section.

"Look, Martin," he says. "One Sherill Baumwort is holding her nuptials. Hold them high, Sherill. Wave them proudly around. From your looks I can tell you are full of babies, a regular egg-case. May you be as fertile as the prize cow in the State Fair. May you and yours enjoy tremendous bliss as you go forth to populate the earth. May your fiancé, Irving J. Clippstok of New York and Detroit, warm you like a candle. Good luck to the whole family."

Lester Pig loves coming-together in any shape or form. It was through his conniving that, at the first trumpets of spring, I met Irene Bell, an impossible girl.

For me, the changing season is a nervous time. The finish of summer seals the book of summer like a full ledger. And what have you got? Memories. Comparisons. A few wilty flowers. Then autumn comes and you go out to meet it crisp with appetite.

Autumn, full of nostalgia, romances the whole idea of dying and parting. Then, like a sick undertaker, autumn itself dies and departs. So what's left besides pressed leaves? Bills for pants and a jacket; a remembrance of the September surge of ambition, which is December's guilt feeling; and maybe one or two good moments.

You think, enough, enough. Then lousy winter wakes the flesh with the touch of a wool sweater. Dreams stir. Winter passes, good or bad, and where are you? Suckered in by the worst time of all for tempting and teasing. The ice is still hanging from your nose and already you are smelling violets. What a rat race. What the hell, can you resign from the seasons? Spring bugs Martin Stein like nature's alarm clock. The lion is sleeping and snoring, then bang, he is itchy again, thinking where to scratch.

In April, Lester Pig, a human barometer, knew I was restless before it showed even to me.

"Hibernation is over, Martin," he said. "Last night you sang 'The Marseillaise' in your dreams. It was inspirational. I almost got up at four-thirty to go Bastille-storming."

"How was my French?" I said, unimpressed.

"What French?" he said. "Don't flatter yourself. You sang in a hectic Yiddish except for the part about the citizens' forming battalions."

"As one subconscious to another," I said, "what does it all mean?"

"In the remote past was there a dentist in your family?" Lester said.

"There was," I said. "An uncle on my mother's side. He practiced in Staten Island."

"I suspected," Lester said. "I have interpreted your dream. You will have seven lean years and seven fat years, but the important thing right now is for you to fill a cavity."

"Listen, doctor," I said. "You know how I feel about your genital prescriptions. Sex is for making babies."

"My theory is simple," Lester said. "I am pro-body rather than anti-body. Try it for fifty years."

"I know," I said. "Now tell me that if you had my voice you could make out, reading the Yellow Pages."

"It's true," Lester said. "You have a special responsibility. Western civilization is on the block. Think of your equivalent Russian. You've got to be more active."

"Storm your own Bastille," I said.

"Come off it," Lester said. "I know by the shape of your head that you are a classical lecher, a human phallus, the kind that goes into stud right after the big race. All the joys of the republic are concentrated in your Adam's apple. You are the living spirit of Passing Puberty. Is it the women that scare you, or are you too lazy about taking showers?"

"Everything scares me," I said.

"Don't give me the shyness crap," Lester said. "I have great plans for you."

"I don't need your help and I don't want your help," I said.

"I'm a sulking all-or-nothing person. I'm interested exclusively in deep, tragic love affairs, not transient pleasures."

"Hold on," Lester Pig said, jumping up and down on his bed. "Don't you believe that getting there is half the fun?"

"No," I said. "I hate getting anywhere."

But Lester Pig was determined. Later that day I found a bottle floating in the bathroom sink with a note in it that said, "Should people be cold and shaking on the way to destiny? What's wrong with mature males and females touching each other with warmth and tenderness on a part-time basis?"

I took a pencil and wrote, "Not for me," and floated the bottle again.

He telephoned at midnight from a bar downtown.

"My date is cold in the car," he said. "But I wanted to ask you, what memories will keep you warm in the grave, bubbie? The girls you fondle today are the companions of your future senility. You want to sit with me, grinning in the Florida sun, don't you? So what will we talk about, pension checks? Social Security? You need friendly ghosts to share your declining years."

"I'm declining right now," I said. "I passed my peak at thirteen, the second I was Bar-Mitzvahed. Anyhow, what girl would want me? I have achieved nothing."

I heard his dime drop.

"They're trying to cut me off," Lester said. "But to answer your last question in the words of better mountain climbers, a girl will want you because you are there. Martin, you need a Sherpa guide to get you uphill. Fortunately, you've got me."

"Find another hobby," I said. "If God meant for me to be a lover, he would have given me a sign."

But I was talking to the operator who wanted money for the next five minutes.

It had come to pass that, coincident with the vernal equinox,

I was taking a peculiar course called Existentialism 104. For learning about this relatively new philosophy, the university granted one golden credit, a credit usually reserved for Gym. But there was no gym. It burned down in January, on my birthday.

I imagine this was purely coincidence, as I must to keep sane, though I am Capricorn and the Director of Athletics is Aquarius. Since he saw me buckle during a freshman push-up, we never got along. But Gym was compulsory, and I accepted it without visible protest until the building came crashing down in flames.

I remember the morning it happened. We went to watch the fire. The Director of Athletics was there, staring into the embers, looking cheated and deserted. I was sorry for him but so relieved that I couldn't help rejoicing. I was rejoicing noticeably. I was laughing out loud. I saw the Director whisper something to a fireman, who came over to examine me. He was looking for the bulge of kerosene cans in my clothes, or at least a detonator cap.

"Don't mind his hysterics," Lester Pig said to the fireman. "He was just beginning to build himself, and now this. The boy is all smashed up."

No matter. The thing being that after the gym sizzled there was one credit to account for, and the university announced a choice of emergency courses.

I took Existentialism 104 because I like the common-sense-pay-as-you-go-look-under-rocks-no-horseball approach it sold. And as I am a galloping optimist with overtones of the millennium, the depressive parts of the doctrine worked in reverse to cheer me.

When the professor painted black pictures of man's destiny, I thought of things like bagels, lox and the Ivory Soap baby. These buoyant images, my personal life jackets, floated me back up to the surface.

As I wrote in my term paper, "A splash of seltzer and chocolate syrup turns the sea of despair into a first-class egg cream." Not that this is the answer to war and pestilence, but it is at least to be considered before taking the gas pipe.

Existentialism 104 had complications. First, since the class was really a sublimation for Gym, the students gathered there were not exactly a selected group. Mostly there were girls who knitted Argyle stockings out of Kierkegaard's guts. There were Bus Ad majors like Lester Pig, a few scattered Poly Scis, many Anthrops and a clutch of Psychs who asked questions about Sartre's toilet training.

The class was like an ark dispatched to save the Liberal Arts, and because it was associated with knee bends and rope jumping, everybody was a little too festive.

Secondly, the teacher was a problem. His name was Max Pierre, a tiny, tense Algerian genius. He was in trouble and we all knew it.

Max Pierre wanted to stay in America, but he was on a temporary visa due to run out of time. He wanted to marry an American girl citizen of any quality or size as soon as possible.

Max Pierre was not too particular the way things were, but neither was he a Rudolph Valentino. Vague, finicky, highly keyed and broke, he resembled a used coffee bean, couldn't speak much English and didn't like women. Out of sympathy we all wanted Max Pierre to win his dream. So we rooted for him. We watched him direct his lessons at eligible girls in the room, looking for a kindred spirit among the knitters. We heard him make embarrassing slips like, "Tomorrow we dis-gus man's yearn-ning for ze statue of lib-er-ty . . . er . . . ah . . . stat-us of lib-er-ty."

I did not learn too much, except about love and politics, and a kind of unnecessary suffering.

Finally they imported a blind date for Max Pierre from the Hackensack Institute of Animal Fat and she married him the next week, because as strongly as he wanted to stay in America, she wanted to stay in shape.

There was a happy ending. The underdog came out barking after a honeymoon visit to the State Department. Max Pierre really let himself go, and I filled a book with the damnedest notes.

Along with the mass, Miss Irene Bell was driven out of her Modern Movement seminar by the Great Locker Room Blaze which the fire department finally attributed to spontaneous combustion in a wet leotard. She too was wafted into Existentialism 104.

My mistake was, I wrote a poem for her after observing her magnificence from a distance for seven or eight weeks. I wrote the poem on a napkin from the cafeteria, and Lester Pig found it in the breast pocket of a shirt he borrowed.

Lines for Irene

Like a Phoenix, draped in flame,
From the ashes of the gym,
Irene Bell in sadness came;
Soft and sensual, yet trim.

Saved from lechy tongues of fire
To dance again in future hours,
My supermarket of desire;
My own bouquet of winter flowers.

Twirl in pagan passion red,
O torch to melt the bluest ice;
While I, unworthy, smash my head
Against the door to Paradise.

Lester Pig confronted me with the poem while I was indisposed and could not punch him in the face.

"Martin," he said, "either your laundryman is amorous or your corpuscles have come back from Capistrano. Hearty congratulations. This document is another *Hiawatha*, only gitchier and goomier. It wails."

"Give me my napkin," I said. "That's not for human eyes."

"This napkin is for the Smithsonian," Lester said. "A special glass case. It's like Hallmark himself came from heaven and kissed your head.

"Twirl in pagan passion red,
O torch to melt the bluest ice . . .

I dig, Martin, I eat it up."

"Ten thousand alligators should chew your entrails in Times Square on New Year's," I said.

"Of course, the poem doesn't square with the facts. I know Irene Bell. She was nowhere near the gym when the fire broke out. She was on a weekend at Cornell."

"May your ancestors swim in warm milk," I said.

"But who cares for facts? A poem makes its own facts, right, Martin? The important thing is, she was

"Saved from lechy tongues of fire
To dance again in future hours . . .

That's the essential truth of it."

"Glob on the sidewalk," I said, "hang by your toes until your hairs fall out."

"Soft, she is. Also sensual and trim. But this part about sadness, Martin. Irene is a swinging girl. She laughs a lot, I am sorry to inform you."

"Prince of bastards!" I yelled. "Hitler!"

"To carry on, this business of

"While I, unworthy, smash my head
Against the door to Paradise

shocks me. Partly because I never heard it called the 'door to Paradise,' though I can buy that. But mostly because of the negative thinking."

"Your navel should fall off, Lester Pig," I said.

"What I say is sound literary criticism," he said. "Stop banging your head on the door to Paradise."

"Wait," I said. "Just wait."

"Again, Martin, your ego is selling you short. My own feelings are, it's better to make keys than bang your head on the door. Can you argue with me? Quit hanging around outside Paradise and concentrate on getting in."

"Where is your dignity?" I said. "Don't you respect anybody's borders?"

"Be nice, listen. Think of yourself as a head-smasher and you get black-and-blue brains. Think of yourself as a keymaker and you get goodies beyond your wildest dreams."

"Cell by cell, I will decompose you," I said. "I will hang your leftovers from the Home Economics clock tower."

"You are nonviolent," Lester said. "Sticks and stones. Martin, life is a matter of self-concepts. Act like you deserve a medal. If it's Irene Bell you want, Irene Bell you'll get. Leave the details to a crass arranger like energetic Lester Pig."

"On your grandmother's candlesticks, promise me," I said. "Swear not to interfere. Promise me. Don't drive me to eviscerate you in your sleep. Pledge on your heart. Promise me."

"What girl wouldn't be glad to have such a tribute?" Lester said, fluttering the napkin. "Immortality for our own Irene."

"You wouldn't," I said.

The next morning he gave my notebook to Irene Bell, with the napkin in the front cover, sticking out. In rage and pain, I refused to talk to him over supper, which bothered him, because Lester Pig has no tolerance for silence or hatred.

"She was behind in her notes," he said, sipping soup. "So I said, poor Irene. My roommate, Martin Stein, has a complete set, practically verbatim. He'll be glad to lend them to you. And she said, are you sure, Lester, that he wouldn't mind? I heard he is a brilliant chap. She called you a chap, Martin. So I said, here, Irene, take and enjoy. Every word is a gem, every idea clearly outlined for easy reading. But I understand there is some personal stuff in the book which you must not read under penalty of death. You know how artists are about their outpourings. Very possessive and touchy. And she said, do I look like the kind that pries?"

Looking neither left nor right, I stuck my fork into a veal chop.

"Admit you're glad," Lester said. "A writer needs his audience. Besides, would you want her a little behind?"

I winced.

"Accept me back into your graces, Martin. I can't endure a man and his beloved kept apart by silly shadows. Have pity. You know I'm a sick boy. If I last the year it's a medical miracle. I need forgiveness for the terrible thing I've done."

"Sick?" I said, basso profundo. "Sick?"

"Watch your decibels," Lester said. "You want the walls to tumble down?"

"The infirmary takes blood from you to boast with. You are as healthy as the pet hog in a children's zoo. What sick?"

"I'm sick of being persecuted for my humanity. Can I help if I'm not sensitive? Should you drive nails?"

"What am I going to do with you?" I said. "Lester Pig, you are unhateable."

"There," he said, perking. "Now I can digest with a free mind."

All this happened on Friday, so I had about fifty-six tortured hours before I would have to face Irene Bell again. Lester Pig began a series of maneuvers to shore up my ego and teach me technique.

"They have devices you put under the pillow," he told me while walking along, "that tell you all night what a fine person you are. I read about them in *Business Week*. Salesmen use them. Maybe we should get you such a machine and make an LP especially for the occasion. There is one trouble, though. The article said that this stimulation causes certain people to micturate an extraordinary amount."

"I would be such a person and drown," I said. "Forget the nocturnal music."

"We agreed," Lester said. "No negativism. Plan ahead. Be prepared. Dig we must."

"I don't like to blueprint my life," I said. "I prefer the natural unfolding of relationships."

"I know there's no substitute for impulse," Lester said. "But this is not like wearing falsies. It's simply a matter of dry cleaning the personality, pressing a crease in the cortex. You're revving up, warming your motor. Is that immoral?"

"Yes," I said.

Lester Pig put his loose-leaf under his chin and pretended to play it.

"Irene Bell is a genuine Stradivarius. Shouldn't you limber your digits before the concert?"

"I'm not ready for Carnegie Hall," I said. "You give yourself a girl like her after you write the novel or the Broadway play. You earn such a girl with work produced. I'm not going to Existentialism 104 on Monday. Instead, I'll kill myself."

"Nah, nah," Lester said. "Lejoordegloryetarivee. Did Robespierre or Max Pierre talk like that? The year of your birth was splendid for poets, Martin. You're vintage, ripe, ready. Besides, I have a five-dollar bet on your nose, so to speak."

"A bet? What kind of a bet?"

"With Gus Gum in the grocery."

"Gus Gum?"

"He bet me sight unseen. He doesn't even know the girl. He knows you, though. That's how people think of you, Martin. Inscrutable, if you know what I mean."

I didn't sleep Saturday night and I didn't sleep Sunday night. Irene Bell possessed my brain, cool, tall and superior. Her hair had a glow, a red-brown earth color that made me think of planting seeds. Her adorable face had green eyes wide apart so that looking into them was a delicious effort. Her cheekbones were sharp, the cliffs in a Japanese drawing. Her lips had separate lives of their own.

She had a long neck with a thin blue vein under the skin so that you could almost watch her blood circulate, which sounds frightening but was tantalizing. A little pulse in the vein showed her heartbeat—slow, regular, strong, pumping like the drum in a jazz parade. Her body's miracle was how she held together. She curved in several directions softly, as if stuffed with feathers, but her dancing gave her tendons I never knew existed. She had a waist as fragile as Panama on the map, but it joined her top to a marvelous bottom, better than Greek fragments. And her legs. Rapture, her legs. I hurt to think of them, those nutcrackers of the soul.

Irene Bell. I held a mental miniature of her in my hand. I stroked her with the fingertips of my being. I sat stark naked in front of a mirror looking at myself, feeling nothing but pity for her. Each time she flipped a page of my Existentialism 104 notebook I felt delectable chills. To sense her wide-apart eyes reading my penmanship, appraising my doodling and, above and beyond, reading my poem, brought hot flashes.

And Martin Stein had never even spoken to Irene Bell, not a good morning, not a word.

I prayed for the world's end. I fought the clock. But in spite of me, Monday came on schedule.

I will remember that Monday to my last and final bone.

I was in on its birth. It came into the world kicking and screaming, yelling for historians to wake up.

It began with a heavy moment of darkness. The town was a lump of quiet. Then a train came through. I could feel its power and speed. I looked out my window. It was snowing. The flakes were big, like parachutists taking over. Then the sun forced arms of light across the sky. High up, the clouds broke into a jigsaw. They moved fast, toward the west. A piece of moon shared the field with the young sun. The moon was weak, the sun gained courage. It was no contest.

A wind came up, carrying an April ocean smell. I opened the

window. Air gushed in, fresh and sweet, better than a cold shower.

Outside it was both spring and winter, a crazy mixture. The weather reminded me of me, all opposites, and I greeted it.

Lester Pig woke from the wind in his face.

"Monsoon, monsoon," he yelled. "The volcano is erupting. Quick, get a spoon."

"Shut up," I said. "It's only an omen, a sign from the gods."

He fell asleep again with his head under the pillow, returned to private playgrounds. I stretched my arms and breathed. My lungs had not been treated to such a party since the gym spontaneously combusted. Stale air hissed out. If I were vacuum-packed, the sound would have been identical. The effort was much too much. I lay down on my bed and conked out from abundance of oxygen. It took Lester twenty minutes to coax me back to the vertical.

He was standing over me, all dressed, on his way to an eight-o'clock.

"You'll show up in 104," he said. "We're having a fascinating lecture on Maurice Chevalier's politics."

"I'll show up," I said.

"Amen," he said, and ran for the door.

I considered a suit, white shirt and tie, but when I shaved I saw a bush of hair and foamy face looking out at me, so I gave up fancy ideas.

But to give myself heart and for personal amusement, I turned my head side to side, roaring and saying M-G-M, M-G-M, M-G-M. It was a kind of incantation, a war dance.

I put on the usual outfit. The one carnival touch was a cap my aunt sent me to celebrate her AT&T dividend. Whenever I wore it, which was rarely, I felt like an Irish intellectual of the Republican Army on the way to blow up Noel Coward.

Walking into Existentialism 104, I looked as if I'd emerged from a cesspool that morning, chasing after evolution, a throwback to our fishy beginnings.

I went in, focusing on the floor.

First I was conscious only of many hostile feet. I found a seat in the back corner of the room, took a pad out of my briefcase, wrote the date in curly letters and poised myself. When Max Pierre made his entrance, all was quiet except for the odd swish of wool and the click of knitting needles. He started to talk about absinthe, and when everyone was safely concentrating, I raised my eyes.

Not ten feet away was the back of Irene Bell, sitting next to Lester Pig. And on the wide arm of Irene's chair was my notebook, with the napkin no longer showing.

She read it, I thought. My poem is now part of her very essence. Oh, glory, hallelujah. Marvel of marvels. Cherries and plums. Yes, yes, Virginia, there is a Martin Stein. But why do my innards rejoice? Now she will certainly despise me. I have no talent. No future. An empty past. Poor breeding. I will be bald any minute. I eat no wheat germ. My rhymes do not scan. T. S. Eliot wrote better when he was nursing. Is there time to become the chiropodist my family dreamed I would be? I am a terrible person, protoplasm without purpose, yesterday's newspaper. However, there are some provocative images like the line about lechy tongues of fire and my supermarket of desire, and the poem is not bad if read with conviction. It could conceivably be the only thing found in good shape after the sun destroys earth. Things seen in perspective, Irene Bell should be honored, as Lester said, and if she is too goddamn blasé, let her go make time with Percy Bysshe Shelley.

My stream of consciousness bubbled along in that ditch, and what stopped it was I bit the eraser off my pencil. For a person like me to have no eraser is nerve-racking, because at any given minute I might revise my whole philosophy of life.

I got the wet eraser out of my mouth and held it ready between two fingers, which occupied my time as Max Pierre went on, talking now about the expression on the face of Mona Lisa, which he said he always thought was too obvious.

Once Lester Pig turned around to wink at me. I pretended that he was a stranger's garbage, ignoring him completely. Irene turned, too, and, I swear it, she smiled. I was crucified.

I made plans to escape. There were eight legs between me and the door, and I reasoned when the gong clanged I could make it by miles before the Pig and the Bell even started. But I was thwarted by a fat girl who tangled in her parka. She blocked all human progress.

When she finally organized, Lester and Irene were waiting for me in the aisle.

We were introduced. She held out her hand with a lovely gesture, bending just right at the elbow. I shook her glove. The glove was just as well, because I still had the eraser, which made a slight bump in my palm.

"I'm off," Lester said. "I've got to get down to the post office. There's a new issue out today commemorating Molly Pitcher's change of life. And there is an obscene letter from the *Reader's Digest* which I must report to my postmaster."

When Irene Bell spoke her first words, I reacted like a tuning fork, but she went right on as if I were the calmest ape in Africa.

"I think Max Pierre is a darling lamb," she said, "don't you, Marty?"

"Yes," I said, grimacing. "I really do. I mean, who wouldn't?"

"That's right," she said. "What kind of person?"

We walked into the hall.

"I want to thank you for your book," she said. "It was very useful. It saved me."

"Nothing," I said. "Forget it."

"I never knew notes could be so stimulating."

I shrugged.

"In fact," she said, "I have a request. Could I keep the book this afternoon? I'm still transcribing."

"Keep it," I said. "Why not?"

"Thank you, Marty," she said. "You can come over tonight to pick it up."

"Come over?" I said. "Well, I really don't need the bloody thing. I have this photographic memory. I mean, I can repeat everything from *Uncle Wiggily* on down."

"Everything you ever read?"

"Since the cradle."

"How wonderful," she said. "And awesome. But come anyway. Mama, Teddy and Chan are looking forward to you. They know all about you."

"They do?" I said.

"Even if it sounds aggressive," she said, "I admit it. I'm one of your fans."

"Aggressive? You, Irene? No. The truth is, you're extremely feminine."

"Bless you for saying that," she said. "I hate pushy women. I'm glad I'm a girl like in the song."

"Good," I said. "That's nice to hear. I think a person should be proud of her biology."

"You are sensitive," she said. "I knew it the moment I heard you speak."

"It's just a voice," I said.

"Do you have a class?" she said.

"Not for an hour."

"Let's walk, then. It's so stuffy in these buildings."

"The gathered perfume of scholarly generations," I said. "The class of '60 was supposed to donate an Air Wick, but they couldn't raise the gold."

"You're so cynical," Irene said.

"Not really," I said.

"I know not really," she said.

We walked down to Mingle Street, where the restaurants and stores line up.

"Let's go listen to records," Irene said.

So we went into the Stack, but the booths were all crowded.

"I did want to hear some Gregorians chant," Irene said. "I had a yen."

I had a small inspiration.

"Come with me," I said.

"Where to?"

"Monte Carlo."

She came along. I took her to Gus Gum's Grocery.

The grocery was a grocery by virtue of one box of Rice Krispies, prewar. The rest of the place was given over to pinball machines, electronic geishas who gave back more for your nickel than even Hershey's.

The illegitimate sons and daughters of Univac and IBM were all busy, so we waited for a vacancy. Irene was entranced by the bells and lights, by the banging, the pushing and the masculine dedication. Her eyes were wide with wonder.

I saw Gus savoring her, ankles up, through the smoky light, and I was proud to be with such a girl. A young man, impatient with fortune, tilted. We took over his still-warm machine, a charmer called Maiden's Revenge.

Maiden's Revenge had a stained-glass picture of a solid maiden holding a club over a villain's head. The idea was, if you scored 750,000 she boffed the villain, he lit up green, and Gus Gum gave you fifty nickels.

Meanwhile, the action had the maiden running around the edges of the glass with the villain chasing after. With each bong of the steel ball they moved like a slow-motion movie.

"Go ahead," I said. "Try your luck."

"I could never do it," Irene said.

So I stood behind her and helped her aim the plunger. Being a neophyte, she did not bang the box or urge her ball. After she shot it, she stood back, leaving everything to chance.

The ball bonged passively around, racking up a fairly good score, then plonked into the trap. So we shot another.

Our maiden never got her revenge, though we gave her six opportunities.

"Maybe she really loves him," Irene said.

"There's a consideration," I said.

"I've had a beautiful experience," she said.

"I'm glad you liked it."

"Exciting," she said. "Slice of life."

We walked outside, past the Krispies.

"This was invigoration," I said. "Thank you for your company."

"You're welcome for my company," Irene said. "But you've got to come over tonight. I insist, Marty. Should I write my address, or will your memory photograph it?"

"Write it," I said.

"See you around nineish, if that's not too late."

"Late?" I said. "No. I'm a regular owl. Nineish is just right."

"Do you like bleu cheese?"

"Bleu cheese? Yes. Bleu cheese is splendid."

"We'll have bleu cheese, beer and assorted tidbits. It's not every night that we have a poet over to nibble."

Then she waved and I waved and we parted.

"Martin Stein, the nibbling bard," Lester Pig said, after I made the error of telling him. "The bleu-cheese Beowulf. What a concept. Beautiful."

"Gargle with Drano," I said.

"Mama, Teddy and Chan," he said. "That's a curve, but you'll have to live with it. Who in hell is Chan? The houseboy?"

"I don't know," I said.

"But you'll find out," Lester said. "Martin, you were immense."

"I just stood there," I said.

"That's the secret," Lester said. "Stand there and sooner or later every woman will tell you how she wants to be fulfilled."

"Fulfilled?"

"The two rules for basic fulfilling are: one, stand there and two, beware of key phrases. For example, D. H. Lawrence. If she asks you about D. H. Lawrence, get immediately excited. D. H. Lawrence is a vital point of communication. Also J. D. Salinger, which is a different kind of reaching, but reaching nonetheless. Even bleu cheese, which to Irene Bell was a winged messenger from where she lives. If you had turned down her bleu cheese, the whole thing would have gone bosh."

"Bosh?"

"It's my word, so live with it. Language is inadequate to hold me, Martin. Did you know that in Greek plays at moments of high tension the actors burst into song? That's how I feel now out of envy and empathy."

He started to sing.

> "Stein, you don't deserve such a nibble
> Since you are basically anti-pipple."

"I am not anti-people," I said. "What gave you that idea?"

"You did," Lester said. "You, a man of optimum conditions and rigid rules. Though you think of yourself as downtrodden, you are more a judge than life's victim."

"Go back to your accounting charts," I said.

"I am a Renaissance boy," Lester said. "I travel with ease from gross national product to *Oedipus Rex*. Don't curb me."

"Express yourself someplace else," I said.

"All right, Kimosabe. But while you are evaluating, fantasizing, and mapping strategy despite yourself, remember to wash."

"Thank you, little mother," I said.

"Don't thank Lester, thank Prometheus," he said. "Without him there would still be der gymnasium."

I washed. I even shined. I was ready by five and read some Alexander Pope to relax and pass the hours. But Alexander's iambics,

da-dum, da-dum, da-dum, da-dum, da-dum
da-dam, da-dam, da-dam, da-dam, da-dam

bounced my brain like bedsprings, so I put on some Lennie Tristano and absorbed the music, which was refreshing and clean.

My weather came back at seven-thirty. It snowed again, and with lightning, too. Can you imagine? Lightning behind the snow. I never saw anything so majestic. This was unquestionably the highest type of weather. It even thundered, long, rolling booms from the rumbling belly of Zeus. Lightning, thunder and snow in a package. What more could I ask? The night alone was worth a pound of free verse.

Irene Bell lived in town. She was not a dormitory sort, not the least bit communal. She was one of a kind, a girl who needed her own four walls.

She lived on Walpole Avenue, which was up a hill. That hill was symbolic, an obstacle. No Annapurna, but a good-sized slippery hill, and with each step I felt I was accomplishing something.

I got to her house at eight-forty-seven, which qualified to my impatience as nineish. The storm was worse. I walked under flash bulbs and explosions, my soul churning. Her home was simple, a two-story frame house with three steps and one tree in front. To me, city-produced, a separated house was some kind of miracle, and I swallowed as I pressed the bell. Such chimes rang out as if they were crowning a Holiness inside.

Then a peephole opened, and a voice said, "Who is ringing the Bell bell, friend or foe?"

"Friend," I said. "I'm Martin Stein."

"Of course," the voice said, and the door opened.

Her mother. I knew this because the lady standing there kissed me on the cheek and said, "I'm Irene's mother."

"Delighted," I said.

"Are your feet wet?" she said.

"Yes," I said.

"Leave your shoes out here," she said.

"You mean take them off?"

"Both sneakers," she said.

"All right," I said, already feeling compromised.

She took my coat and cap and hung them in a closet.

"Irene is in the living room," she said.

I followed her in. From behind, she was a chunky woman, no more than five-three, fiftyish and healthy. She had none of her daughter's grace. If Irene was a supermarket of desire, her mother was more of a delicatessen.

Padding along in my socks, which were damp and clammy, I made no noise whatsoever. Not hearing myself was an eerie experience, and you could have convinced me that I really didn't exist.

The mother made a sharp left without signaling, and, through an archway, I saw Irene. She was lying on a couch, wearing a black creation, elastic and skintight, turned stomach down with a book under her face, one leg waving hello in the air. When I went in she wiggled into a normal sitting position, pulled her knees up to her chin and grinned.

"Hello," I said.

"Marty," she said.

She patted the cushion beside her and I started over there, but her mother took that seat and smiled at a flower-covered easy chair.

So I went to the chair and began to drop, but there was a rapid movement under my buttocks and a wild scream. A black, muffy beast jumped into the air and came down on the rug.

"Chan," Irene said. "You nearly sat on Chan."

Chan looked up at me from the floor. He was the biggest, hardest cat I ever saw, a bundle of muscles and fur.

"Poor pussy, pussy," Mrs. Bell said. "Go to the kitchen."

Poor pussy, pussy stayed where he was, with yellow eyes eying the skin where my collar parted.

"Nice cat," I said, out of strained love for the species. "I'm sorry I almost pulverized you."

"It was naughty Chan's fault," Irene said, pointing the finger of guilt. "Bad puss cat shouldn't be on the furniture."

Chan took her admonition with a huge yawn. His mouth opened so wide he almost turned inside out. I could see down to his tail, past a full set of fangs.

"We love our Chan," Mrs. Bell said. "He's so loyal to Irene he brings her dead birds."

"Mama," Irene said. "That's ghoulish."

"Yes, I suppose it is," Mrs. Bell said. "But it's Chan's way of saying I love you."

The muff broke wind.

"Chansy ate too much and ate too fast," Mrs. Bell said. "Does Chansy want a Tums?"

"I can't believe you're really here," Irene said. "It seems so strange."

"To me, too," I said.

"Well," Mrs. Bell said, "people have a way of meeting people, especially if they have common interests. Irene tells me you're something of a notetaker, Martin."

"I'm just compulsive," I said.

"It's nothing to be ashamed of," Mrs. Bell said. "Mr. Bell was thorough. You're from New York City, aren't you?"

"Yes, ma'am," I said. "The Bronx."

"That's fine," Mrs. Bell said. "I'm sure your parents are lovely people. Professional people, I suppose."

"Mama," Irene said. "Don't pry."

"Nonsense," Mrs. Bell said. "Martin understands. It's just natural that I want to know all about him. Irene is a fatherless girl. And so pretty. I like to know her friends."

"My father is an optometrist on the Grand Concourse," I said.

"An eye specialist," Mrs. Bell said. "Do you know it's been five years since I had my glasses changed?"

"Checkups are important," I said.

"An ounce of prevention," Mrs. Bell said. "He owns his own establishment?"

"He works for a Mr. Bimberg," I said.

"That's very sensible," Mrs. Bell said. "Let the proprietor have the worries."

"Pa is a worrier," I said. "He worries about Mr. Bimberg."

"We all have our concerns," Mrs. Bell said. "Life is not all roses. You'll come to realize that."

"Martin knows about roses," Irene said. "Stop quizzing him."

"We're getting to know one another, dear," Mrs. Bell said. "Aren't we, Martin?"

"Yes," I said. "We are."

"And you were right, Irene. He does have a gorgeous voice."

Chan yowled.

"He must be having a nightmare," Mrs. Bell said. "Or is he jealous? Chan, are you jealous because I complimented Mr. Stein?"

Chan got up and walked to the wall, where he sat scratching.

"He's restless. You know what I mean, Martin. I can't bear a fixed cat. But Chan pays a price for being a boy. He feels so cooped up in the house."

I looked over at Irene. She was pink in the cheeks.

"Winter makes us all feel a bit closed in," Mrs. Bell said. "Do you agree?"

"It makes me feel very closed in," I said.

"I thought as much," Mrs. Bell said. "You must be hungry."

"No," I said. "I just recently had . . ."

But she stood up and went toward a door which I assumed led to the kitchen.

"Don't mind Mama," Irene said in a low voice.

"I don't," I said.

"Since Papa left us . . ."

"I know," I said.

"You're sweet," she said.

"Thank you," I said.

"This is so cozy," she said, shifting her body.

Irene and I locked eyes. Our eyes glued across the space between couch and chair. Her mouth opened just enough to let in supplementary air, and my lower lip twitched. We sat that way, mutually numbed.

"I hear tell you love a good cheese," said Mrs. Bell as she came back, carrying a tray full of glasses, beer cans, potato chips, crackers and a wedge of bleu.

"I do indeed," I said. "Give me a slice any time."

Mrs. Bell set down the tray. "Help yourself," she said. "We're all a family."

We helped ourselves. I ate a cracker and poured a beer.

"That's tasty," Mrs. Bell said. "It hits the spot. You don't drive, do you?" she said, after wiping her mouth.

"No," I said.

"A machine is so much trouble," she said. "And expensive. I don't blame you."

"I'm a big walker," I said.

"You're in Liberal Arts," she said. "Isn't that correct?"

"I am," I said. "An English major."

"You'll teach, I imagine?"

"I might. I don't know."

"Teaching is nice," Mrs. Bell said. "So necessary."

"I want to write," I said.

"I love television," she said.

"Books," I said.

"Books. How fascinating. Irene didn't tell me. Books."

"I didn't know," Irene said. "You know Marty better than I do."

"A best seller can happen to anyone," she said. "I'm sure

you'll have a best seller, and then a moving picture. We'll be proud to say we knew you."

"Know you," Irene said.

"Books of poetry," I said.

"Ah," she said. "Would you like a potato chip? They're a little soggy, but that's the weather."

I ate a soggy chip and drank more beer.

"College friendships are lovely," Mrs. Bell said. "They can last for many years. Irene has such nice friends. Like that young pre-medical fellow."

"Is the cheese good?" Irene said.

"Delicious," I said. "A diamond."

"It melts in your mouth," Mrs. Bell said.

For the first time in my life, I blushed. Why, I know not, but I blushed. Mrs. Bell saw, Irene saw and so did Chan. He began chasing his tail.

"We have company," Mrs. Bell said. "Peace, Chansy."

There was a heavy stamping on the porch, somebody shaking the snow off his shoes.

"That might be Mr. Vine, the law graduate," Mrs. Bell said. "He drops in unexpectedly."

"It's Teddy, Mama," Irene said.

"So early," Mrs. Bell said. "Is he home already?"

The door opened and Teddy came in. Chan ran out of the room, a gesture of affection.

"Hang your wet clothes," Mrs. Bell said. "And come say hello to Mr. Stein."

Genetically, the Bells were an interesting family. Just as Mrs. Bell and Irene were not look-alikes, brother Teddy was unique unto himself. His closest similarity was to the horny cat.

He came in blowing cold, squeezed Mrs. Bell with a massive squeeze, enough for all the mothers of the world. Then he kissed Irene.

"I'm a snowball," he said.

"Teddy," she said. "You're freezing."

The snowball, all six feet of it, was mostly protein. He stood squared away in a Boy Scout uniform, his head topped with a crew cut that made him look like a headache brush.

"Teddy is Irene's baby brother," Mrs. Bell said. "He's sweet sixteen. Teddy, this is Mr. Martin Stein from the University."

"Yeah," Teddy said.

I stood up, wishing I had shoes, and we shook hands.

"I see you're a Scout," I said.

"A Scout," he said. "I'm practically Eagle."

"Terrific," I said.

"I'm doing my next merit badge in wood carving."

"Not everyone is academic, Martin," Mrs. Bell said. "Teddy is more the physical type."

"Physical," Teddy said. "I like sports."

"He can't wait for the Army," Mrs. Bell said. "Can you, brother?"

"Marines," Teddy said. "I can't wait for the Marines."

Teddy sat on the rug. Chan came back into the room and squatted near the artificial fireplace.

"Isn't this homey?" Mrs. Bell said. "Here we all are. We used to sit like this when Irene was a wee girl," she said.

"Mama, no Little Irene stories tonight," Irene said.

"To look at her now, it's hard to believe," said Mrs. Bell. "But she was once so tiny. Both of my children were incubator."

"Me?" Teddy said.

"Irene used to sit over there, where Chan is now, telling her father how she would marry a royal prince and take care of us all forever after. Remember, Irene? It's like yesterday."

"I don't remember," Irene said.

"Little did we know that Mr. Bell would leave us so soon," said Mrs. Bell.

"Rest in peace," Teddy said, reaching for the cat.

"Now we take care of each other. It's hard, Martin. It has been a struggle. But we're all for one."

Teddy caught Chan, but pussy did a flip, which was especially impressive for his dimensions, and escaped.

"Don't torture a dumb animal," Mrs. Bell said. "All for one, and one for all, Martin. We pull together. Teddy was a late child, but now that he's grown up so nicely he helps, too."

"I work part-time," Teddy said.

"And he's a real Bell," Mrs. Bell said. "He loves his sister. They're so close. I instill closeness in my children. Why, if anyone hurt our fairy-tale princess . . ."

"I would kill them," Teddy said.

Chan leaped onto an empty dining-room chair, clearing at least fifteen feet from a standing start.

"It's ten o'clock," Irene said, after a ship's bell went off somewhere upstairs.

"Teddy must be famished," Mrs. Bell said. "Irene, go fix brother some cocoa, I've been running all day. I'm exhausted."

"Marty and I have studying to do," Irene said.

"It's the last demand I'll make," Mrs. Bell said. "Before taking myself to bed."

Irene got up, did a knee bend without cracking, and went to the kitchen. I sat there with Mrs. Bell, Teddy and Chan.

"Yes, Teddy is the man of the house now," Mrs. Bell said. "He's our bodyguard. I hate to think what would happen if anyone hurt Irene in any way."

"I would break them in half," Teddy said, slamming a fist into an open palm.

Chan was unnerved by the sharp slap and stood on his hind legs, pawing.

"Teddy is such a powerful child," Mrs. Bell said.

"He seems in good shape," I said.

"Go and get my green box," Mrs. Bell said.

"Now?" Teddy asked.

"It's on the dresser upstairs," Mrs. Bell said.

Teddy pulled himself upright and headed, sulking, for the hall.

"Isn't he a young brute?" Mrs. Bell said. "A bull. I worry about his strength, Martin. How he emerged from my loins is a curiosity. We're all small-boned, you know."

"One of those things," I said. "I have an aunt with red hair whose . . ."

"It's amazing, Martin, but I feel I know you so well," Mrs. Bell said. "You are a bright, warm person. Irene raves about your ability. And I know just why. I went through your notebook myself."

"You did?"

"Of course, I didn't understand everything, not being college trained. But I understood enough."

"You did?"

"Yes. I understood quite a lot. Existentialwhateveritis is stimulating, isn't it?"

"Stimulating," I said.

"Would you like a napkin?" she asked.

"A napkin? No. Thank you."

"I thought you might," she said.

She got up and emptied an ashtray into a plate.

"To think that Irene will marry soon," she said. "It makes all the sacrifice worthwhile. It's a kind of reward, don't you know."

"I see," I said.

"She is beautiful," Mrs. Bell said. "A real princess. She'll make some happy boy a fine wife."

I squirmed.

"Possibly a prince," Mrs. Bell said. "Like that Grace Kelly. It's not impossible, is it, Martin?"

"Not in America," I said.

"You don't know my daughter very well, Martin. She's an accomplished girl. A common-sense girl, too rare nowadays. But she
does have her flights."

"Does she?"

"I think her dancing lessons did it," Mrs. Bell said. "They
changed her."

"How?"

"Let's just say she's attracted to intelligence, Martin. She picked
you out of the crowd. You should be flattered."

"I am," I said.

"You're an interesting boy," Mrs. Bell said, "with potential for
grand success. But it takes years to establish oneself as a practicing poet."

"About two hundred years," I said, "give or take a century."

"Time, time, time," Mrs. Bell said. "Time is such a problem
to a girl."

"There are always problems," I said.

Mrs. Bell pst-pst-pst'd for Chan, who came over and arched
while she stroked him.

"Have you read about the population explosion?" she said,
pouring another beer.

"Here and there," I said, getting interested.

"Isn't it shocking? They say in sixty years we'll all have one
square foot of space."

"We're very prolific," I said.

"All that sex," she said.

"Yes."

"Those underdeveloped areas are the worst. They have nothing
else to do. And Uncle Sam supports them."

"They say television is going international," I said. "And there
might be hope in that. Television is a kind of acceptable form of
birth control, you might say."

"Chan is so restless. Look at him. I'd let him out, Martin, if I knew he wouldn't come back and smudge the rug. Do you think that's an unfair attitude?"

"Very fair," I said.

"If I only knew for certain that Chan would wipe his four soft paws, I would let him out to find his ladyfriend."

"You would," I said.

"Cats will be cats," Mrs. Bell said. "We can't change that, can we, Martin?"

Chan yawned again, showing his cave.

"I'm liberal-minded," Mrs. Bell said. "I'm humane. I feel for my own cooped-up Chansy."

"I see that you do," I said.

"You like our Irene, don't you?" Mrs. Bell said.

"Positively," I said. "I like her very much."

"She has her flighty periods," Mrs. Bell said. "But she always comes to mother and mother helps her back to terra firma."

"She's lucky to have you," I said.

"Yes, Irene always comes back down to earth."

"Like Chan," I said. "Right-side up."

"Exactly," Mrs. Bell said. "Very well spoken. I couldn't have phrased it better. You're alert, Martin. Nothing passes you by."

There was a booming on the staircase and Teddy came in holding a small steel box. Mrs. Bell opened the box which held an A-Z file inside and took out a clean, lined card.

"This is going to be your card, Martin," she said. "I like to keep a record. It's like having pictures for Irene's memory book."

She flipped the cards. I could see writing on many and numbers on some.

"I'll write you up as the sensitive boy with the wonderful voice. The boy with promise. I'll give you an excellent review."

"I would like to be remembered that way," I said.

"Cocoa," Irene yelled.

"I'll take my cup up to bed with me," Mrs. Bell said as Irene

walked in with another tray and four cups. "Martin and I have
had a marvelous, folksy chat. But I need my beauty sleep."

"I hope you two settled the world's problems," Irene said.

"We did, dear," Mrs. Bell said.

"Take your warm drink up to your room, Teddy," Mrs. Bell
said. "The children have their studying to do."

Teddy took a cup, leaving the saucer, and stuffed two cookies
in his craw.

"Night," he said, through his Oreos. "See you around."

"Good night," I said. "Nice meeting you both."

"Martin is a lovely boy," she said. "We'll definitely add him to
our cards."

"Sweet dreams," Irene said.

Mrs. Bell and Teddy went upstairs, carrying their cocoa.

Irene put the two cups on a coffee table near the couch.

"Come sit by me," she said. "I hate talking from far away."

I moved over beside her.

"So you saw the cards," Irene said. "Isn't Mama the most eccen-
tric woman you ever met?"

"Is that what she is?" I said.

"Did she upset you, Marty?"

"Upset me?"

"You seem disturbed."

"Confused," I said. "But not disturbed."

There was a buzz between my ears after the extended conversation with Mama, and the buzzing lasted until Chan took up a
position across from us, in flying distance.

"Your cat makes me self-conscious," I said. "I feel like an off-
shore island."

"Nonsense," Irene said. "He's just behaving."

"I feel threatened," I said. "I feel in danger of being consumed."

And when I said it, I realized that I meant it. What was more
peculiar, I didn't understand why. Because it dawned on me that

what Mrs. Bell had given along with her beer, cheese and cocoa was full clearance.

There was a treaty between Mama and me, so long as I promised to wipe my paws and keep Irene comfortable but handy for her forthcoming prince. I went along with her terms. Me, Martin Stein. So by the rules of the Geneva Convention that fink of a cat should have lowered his guns and gone upstairs with the rest of them, including the incubator brother who couldn't wait for the Marines.

Wasn't Chan in on the deal? Wasn't Irene?

Well is she or isn't she, I asked myself. Or am I merely stir crazy from double meanings?

I looked for a sign.

But Irene showed nothing. She sat sipping her cocoa, radiant and supple, the heroine of my poem, the queen of the index cards.

"Marty," she said, "I don't feel like studying. I want to dance for you."

"Dance," I said. "But don't ask me to cha-cha."

"I mean interpretive dance," she said. "Wait."

She bounded into the kitchen in three enthusiastic giant steps and came back with a cookbook.

"The idea is, anything can stimulate the emotion of motion," she said. "Even a recipe."

She flipped the book.

"Read me this," she said, "and I'll improvise."

I read.

"Curry of Pork, Belgian."

Irene stood with her arms in the air.

"Mince or grate a Spanish onion," I said, following the text, "and cook in one-quarter cup butter until delicately colored."

Irene spun and bent, mincing and cooking, and she was delicately colored, oh so delicately.

"Season with a pinch of celery salt, three whole cloves, eight peppercorns and a generous pinch of thyme leaves."

The spices moved her. Although I'd never tasted Belgian Pork Curry, it became my favorite dish.

She stretched her legs until I felt her splitting, then jackknifed and rolled on the rug, then zoomed onto the easy chair, crumpled, stood and whirled. Her hair came apart and spilled over her shoulders, the top of her outfit separated from the bottom, exposing a middle of moving muscles. She breathed in gasps and fell on the floor between my legs, looking up at me.

I took her face in my hands and pulled her toward me without a thought in my skull but to taste her and take her. Me, Martin Stein.

"Stop it, stop," Irene said. "Oh, Marty, I never expected you . . . we hardly know each other."

I stopped. Old guilts drowned new courage. I felt like a fool. I stopped all right.

"Irene," I said, "forgive me. I felt a suspense all evening long with you here and your mother never leaving. I mean, when you went into the kitchen she . . . Irene, I knew that when two people . . ."

Then I saw that Irene Bell was not listening to my shaky apology. She listened to something else and smiled at what she heard.

It was a music box. A tinkly music box from Mama's room signaling the end of day, and maybe more. It played "Auld Lang Syne," but it meant taps for the eyes and ears upstairs.

The cat heard it, too. Chan looked me over. He was beaten, but a good loser. He yawned again, then ran toward the plinky tin sound, his mistress' voice.

Irene got up and turned out the lights. Outside, the lightning was bad. The thunder was loud. It was spring militant, and no doubt about it.

The music box wound out. And when it finished she was in my arms and we wrestled on the floor. If not three cloves, then two cloves. If not eight peppercorns, then six peppercorns. As long as the dash of thyme was generous. And it was generous, all generous.

The lion, full of longing, ate and drank and said thank you, thank you. The dancer, pledged to her noble cause, moved with abandon on lubricated joints. Irene Bell and Martin Stein, express trains on different tracks, came crashing together. And the story will never make the papers.

How we cried when I said goodbye.

I walked home in slush. There was a candle in the window waiting for me. An honest-to-God candle, like the kind they light on Friday night to mark the happy Sabbath. Lester Pig held the candle when I came in. He put the little flame under my chin and he said:

"Look who's here. It's Martin Stein, a person of increased value. Come, Marty. Say a few words to the universe."

A DISTURBANCE OF THE PEACE

Mary and Jim lived happily
In a cozy house with their family.
Then trouble came—
Here's what they found:
Water in the drain that wouldn't go down.
—Roto-Rooter TV commercial,
The Late Late Show

ODAY IS FRIDAY.

The E train to Manhattan is jammed with workers heading toward their jobs. Above them, fans with thick black blades turn slowly. A sudden drain on the supply of electricity has broken their motion. They circle with exasperating rhythm. A thick heat rises out of the sharp, grinding sounds of the express. The steel wheels against steel tracks give off shrieks of friction. The train enters the tunnel underneath the East River.

Floyd Copman has no seat. He is standing wedged against a girl who reads the *Daily News*. Their bodies enjoy a city intimacy. He feels her breasts and hips against him.

Sounds change as pressure builds against Floyd Copman's ear. He opens his mouth slightly. Mouth open, gulping air, Floyd Copman thinks now of a recent visit to the new vaults his bank is building in the heart of a mountain a hundred miles from New York. With other clerks from his branch he was led on a tour through huge man-made caves. He walked through rooms of stone. He followed his guide along cool corridors. Thick steel doors parted for him.

186

A little snap inside his ear brings sound back into focus. The train stops. Floyd Copman is thrown forward. Noise drains from the tunnel. The fans labor.

From somewhere in the car a remark is made about the transit system. No feeling of communion springs up among the travelers. It is simply too hot. The train waits.

Floyd Copman thinks of the planning and engineering that went into the construction of the bank's mountain vaults. He has been told exactly how many tons of rock were blasted and removed, etc., etc., but his memory is not exact on the details. He marvels at the project. Treasure Mountain is the name the vaults will have. The name is catchy and appropriate.

A gush of air and the hum of current from under the train indicate that movement is imminent. Floyd Copman braces for the jolt. But the delay continues. Lights dim and flicker.

Floyd Copman's thoughts are complicated by the memory of a late-night radio broadcast. In an interview with a successful writer of science fiction, Floyd Copman heard that life on other planets will take forms beyond human imagination, that earthly ideas of size and shape are inadequate, that a new understanding and a new tolerance will be necessary when the time comes to cope and communicate with these creatures.

As the train waits under the river, Floyd Copman speculates on the nature of extraterrestrial life. Suspended in the heat, his mind fashions a battle. Strange shapes advance on Treasure Mountain. Floyd Copman's fantasy follows two roads.

One road has no ending. The guards in the mountain find their bullets useless. The attacking enemy ravages the mountain and its catacombs, room by room, sucking defenders, jewels, stock certificates, microfilm records and priceless miscellany into pulsating bags of savage stomach acid.

The second road is happier. The guards of the mountain discover, accidentally, that they can think their enemies dead. Thought waves bloat the slime-flesh of the invaders and they pop, collapse and dry. The mountain is saved, though there is much cleaning up afterward.

Now the train creeps. The girl pressing against Floyd Copman asks the time. Her question suspends the war of the worlds. Floyd Copman gives her an answer, correct to the minute. She tells him that she will be late for work.

Go back to Monday.

The old man had been in the bank for hours, standing and watching the transaction of business. He stood like a dirty statue. Two guards came up behind him. They took his arms and dragged him toward the door.

The old man fell backward to resist them with his weight. The guards cleverly linked hands and pulled him along. He hissed and spat.

With the help of the janitor the guards forced him through the revolving door.

Those in line at the tellers' windows watched with disgust. When the guards had the old man outside he sat on the sidewalk. They raised him and walked him down the avenue.

Later Floyd Copman was told that they had taken him for three blocks, across streets and around corners. They reasoned he would not find his way back.

When the guards returned to the bank, those clients who had witnessed the incident were serviced and gone. Floyd Copman saw Mr. Munrose, the Vice-President-in-Charge, take a tour of the premises. He knew that the executive decision to oust the old man had been carefully calculated. There is always the danger of repercussion in a public place.

Mr. Munrose appeared satisfied. There were no stains or echoes. His decision had been absolutely necessary.

Floyd Copman shared his superior's satisfaction. The city is full of grotesques, he thought. Bad enough that they come out at night to eat from garbage cans and spread filth. Not in broad daylight. Not in a place of business. Especially not in a bank which trades on an image of strength and dignity. The guards had done an efficient, humane job.

At two on Monday afternoon the old man returned. Someone brought him in a taxi. He walked in quietly, as before, and took up his position across from the tellers. Everyone had been alerted to expect him.

And along with the news of his return came the whispered message that this very old man was the father of ———.

Floyd Copman was amazed at the circumstance. It was more than fantastic. The father of ———. That ——— should have such a father!

Of course, the old man was harmless. He bothered nobody and said nothing. Until the guards came he stood watching the bills pass over marble counters and listening to the coins. He was certainly harmless. He was safe as a child.

The father of ———. Then why wasn't he in an institution? It was certainly not a question of funds. Not if ——— was involved. If there were any danger, the smallest trace, he would be put away. Nothing else made sense.

His look was frightening. But who could condemn him for the disease of senility?

Better dressed, who would notice him there?

What a burden for ———. Was the condition hereditary? Would ——— end up standing, with an idiot grin, watching the movement of bills and the flash of coins?

No, of course not.

Floyd Copman found deep sympathy for them both. This was not the kind of thing you read in the papers. This was a toilet secret, floating, ignored.

Imagine that ——— had courage enough to telephone *himself*. It took courage, no question. Others, with much less at stake, would insist on a Home.

The father of ——— stood in the shadow of a marble column.

Floyd Copman knew that now the old man would be a constant visitor. He would come every day.

A guard stood near him, not ten feet away. It was one of the guards who had banished him. The old man was tranquil. His mind, Floyd Copman thought, must be a dry sponge. If he cannot remember so recent an enemy as the guard, his brain must be rotten to its center.

At ten of three Mr. Munrose toured again. Floyd Copman saw that his cheeks were red. He had been whipped, and for no reason. He had been forbidden to clean his own house.

At one minute to three, the guards gave the closing signal. As the bank emptied, the old man went too, with no protest. Floyd Copman saw a wet stain spread on his trouser leg.

The old man wet his pants. But was that a ragged action? The rancid ladies who came each day to sit alone with their safe deposit boxes probably did worse in the cubicles downstairs in the vault.

The old man only stood watching money change hands. Where is the cause for retribution in that? Who would say to ————, "Come and get your father. He made wee wee on the floor"?

All that happened on Monday.

Now the train passes a bank of bare lights hung in the tunnel. Floyd Copman can see repairmen pressed against the tunnel's sides to let the train pass. The obstruction is finally navigated. The train picks up speed. The speed brings a breeze. The fans whirl to blurs.

At Lexington Avenue the crowd thins. Floyd Copman continues downtown.

At Times Square there is a seat. Floyd Copman rushes for it. Relaxing, he feels much better. The man next to him gets up to exit at Thirty-fourth Street and drops a *Herald Tribune* behind him. Floyd Copman quickly picks up the paper, folded inside out.

The first story he reads is about a strange new virus causing an epidemic in Pakistan. Floyd Copman remembers how Asian flu crept from page twenty to page five and then to the front page. A team of American scientists has been dispatched, the story says. Last winter Floyd Copman caught Asian flu but he had been vaccinated and developed a mild case.

Why is it, he wonders, that a bug which kills in Asia merely gives New Yorkers wet eyes and stuffed noses. Still, some died of the Asian flu even in the five boroughs, and some will die of the virus from Pakistan. But not before the cold months.

Floyd Copman turns to the financial page. His eyes wander columns of numbers. He becomes absorbed in the language of plus and minus. Defense issues are up. Oils are down. Polaroid is researching a new film. The price of drugs is under investigation. Leisure industries are booming. Bowling and boating attract new millions. So it goes until the train reaches West Fourth Street.

There Floyd Copman leaves the train and walks toward the Third Street staircase. It is nine-ten. Floyd Copman's lateness is the fault of the subway. He walks quickly.

No familiar faces greet him in the crowd at the base of the stairs. The population of the subway changes with minutes. He is of the eight-thirty people, except in cases of unavoidable delay. The nine-o'clock people are strangers.

As he climbs the metal steps he sees a fellow clerk, a perpetual latecomer. The clerk, hurrying ahead, is folding a newspaper as he walks, making it smaller and less obvious. Floyd Copman's own paper, a gift of the subway, is folded under his arm.

Near the top of the steps Floyd Copman sees, scrawled on a billboard, the handwritten phrase "An Onion and You."

He has seen the message before, in fact for several months. By now he is more annoyed than curious. Many times in his life Floyd Copman has been tempted by advertisements which read "Soon It Will Be Here." After a matter of days, the it has been revealed.

But "An Onion and You" has remained a mystery through the

spring and half the summer—far too long. And now Floyd Copman wonders if it really relates to a movie or product or anything worthwhile. He is suspicious that the scrawl is only the work of a lunatic filling public walls with some private complaint.

The air covers Floyd Copman like a wool blanket. The avenue swelters. Dust from the crater where the bank is constructing its annex has been tracked onto the pavement. Sand granules flick against his eyes.

He sees that wooden planking has replaced the sidewalk near the excavation. A gangplank now leads to the door of the bank. The feel of wood boards under Floyd Copman's shoes is peculiar. He hears his own footsteps.

Beneath him is a pit. He can see wires and pipes uprooted. Floyd Copman marvels that the whole island of Manhattan is a shell. Looking into the opened earth is like observing surgery. He notices a pool of brown water in the temporary canyon. There is always water. He wonders at its origin. There has been no rain.

A bulldozer is moving in the excavation. On its iron mouth is the name "Lorraine." The trademark strikes him funny. He remembers the elephants in Central Park Zoo with delicate lady names and the female walrus at the Aquarium showing huge organs to the crowd through a glass-walled tank.

The foundation for the annex is coming along. A scale model of the new building is displayed in the bank's lobby. It will be of steel and glass. Everything will be in the open. Even the vault will be visible from the street.

The model looks pleasing but insubstantial. Like modern furniture, everything seems poised on insect legs. Of course, the structure will be solid enough. Leave it to the bank.

Floyd Copman is pushed from behind. He turns. It is the old man shoving past him. They are side by side on the planking. The old man is breathing hard, wheezing air. His face is a brutal red. He is Floyd Copman's height. Their faces are inches apart. Floyd Copman presses against the railing to let him go by. He pushes through the revolving door. As the door takes him, he smiles. Floyd Copman sees him smiling as he is whirled inside.

"Mr. —— is full of oats today," the guard says to Floyd Copman. The guard laughs. Floyd Copman grins back at him.

The guard is at least sixty. He wears a blue uniform with a black leather gunbelt around his middle. Floyd Copman and his associates often joke about his usefulness in a holdup. Floyd Copman has said that if it came to that, the robbers would lay him belly down and empty the place while he tried to turn himself over. And what of the old man in a robbery? What would happen to him? Nothing, probably. He would stand peeing while the robbers worked.

The bank is already active. Floyd Copman wants to go to the men's room to wash up and brush construction dust from his suit. But he goes right to his cage, slips his nameplate into place and opens his windows.

His first customer hands him a check. The customer is known to him. He cashes the check. The next customer makes a small deposit. Floyd Copman's business day has begun.

The morning moves smoothly. Floyd Copman notices that the old man has taken up a different position, directly across from his cage. This does not surprise him. Quite the contrary. Floyd Copman has expected this to happen.

A customer asks for five hundred dollars in small bills. Floyd Copman counts out the sum. The old man is watching, blinking as Floyd Copman handles the crisp bills. The old man locks his hands across his stomach, leans forward and waits. Floyd Copman's agile hands make the new bills crackle. With the noise, the old man's lips jerk into a spasm smile. His body actually sways.

Floyd Copman and the old man have watched each other all week. Floyd Copman realizes the bounty of pleasure he controls. He knows that the old man loves his hands.

Floyd Copman performs brilliantly. He manipulates the bills and coins like a magician. He snaps new bills, stacks the old, moves silver and copper against cool brown marble. Really, it is a game. Floyd Copman has lost all feelings of malice toward the father of ———. Really, it is hide-and-seek.

Floyd Copman shows the money, makes the money sing. Floyd Copman conceals the money, the money is silent. If Floyd Copman chooses, six or seven customers will conduct their business at the window and the old man will never see so much as a penny, or hear the slightest whisper of paper. Or, if Floyd Copman wishes, his generosity makes the old man shuffle his feet with happiness.

During stretches of deprivation, Floyd Copman sees the old man dry. The fluids seem to evaporate from him. Still he does not abandon Floyd Copman's cage. He stays. He waits. And Floyd Copman rewards him with a sudden *thok thok* as the pads of his fingers rub violently at banded groups of bills, and the birthday jingle of nickels, dimes and quarters rises like a bell song. Then the old man drips saliva through his lips and sucks it back again with his tongue. Like those fountains that use their own water.

So silly. Fantastic, this game they play. But it makes the day fly. Floyd Copman is surprised when his noon relief comes. As he leaves his cage he notices the look of gray fear on the old man's bulging face. He smiles to say, "Don't worry. I'll be back."

Floyd Copman sees that his luncheon companions, Marvin Ash and Jack Boyd, are already waiting for him. He waves toward the men's room. They signal him to hurry. Floyd Copman hurries into the bathroom.

Inside, Floyd Copman sees Mr. Munrose standing at the sink. Mr. Munrose is washing his dental plate under cold water. The vice president looks around at Floyd Copman.

"Caught with my choppers down," he says. His voice pushes out over bare gums. His upper lip is a hanging flap.

Floyd Copman is embarrassed. He turns to the white urinal. He hears a wet suction sound, then the click of teeth. The vice president comes up beside Floyd Copman and together they stand, facing the wall.

"Hang on to your teeth," his superior says. "Take care of your teeth. You have no idea how important they are."

"Yes," Floyd Copman says.

"There's no substitute for them."

Floyd Copman is trying to relax the muscles below his stomach. He is waiting for his bladder to function. He feels ridiculously shy. Mr. Munrose is already flushing. As he zips up his fly the vice president sighs.

"What a week. This is one weekend I'm looking forward to," says Mr. Munrose.

Floyd Copman still stands at the urinal. Mr. Munrose is washing his hands.

"How's the missus?" says the vice president.

"Getting along fine," Floyd Copman says.

"It's your first, isn't it?"

"Yes.'"

"She's getting close, isn't she?"

"Eighth month."

"Wonderful. Wonderful," says Mr. Munrose.

Left alone, Floyd Copman empties his bladder, washes, combs, swishes water in his mouth, dries his hands and goes to meet his lunch buddies. Marvin Ash and Jack Boyd are waiting outside. Floyd Copman is nearly across the bank floor when he realizes that the old man is moving after him. He walks faster. He does not wish an encounter. But it seems inevitable. The old man, moving at an angle, will cut him off. The guard is facing in another direction, unaware of Floyd Copman's situation.

Floyd Copman rushes for the door. The old man hurries too. Floyd Copman sees the confusion in his eyes. A foot from the door they are together for an instant. The old man puts his head forward, taking a deep inward breath.

Floyd Copman is through the door now. His friends, who have been watching, hail him. He turns back to see if he is followed. No. The old man has stayed in the bank. The revolving door is still.

Floyd Copman and his friends go down the gangplank and across the street.

Marvin Ash is laughing loudly. He leans toward Floyd Copman and pretends to smell him. Jack Boyd is laughing too.

"That's what he was doing," Marvin Ash says. "You know, that's what he was doing. He must think you're some kind of hydrant."

Floyd Copman joins their laughter. He knows that Marvin Ash is correct. The old man was smelling him. He feels a wave of nausea. No question. The old man was smelling for the odor of money, the green algae smell of bills, the pungent metal smell of coins.

"Floyd found a friend," Marvin Ash says. "An influential associate. Floyd, you've got it made. Tell him to ask his sonny about making you president."

"I'll send you a postcard from Washington."

"It takes all kinds," Jack Boyd says. "Onward and upward."

The three men walk up Sixth Avenue to Eighth Street. They feel the heat filling their lungs.

A young girl goes by pulling a shopping cart. She is wearing shorts and a light cotton blouse. Her feet are strapped into sandals. Her hair is loose and long, pitch black, a river of ink. Her breasts hang low in the blouse. They look free and fleshy. Their nipples make little pimples in the fabric. Her waist is held tight by a wide leather belt with a large silver buckle. She holds her trunk and head very straight. Her bare legs are too short for her top. They move too quickly and cover too little ground to carry off the image of tranquillity. The shorts hug her thighs and outline a soft rise under her belt and the tight triangle between her legs. Her face is damp with perspiration, pale in the sharp sun.

"Melon for dessert," Jack Boyd says.

"Too much ass for summer," Marvin Ash says.

"I personally like it," says Jack Boyd.

"Too much tit for weather like this. Give me an Emily in the summer. Cool. Small. Nice boobies. Short hair on her head. Emily in an air-conditioned hotel room someplace where nobody knows you or gives a damn about who's who and a bottle of ice-cold martinis."

"I like that one," Jack Boyd says. "Do me something."

"Your trouble is you like everything," says Marvin Ash. "The rest of humanity divides up. Tit men. Ass men. You are a tit-ass man. You should be ashamed of yourself. You're not even married a year."

"I can't help it if I'm a lecher. Besides, you were my teacher. Really, Floyd, I was a virgin when I first came here. This man corrupted me."

"Say that again," Marvin Ash says. "I can still teach you plenty."

"When I'm your age I hope I know as much," Jack Boyd says. "Floyd, here comes the story of how he got it on the BMT subway or how the girl came to sell him a subscription to the *Saturday Evening Post*."

"Talk to yourself," Marvin Ash says. "I can still tell the difference between a hot sloppy oven and a nice breezy summer nosh."

"So go. Emily holds it on a platter every day. You've been talking for a year, you phony baloney."

"It's not so easy," says Marvin Ash, deeply serious. "Where? Where can I take her? A good hotel wouldn't rent to us. She's too dark. A flea bag is dangerous. The house cops shake you down. The thing to do is rent a furnished room for a week or two."

"So rent. Rent, big daddy. Floyd and I will chip in. Ask her today."

"She'd say yes," Marvin Ash says. "She's got a tremendous case of the hots for me. She practically asked me up to her place. But

I don't want no knife in my gizzard. Who knows what she lives with."

"Floyd," says Jack Boyd, "be my witness. I'm calling his bluff."

"Listen, I'm married fifteen years. I've got two wonderful children. I've got to be careful."

"Be careful. I'll stand in the corridor throwing body blocks."

"It's no joke. This is a century of men with cameras. Take the Queen Mother of England. There's a woman with plenty left. But she's in a trap. She can't make a move. I'll bet she hasn't had it since her husband died."

"Where in hell did the Queen Mother come from? We were talking about a spic waitress in Howard Johnson's."

"Be nice, don't fight," Floyd Copman says. "It's too hot for sex."

"Not by me. This heat brings out my seminal fluid," Jack Boyd says.

"He's still a boy," says Marvin Ash. "A young consumer in his acquisitive years. All his pores are open. Let him rave, Floyd."

"I'm horny, that's all. Every man has a tragic flaw. Besides, you're worrying about the Queen's mama and I'm raving?"

Floyd Copman, wilted with heat, usually enjoys the banter between Marvin Ash and Jack Boyd. Marvin Ash, like an old rhino, snorts and grumps in the jungle, belching and farting over ancient outrages, too careful to risk a charge in any direction.

Jack Boyd, an antelope, dances around him, spits liberally in his eye, jumps back and forth like a flame. The two exist together. They follow the same path.

Jack Boyd is closer in age to Floyd Copman so that Floyd Copman feels an easier kinship with him. Both joined the bank in the same year, both married in the same season. But they are not tight friends. Their only social contact is at lunch—Marvin Ash, already in his forties, already beyond certain hopeful optimism, acting as a fulcrum for their relationship.

Their noontime conversation is remarkably similar day after

day. Floyd Copman finds this entertaining and undemanding. He enjoys listening. Marvin Ash and Jack Boyd enjoy an audience. But today, Floyd Copman is out of things. The incident at the bank has left him disturbed. Besides, when the talk turns to women, he thinks immediately of his wife. He sees her alone in their apartment, uncomfortable in the heat, very pregnant, waiting out her time. Since the beginning of summer, Floyd Copman has felt a suspension of desire. He feels heavy himself, too clumsy for movement.

Inside the Howard Johnson's, refrigerated air bathes over them. Floyd Copman's shirt sticks to his back. He waits uncomfortably for a table. The restaurant is noisy and crowded. Jack Boyd tugs at his arm and nods in the direction of the counter. Marvin Ash is there talking with a tiny waitress in yellow and green. She smiles while he talks and waves an ice-cream scoop at him. Marvin Ash points to the scoop, then to the girl's thin chest. The girl laughs and goes to serve a customer.

The headwaiter gestures. The men follow him to a table. They wait while the table is cleaned, sponged and set. The leather seat feels cool to Floyd Copman, chilling him through his wet jacket. He is seated opposite Marvin Ash and Jack Boyd. He notices that Marvin Ash's seersucker has a crumpled look. His shirt is wet in patches. His tie, a blue dotted swiss, is hanging loose. Marvin Ash wears his clothes hard. In contrast, Jack Boyd's palm beach, starched shirt and striped tie look fresh and neat. His slender build and thin face add to his crisp aspect.

A new girl comes to take their orders. She is all business. There is no joking with her. Each orders the daily special, filet of sole, with potatoes and vegetables. Floyd Copman remembers that Marvin Ash usually eats the same amount of food as himself. Yet Marvin Ash is fat. He must eat great quantities between meals, or at home.

The waitress brings tomato juice for each of them. Jack Boyd raises his red glass.

"To Marvin Ash," he says, "and to Mamma Queen. Salud."

"To Mr. ———," says Marvin Ash. "The happy moron. May he and Floyd enjoy a long and happy relationship. Floyd, you do smell delightful today."

Floyd Copman drinks his juice, then excuses himself. He has forgotten if he washed his hands back at the bank. He goes to the lounge, scrubs himself, and dries by wringing his hands under ultraviolet rays. When he returns to the dining room, his food is waiting. Marvin Ash and Jack Boyd are eating their fish while they study a booklet prospectus for a mutual fund.

"I see your point," Marvin Ash is saying as Floyd Copman settles into his seat. "But I maintain that this is no time to enter the market. If you ask me, this is a time to retrench."

"I can't agree with you," Jack Boyd says. "It seems more sensible to build a portfolio with a long view. I believe in dollar averaging. I'm not that much of a speculator, Marvin, but the trends have held up over the last twenty years."

"I'm not out to change your mind, Jack. Nothing I say is going to change your mind. And the half-hour I spend on the *Wall Street Journal* doesn't make me Bernard Baruch. But to my way of thinking, when elevator boys and Mr. Shmendrik's secretary run to buy stock, that's the time to bye-bye baby."

"A sensibly planned portfolio . . ."

Floyd Copman slowly chews his fish, feeling for bones. He listens intently. He owns a few shares of AT&T and has considered investing a portion of his savings but he has not reached a final decision.

"Tri Continental or the other closed-end funds have a certain merit," Marvin Ash says, "but just because the widows and orphans buy them doesn't mean that the wise boys won't. . . ."

Marvin Ash is speaking well, with conviction. Jack Boyd is making a good case too. Floyd Copman feels a satisfying sense of unity with them. He thinks of the long columns of numbers on the financial pages, where fractions determine fortunes.

"I've sent for a book on warrants," Jack Boyd says. "The leverage is fantastic. Not that razzle-dazzle manipulation is for me. But a certain amount of risk capital . . ."

"You'll break your back on warrants. If you want to play in those leagues, go with commodities. Last year, a cousin of mine . . ."

The discussion continues through lunch. The men order coffee, smoke cigarettes and get up to leave. On the way out, Floyd Copman notices that Marvin Ash does not turn to wave at his waitress. She is standing at the counter, her wide-nosed, thick-lipped, black-eyed face watching as they pay their checks. Marvin Ash is still holding the prospectus as they venture into the street. The heat storms over them as they walk toward the bank.

The sky is white. A sharp line of shadow divides the avenue. They walk into the sun. Floyd Copman sees pedestrians on the outer rim of the sidewalk as burning black shapes eclipsing light. He focuses on the pavement. Its glare is easier on his eyes than the silhouettes that populate the sun-drenched avenue.

Floyd Copman has a sudden urge to tell his friends about his curious game with the father of ———. They can watch. He will have two allies for the rest of the day.

"No," Marvin Ash says, from a profound part of himself, as if predicting a death. "I do not like the stock market in its current state."

Somehow his pronouncement is terribly final. Floyd Copman decides to keep silent.

They reach the wooden platform and mount the boards. The tat-tat-tat-tat of a drill hammers their ears. Floyd Copman sees the bulldozer crawl toward a pile of debris.

The three fellows separate with a wave and a wink. Each heads for his own window. Floyd Copman walks smartly across the marble floor.

On the way to his cage, Floyd Copman passes Mr. Munrose's office. Its cool walnut door is closed. Outside the door, on an

island of blue carpeting, is the domain of Miss Vlachek, whom
Floyd Copman has heard called the Business Nun. In her small
kingdom, Miss Vlachek searches her desk. She is looking for some
document. The carpet island hardly contains her search. The con-
cave face of the secretary, arched like a hangnail moon, communi-
cates Mr. Munrose's moods. The crescent is troubled. Floyd Copman wants to know if any more calls have come from ————. But
Miss Vlachek is in no mood for office gossip.

Refreshed by the lunch break, Floyd Copman finds himself an-
ticipating the afternoon. He is eager to resume his game of hide-
and-seek. He has deliberately avoided the old man's eyes, but he
knows their play has already begun.

Floyd Copman enters his cage. His relief is a trainee, a city
cherub with pink, puffy cheeks and oily hair.

"Good afternoon, Mr. Copman," the trainee says. "I'm glad
you're back. Mucus face has me shook up. I'm absconding to
Brazil."

"What's your problem?"

"Mr. ———— and me do not get along. Not that I don't respect
elder statesmen. But mucus face keeps looking at this window.
I think he thinks this is the zoo. I think he wants to feed me
peanuts."

"I don't like that 'mucus face' expression."

"You're right, Mr. Copman. It is pretty pathetic. I'm sorry."

"Was he here all the time?"

"He didn't take a lunch hour, if that's what you mean. I think
he lives off air. He stands around dribbling, which is one sight
that gives me the heaves."

"He's a sick person."

"I'm sick too, Mr. Copman. I have no appetite. I'm going out
someplace to throw up. I don't envy you putting up with that all
day. I don't see why Mr. Munrose can't have him thrown out no
matter who he is."

"I'll tell Mr. Munrose you said so."

"He's all yours now."

The trainee goes and Floyd Copman takes over his station. He tidies up his implements. In just an hour the trainee has managed to upset things. After five minutes Floyd Copman suddenly raises his eyes. They crash into the old man like headlights. Amazingly, Floyd Copman can see the result of his stare. His play partner is covered with a purple blush, as if blood seeped through his arteries and veins and spilled under his skin. The slit of mouth opens, panting wet sucking sounds. A woman writing in her checkbook gathers her papers and moves to another table.

The very fact of recognition startles Floyd Copman. It is brought home to him that the old man has a mind or at least the shreds of a brain. Floyd Copman has considered him as a totally sensual creature, fat, bone, saliva, gelatin eyes. His game has had the quality of teasing a worm with a stick, of prodding a sunfish on the beach. Now he sees that the old man has the capability of re-membering shapes.

As Floyd Copman services a customer, he conjures an image of a room filled with burned wires and blown tubes. He imagines his image behind the old man's eyes. His imaginings have a moist, live feeling. He feels his picture drawn into gray quicksand pools.

This quality of mind makes the old man less predictable. Floyd Copman questions his wisdom in encouraging the affair. The joke has gone out of it. Floyd Copman sees that it is a serious matter.

Floyd Copman remembers being followed home by a cretin of a night creature who chewed on a handkerchief. It happened after a meeting of his lodge. The creature fastened to him as he waited on a subway platform. It watched and followed him. It entered the same car. It left at the same station. Outside, Floyd Copman saw no one following, but he sensed pursuit. Even in the halls of his apartment house he felt thick shadows. Locked in his own apart-ment, he woke his wife to tell her the story. Sleep weary, she took his hand and put it on her belly. She was hot with blanket heat. In the morning she remembered nothing of the incident, so he told her again over breakfast.

The next customer asks Floyd Copman to check his balance. Floyd Copman explains that there is a charge for this service. The depositor agrees to pay the charge. Floyd Copman goes to the records in search of the proper coded card. He telephones for information.

This bit of business interrupts his thoughts. The intrusion is disturbing. His thoughts have been leading somewhere and he would like to discover their destination. But the task at hand must be served. Floyd Copman secures the balance figure, writes it on a slip of paper and returns to his window. The customer takes the slip, is satisfied, and leaves the window.

Floyd Copman sees that the father of ———— is standing quietly. He has learned that each disappearance will be followed by a return. Floyd Copman senses that this grain of sophistication will complicate his game. The old man laughs.

The day goes on. Floyd Copman does his work. In the last hours the bank grows busy again. More customers come and wait in line. Floyd Copman, on the verge of the weekend, has his work cut out for him. There is much to do before three. He works fast. Customer after customer comes. The guard makes sure each teller's line is supplied. New bills crackle. The changemaker punches out a flow of coins. Floyd Copman moves in a continuous, energetic rhythm. He does his work step by step, steadily, easily. He is absorbed in his efforts, carried along. Looking up quickly, he sees that the old man is submerged in his hands. Floyd Copman finds things to do, new important things. He opens and closes the metal drawers of a cabinet. He stacks a roll of half dollars against the marble tray. He sharpens a pencil in an electric grinder.

Floyd Copman builds an emotion. He does this beautifully. He pulls the old man after him. With each customer Floyd Copman shifts his weight, moves differently. He sees that the old man is in a sweat, a boil. Like a toy train Floyd Copman pulls his baggage along. The train churns harder, higher, into a land of mountains. Floyd Copman's fingers dance. The money comes and goes, flying, singing.

While he works, Floyd Copman thinks again of the night when he was pursued by the handkerchief chewer. Suppose this old man follows him home. At lunchtime he tried. Why not in the afternoon? Why not for the weekend? It is a risky business. Floyd Copman knows that.

The toy train moves in spurts, pushing wind. It moves along a ledge, through thin air. The guard passes his window. He winks and gestures toward the old man. Even the guard senses their game. And Mr. Munrose must know. He must, by now. Everyone knows.

What can Mr. Munrose think of all this? Mr. Copman, you seem to have an inside track, so to speak. Understand our gratitude. But under no circumstances risk your own well-being. We cannot condone any action that would result in harm. We will support your decision, confident that you will be guided by wisdom, prudence, caution. But reconsider. Reconsider.

The toy train splits a flock of birds. Ahead is another peak, a mountain hollowed to its gut. Its insides are bloated with stored gold. It shines like a light bulb. The toy train heads for its heart. And with the train the old man comes, his spit turning to steam on the molten rails.

The clock is moving toward three. Floyd Copman bands a package of tens. He accepts a large deposit. He empties a sealed bag. He counts and recounts and writes and stamps. He verifies. He phones. He directs.

The toy train roars strain. The old man has moved forward, only a step, pulled by Floyd Copman's marvelous hands. The guard approaches. The old man steps back. Slowly the toy train inches up the final shining mountain.

Floyd Copman is tired. But he moves. He keeps moving. Now

the window is empty. There are no more faces. Floyd Copman clutches a handful of money. The old man leans. Floyd Copman has a single bill in his hand. He snaps it between thumb and forefinger. The old man moans. The toy train touches the mountaintop. It hovers. It splits. Floyd Copman moistens his lips. He licks his cheek. He takes the bill slowly in his mouth and chews it into a ball. He does this, then pretends to chew and swallow.

And the old man screams violent outrage. He screams and screams. He charges the bars. He smashes his face on the bars. Floyd Copman sees the face pushing steel, pushing through.

Floyd Copman, feeling dizzy and sick, walks with Marvin Ash to the Independent subway. Mr. Munrose has detailed Marvin Ash to ride home with him. Floyd Copman has declined the offer of a taxi. He feels capable of taking the train.

"There's no need for you to ride all the way out, Marvin."

"I can't let you go alone."

"I'm fine. I would certainly tell you if I felt I couldn't get home alone. Look, honestly, Marvin, forget it."

"You went out like a light. I would have dropped dead."

"I didn't know what hit me. That face. My God."

"Jesus, Floyd. At least you missed seeing him when they took him away. It had to happen."

"Did they call the son?"

"Of course. Immediately."

"He'll get the treatment he needs. They won't let him go roaming."

"I should hope not."

At the subway entrance. Floyd Copman puts his hand on Marvin Ash's arm.

"Go home, Marvin. I'm OK. I appreciate your walking with me, but I'm in good shape now."

"You're absolutely sure you feel up to it?"

"Yes. Absolutely."

"Because I'd be glad . . . "

"No. Go home."

"I already called the wife."

"Thanks, Marvin," Floyd Copman says sincerely. "I'm back to myself. It was a jolt. I never fainted before."

"Go home. Fix yourself a cool drink. Sit around in your underwear. Let your wife bring the pipe and slippers."

"That's what I'll do. Thanks again, Marvin."

"Rest. You need it. Take care."

"You take care too. Thanks again."

"Take it easy."

Floyd Copman goes down into the subway. The station is not yet crowded but the heat is impossible. It burns his throat. Floyd Copman takes off his jacket and stands on the platform, safely back from the track. His eyes are not yet focusing normally. After the glare of the street, the subway dark contributes to his sense of unbalance.

He remembers waking on Mr. Munrose's leather couch. The father of ——— will not roost in the bank anymore. Suppose he had continued to return day after day and moved into the new building when it was complete. Floyd Copman imagines a little icon of the old man placed inside the scale model of glass and steel.

The train sound fills the station, then the train itself, showering sparks. Floyd Copman enters the car. The doors glide shut.

There are several seats. Floyd Copman chooses one facing in the train's direction. The train rocks his body.

Floyd Copman wonders where they will take the old man. To the vaults, he thinks. What a watchdog he would make. What an alarm. To a hospital. Print George Washington on lettuce leaves and feed him salads for his remaining years. The father of ———.

At Lexington Avenue a crowd of shoppers pushes into the car. Soon all the seats are occupied. A man stands in front of Floyd Copman reading the afternoon paper. Floyd Copman scans the headlines and thinks of the world's pain.

The train is in the tunnel under the East River. It loses speed. Floyd Copman remembers that there is construction. The train waits. Floyd Copman thinks of the train under tons of water. Not water, mud. He knows that this tunnel is probably the safest place in case of atomic attack.

He sees the old man's face. The taste of money fills his mouth. Glossy. Oily. The bill was filthy with germs. Who knows how long it was in circulation? They will find the wet bill on the floor. The cleaning woman will find it. No.

Floyd Copman reaches into his pocket. He has the bill. Yes. He remembered to pocket the bill. It was a cruel thing, a cruel game. A private stupid game.

The train is moving. Floyd Copman thinks of his wife. He thinks of the baby kicking inside her. He remembers a ridiculous story Marvin Ash told about a woman whose baby cried inside her in a movie theater. Impossible. It was nice of Marvin Ash to volunteer to come home with him. Of course, Mr. Munrose insisted.

Floyd Copman thinks it is hard for his wife to be carrying in summer. Better in autumn or winter. The train rushes into Queens Plaza. There is an exchange of passengers.

Floyd Copman thinks of his wife in the apartment alone. He wonders if he will tell her the story. Why say anything?

The baby will be born in September. September, August, July, June, May, April, March, February, January.

Which night in January? Floyd Copman thinks himself silly for wondering. The thing is, one of the wrigglers found his way home.

A BREAK IN THE WEATHER

AMOS HAD A COLD AND MADE SOUNDS LIKE *aieeehoom* EVERY third or fourth breath. It was unnerving. Lisa gave him Hycomine, Triaminic and aspirins on top of the penicillin.

"Look at the little drug addict," she said. "He's so congested. He must be having terrible dreams."

I looked at the little drug addict. Amos twisted in sleep, looking for a comfortable position. My heart went out to him. I am terrified when Amos gets sick. He is our only child. I love him in a way that is painful. He is the best thing I have going for me. But there is only one of him. And I am a hypochondriac. I worry from diseases they might bring back from outer space.

"We got to have more kids," I said.

"Jesus, how brutal," Lisa said. She knew what I meant. She knew that in my deepest insides I was thinking about spreading the base of my emotional investments. Since I began reading the *Wall Street Journal* I tend to think like that, despite my poetic nature. I have developed a conglomerate personality, aggressive and fearful. Lisa read that thought too.

"Diversify. Right?"

"All our eggs, you should pardon the expression, are in one dear basket," I said. "It wouldn't hurt to have more kids around. It would be good for Amos too. Of course, if you're not up to all that fornication . . . "

"Don't punish me," Lisa said. "It's your office dinner party. If you don't want to go, I'll cancel the baby-sitter."

"I have got to go."

"Go yourself."

209

"Go yourself. You're saying that because it's my thing. You know I can't go myself. It would be bad for my image. You are absolutely essential at this dinner party. The whole party is so we can look at each other's wives and have a deeper human sense of one another."

"Very funny," Lisa said. "First you make me feel guilty about leaving Amos, then you make me feel guilty about wanting to stay home. That's some technique. It stinks."

"At least the sitter is a nurse. Almost a nurse. And the party is only fifteen minutes away. God forbid if anything did happen she could call us."

"What can happen? Every kid in the city has a cold."

The student nurse rang the bell at seven-thirty. I answered the door.

"Hello," the little nurse or nursling said. "I'm Amy Pokko. You must be Mr. Craft."

The embryo nurses who sit for us come from St. Vincent's Hospital. They have names like Amy Pokko, where the first name is beautiful and the second kicks you in the stomach. Besides the fact that their names do not hang together, they are all very pert and pretty. And they carry books depending on their term and current course. Amy Pokko did not have pediatrics books. She had kidney books.

"We haven't met before," I said. "We usually use Leslie, Marie, Angela or Sue. Horslip, Didliglia, Xekopolis or Beerbeider. They're all on retreat this weekend."

"I know. I room with Angela Didliglia."

"Ah."

"Is that Amy Pokko?" Lisa said. "Would you ask her to come in, Harry."

"Of course," I said. "Come in, Miss Pokko."

Amy Pokko came, examined the living room, and apparently approved of the furniture because she smiled.

"Take her coat, Harry."

I took her coat. Amy Pokko had a marvelous body, like all of them. The St. Vincent's nurses have a very sensual quality, slightly starched. They look so crisp and cute in their white uniforms and blue capes. But in civilian clothes they are loose and languid. Walking those children back to the hospital at curfew time, you pass a corridor of parked cars in which freshmen, juniors and seniors are kissing good night until the last and final moment of freedom is done. You turn your sitter over to a nun and you get a blank, beatific look, not even a receipt. It is sweetly unnerving.

"Aren't you a pretty girl," Lisa said.

"Thank you," said Amy Pokko.

"When they come out of the ether they must think they're in heaven," I said. "Ha hee."

"Don't mind my husband," Lisa said. "He has an odd sense of humor."

"Angela told me."

I went into our room to finish dressing. I could hear Amos breathing in his room and, in the living room, Lisa telling Amy where the TV was, how to find food, filling her in on Amos' condition, showing her various medications, and listing telephone numbers ranging from our number at the party to our doctor's number to numbers for police emergency, the neighbors and the doorman.

"Double-lock when we go and don't open for anybody," Lisa said.

"I know that," Amy Pokko said.

"You won't have trouble with Amos."

"I hear he's a darling."

"Amy and Amos," Lisa said.

"His respiration is funny," Amy Pokko said.

"What do you mean his respiration is funny?" I yelled from our bathroom. Coming from a student nurse that comment was dangerous.

"Your husband must be some character," Amy Pokko said. "Angela said he's a laugh a minute."

"Sometimes two laughs a minute," Lisa said.

In the bathroom I buttoned and put on shaving lotion. There were two bottles of lotion, Royall Lyme and Monsieur Balmain. A year ago if anybody said I would be using perfume I would have gone into homosexual panic. Now I used lotion. Lisa gave me the bottle for Christmas and I was trapped by the gift. The worst part was, I liked it.

"Smell me," I said when Lisa came in to finish her hair.

"Leave me alone," she said. "You have already ruined the party. And who the hell wants to go to the damn thing anyhow. I'd rather go see *Bonnie and Clyde*. The whole apartment is a mess. I should do laundry. Shit."

"You look disgusting when you're mad," I said. "Look at your face in the mirror. Hide that charming expression under tons of makeup."

"Get out of here," Lisa said.

"I was just making my toilet," I said.

"There's a hydrant down the street," Lisa said. "Use that."

Before we left, Lisa looked in on Amos. I refreshed Amy Pokko on the telephone numbers, medicines and security preparations. *Aieeehoom.*

"He seems to be breathing better," Lisa said.

"Really?" I said.

"Now look," Lisa said. "If you . . ."

"Come on. We're already a half-hour late."

When we left, Amy Pokko locked all three locks on the apartment door. Lisa, bundled in a great fur, waited for the elevator in deep silence. I listened to hear if we could hear Amos breathing better from around the curved hall and behind the bolted doors.

In the car Lisa asked me if I realized that she had not been out of the house since Amos started running fever a week ago. I realized. And I reminded her that I wasn't exactly playing backgammon at Monte Carlo. I was working and on hardly any sleep.

Suffering is mutual in a marriage, especially when there is an only child and he has a cold. I reminded Lisa that she should have expected that.

"Naturally, though, being brought up as a little art genius in Connecticut, there may have been things mummy and dada didn't tell you. All this responsibility may come as a surprise to you."

"Let me out of the car. I'm going to the movies."

"You are going to the dinner party. If you give me any trouble whatsoever I am going to sleep with your mother the next time she comes down to visit. Zap, I am going to ram it to her, right on the new sofa. And won't she be surprised, eh?"

"Harry, if you don't like the way things are, why the hell don't you . . ."

"Because I am sick," I said. "Sick."

We drove as recklessly as possible in New York traffic. Lisa sat in the death seat and knew it. She was too proud to fasten her seat belt. I used that against her.

No words were spoken. Our wheezing baby, a few miles back, was in the car somehow pointing accusing fingers.

We entered the party, in the penthouse of a new apartment building called the Dylan Towers, all warmth and smiles. I browsed among the wives of my fellow workers. Most of them were bland as yogurt. Mine was the best. That was pleasing and also depressing.

The party, predictable, went well enough. At one o'clock we said our goodbyes. Two calls to Amy Pokko established the fact that while Amos was restless, he was still alive. But Amy Pokko had a one-thirty curfew.

"If those seedling nurses are late they get beaten by the Pope," I said.

"Well, that's that," Lisa said in the car. "Another glorious Saturday."

"Come down off it," I said. "It was a nice party. The people were nice. What the hell more do you want?"

"Want?" Lisa said in a wan voice. A hurt voice. A faraway voice.

"Oh, Christ," I said and put on the radio too loud. The speaker faces the death seat and you get it full blast there.

Downtown, we found a parking space fast and there was still some time before Amy Pokko's visit to real life terminated.

"You want coffee?" I said.

"What's the use?" Lisa said.

"That is the stupidest reply possible to a question like do you want coffee," I said.

"You are the smart one," she said. "A laugh a minute."

Again in silence, the marriage weighing heavily, we rode the elevator up. Halfway to our door we heard Amos crying.

And we ran, like tugs seeking a floundering ship, impelled by mercy but with an awareness of salvage rights. Sometimes there is a terrible separation between husbands and wives as they rush to converge on a child with a chest cold. It is something they do not mention in the manuals which tend to be obsessed with positions. New positions may be the be-all and end-all in Rangoon, but in New York they are just so many damned new positions.

"The telephone woke him," said Amy Pokko, holding a warm but not burning Amos.

"He's a sleepy-poo," Lisa said, taking him. Amos snuggled into her soft coat.

"Who called at this hour?" I said. I say lines now that I never believed I would ever say, like *Who called at this hour?*

"A long distance from Rome. Rome, Italy. Madam Vinip."

"Did she say Mona called from Rome?" Lisa said from Amos's room.

"Yes, Mona called. Isn't that wonderful? She called to wake Amos. It's the hot line from some spaghetti orgy."

"You have to call overseas operator twenty-five," Amy Pokko said.

"I wonder what's happening," Lisa yelled from Amos's room, in a voice loud enough to joggle a growing subconscious.

I paid Amy Pokko and walked her home.

"I never took a call from Rome," she said. "It's exciting."

"Yes and no," I said. "Mrs. Craft has this friend from her school days who inherited a bundle. She's a sculptress."

"They have to know anatomy."

"She knows a lot of anatomy. See, Amy, she had this marriage going for ten years, a decade, has a couple of kids and so forth, but she broke up the marriage about a year ago to go into stud, so to speak. Anyhow, she took up with this faun, John."

"Faun?"

I put my fingers up over my forehead like horns, feeling a little guilty about inflicting the story on Amy Pokko. I have a tendency to experiment on living subjects that is certainly evil.

"A human faun. A beautiful boy. You know there are men who live off rich ladies, Amy. Sexual and social acrobats."

"My goodness."

"Right. The thing that's interesting is, the women know it. In the movies they find out and get all upset. But in real life, Amy, they know it and like it. Go explain that."

"It takes all kinds to make the world."

"Uh huh. Say that again. Well, old Mona has this fabulous apartment and a summer house on the coast and a faun. The catch is, the faun treats her terribly. I spent a night with them last year when I went over on business. Mona had these pains in her leg. And all night, in the rain yet, she hobbled after the faun and me going to these night clubs and things."

"It sounds arthritic."

"I don't know. She was wearing this low-cut thin dress and open sandals. And she hurt. She was really in agony. But on she went. And on top of that she paid the checks. Imagine, Mr. Faun sat there looking around for reflections and sulking a little or cracking jokes while she wrote out these checks. It got to me, Amy, and I consider myself broad-minded."

"Anything different is hard to swallow."

"You could say that. I mean, when Mona asked me what I

thought of it, all I said was, it's all very nice but in my opinion she was taking too much crap. And do you know what she said? She said the faun used to sleep with this movie star and he was quite a catch."

"Good night, Mr. Craft."

"Are we at the hospital already? I got carried away. The thing is, Lisa—Mrs. Craft—thinks this Mona is herself with wings. If anybody else called at dawn and woke the kid Lisa would flip. But Mona is another story."

"Well, good night. It was a pleasure sitting for Amos."

"And everytime Mona writes or calls there's an open invitation to go over to the good old Eternal City. Not to knock Rome."

"Mr. Craft . . ."

"Oh. Good night, Amy."

In she went past the Check-in Nun. I lit a cigarette and watched baby nurses pour out of Chevys, Fords and Volkswagens, and run for the door. They were revolved inside where Sister Check-in greeted them with a nod and a smile. There is a tremendously stimulating scene there at the hospital every Saturday night.

I walked home in a slouch heading for certain punishment. It was like going to a dentist without a mouthful of pain. There at least relief is in prospect. Lisa was in a lousy enough mood what with looking after Amos. Now she would be turned on by Mona's call. All kinds of restless winds would blow inside. Who could blame her? Mona the brave, Mona the free, was a powerful symbol. She had probably called to ask Lisa to send her a dress she saw in Vogue or a record by the Fugs or some such. Lisa, mired in domesticity, would trudge slowly up to Bergdorf's or The Record Hunter in between taking temperature.

"He's snoring," she said when I got back. "What took you so long?"

"I slept with Pokko," I said. "Is he hot?"

"Medium rare," she said.

"Did you find time to call operator twenty-five?"

"Not yet. I'm a little nervous about it. It's not like Mona to phone at this hour."

"She called at this hour in 1965 to ask you if you remembered the name of your freshman art teacher. She called in 1966 to ask you to ship her a subscription to the *Village Voice*. She called twice in 1967 for Day-Glo paints and hippie buttons. Always at this hour."

"Just forget it," Lisa said. "Forget the whole thing."

"You might as well call instead of sitting around speculating and savoring."

"Just go away."

I sat on the sofa with an old newspaper while Lisa made the call. While she waited for a connection, she bit her nails. Nail-biting was the start. The storm would last at least three days. At least. Operator twenty-five said she would call back. Lisa began cleaning. She began scrubbing the kitchen floor. She was feeling as much of her drudgery as possible to increase the pleasure of contact with the golden expatriate bird. My blood pressure went up to dangerous levels. I took my pulse. It was fast, fast.

It was nearly three when the telephone rang. Lisa was washing a baseboard. Her knee cracked when she stood up.

"Are you all right?" I said, and she never answered.

"Mona? Mona? I can't believe it. I can never get used to the idea of talking to you . . ."

While I read an editorial I listened for Lisa's side of the international conversation.

"Oh no . . . oh, Mona. It sounds terrible. The doctor?"

Maybe the call was not about a printed panty advertised in *Bazaar*.

"Never said a word . . . is he in pain? No cure? What are you going to do? Oh, Mona . . ."

I admit to a certain curiosity. When the call ended Lisa stood staring at the telephone. I continued to read. She would have to say something soon. A million of years of biology guaranteed that. And finally she did after a commendable struggle.

"It's too late to call Dr. Armon."

"Dr. Armon? Why do you want to call Dr. Armon?"

"I've got to get some information for Mona."

"Is she sick?"

"No. John."

"The velvet phallus?"

"Don't be cute, please, Harry."

"Is it serious?"

"I think so. Mona is very upset."

"Do you want to share the details?"

"We're getting a cable. A long cable. That's what Mona called to tell us. She didn't want us to be shocked by getting a cable in the middle of the night."

"When are we getting the cable?"

"Soon. All I know is, John is sick. He's got something."

"God, I never would have believed it. It's probably nothing."

"Frankly I'm more concerned with Mona. She sounded terrible."

"Ah."

Lisa bit a nail again. The worried look replaced the harried look. It was a softer look. I welcomed it. At least she was more reachable.

"Do you want a cup of tea while you cable-watch?"

"Yes," Lisa said. "Do you feel like making it?"

"Sure, dear."

So I made two cups of Earl Grey and we drank them slowly. After, Lisa went to the window and looked out. If she was looking for the man from ITT or RCA or whoever, it was futile since we live on the twentieth floor. But window habits die hard in the race.

"Really, what did you think of the party?" I said.

From the window Lisa sighed.

"Mona sounded half her size."

"Meaning what?"

"Her voice was thin as a rail."

"She always had a kind of wispy tone," I said. "And it traveled under three thousand miles of salt water with fishes nibbling at it."

"Don't be flip. If she called at this hour to tell us a cable was coming there is something bad going on."

It was probably true. Mona lived on interest. Her luxuries were really infrequent considering the lump of gold that backed her movements. She was careful. Not miserly but cautious. Two hundred years of Philadelphia lawyers were represented in her chromosomes. When I saw her in Rome she complained once about the cost of airmail. It was the same night she gave the faun a handful of lire for a thermal undershirt from Sweden, but she complained about the airmail rates.

"You know you're not going to see anything from the window. Didn't she give you any hint about what was in the cable? It seems kind of peculiar to call and not . . ."

"Accept Mona or don't."

"I accept Mona," I said. "As much as I've had to accept of her."

"She means a lot to me."

Lisa began to cry.

"Come on," I said. "Don't over-react. If there's something we can do we'll do it. Standing there crying is pretty idiotic."

"Maybe it is and maybe it's not."

"It's her thing, Lisa," I said. "At best or at worst it's her thing."

"What are friends for?"

"You've got me there."

"Stop picking at me."

"Go bite your nails for Mona. Wherever she is, she'll be a much better human being because your fingers are bald. Right?"

"Does being vicious give you pleasure, Harry?"

"Scratch my back. Come on, scratch it. With those stubs."

"Screw your back," Lisa said. "Screw it."

"Louder, darling. We'll have Amos in here in five seconds. Then we can all wait for the damn cable. Togetherness."

The doorbell rang. It has a loud, ripping sound. Amos whimpered but he didn't wake up, thank God. I buzzed for the doorman. He told me there was a delivery coming up.

"Here we go," I said.

"Do you have any change?"

I took the cable but Lisa grabbed it from me, then handed it back because she was too nervous to open it herself.

"We are going to do this in a civilized way," I said, and sat on the sofa with Lisa beside me. She was down to cuticle now. I smoke. That kills. Still I do not understand nail-biting. To me it is an abridgment of hostile impulses like a trimming of the claws. When Lisa bites her nails I am convinced it is because she fears tearing me into chunks out of ungovernable frenzy. Maybe it is better to bite nails than tear into chunks but the habit claws at my insides, which is just as bad. Lisa complains because piles of ashes crop up here and there. Give me a ton of ashes against one crescent of chewed nail any day. When we met, Lisa pretended to be a smoker if not an inhaler. After the wedding she abandoned cigarettes. She took up nails. It was a dirty, filthy deception and I have told her so many times.

"Take your hands away from your face and we will read this message of pain," I said.

Lisa pulled her fingers into her lap. We read:

DEAR HARRY ETLISA STOP EXTRAORDINARY TURN EVENTS STOP SURELY ON RETURN NEWYORK HARRY TOLD LISA STORY MY JOHN STOP FAUN STOP WHOLE THING HARRY SAID ALLTRUE BUT STILL IDEAL ARRANGEMENT ME STOP FAUN CHARMING MUCH WANTED SPLENDID PROCLUTCH ETAL STOP NO PROBLEMS BEYOND MY ENERGY LAG STOP NOW ALAS PLENTY TROUBLE STOP FAUN LETHARGIC LAST TWOMONTHS STOP NO GOING OUT

ETREADS BOOKS STOP UNLIKE FAUN ETATTRIBUTED TO INEVITA-
BLE SETTLING STOP AFFAIR RESEMBLES MARRIAGE AFTER WHILE
STOP WRONG JUDGMENT INPART ANYHOW STOP NO OTHER
BROADS STOP NO LIMBO TO CHEMISTRY BUT WORSE STOP FAUN
SUSPECTED SOCIAL DISEASE CAUSED ANTISOCIAL BEHAVIOR STOP
TERRIFIED SEEK MEDICAL HELP BUT FINALLY WENT DOCTOR
DUE CONCERN MEMBER OF WEDDING SOTOSPEAK WOULD FALL
OFF STOP DIAGNOSIS HORRIBLE EYE DONT UNDERSTAND ENTIRELY
STOP SOMETHING LIKE HARPIES HERPES HIPPIES SKINRASH STOP
PRESCRIPTION UNCERTAIN ETSUGGESTION TOTAL ABSTINENCE
STOP REPEAT TOTAL TOTAL TOTAL STOP NO GUARANTEES STOP
EYE IN ODD SITUATION STOP STUCK FAUN WITHOUT SPRING
STOP PLUS CHANCE PERMANENT RUST IN KEY SYSTEM STOP EYE
FRANTIC STOP QUERY PLEASE CHECK LOCAL DOCTOR ON HARPIES
HERPES HIPPIES ETAL POSSIBLE MEDICAL BREAKTHROUGH IN
USA STOP EYE FEELING COMPROMISED DEPRESSED UNNERVED
NOT SLEEPING STOP HE VICIOUS NASTY INSECURE STOP REMEM-
BER HARRY SAID ONE SHOULD ALWAYS DEMAND AFFECTION
FROM PETS STOP REASONABLE STOP DONT WANT BE KIND
WOMAN KICKS MAN WITH HARPIES HERPES HIPPIES WHEN DOWN
BUT LOSING GRIP STOP WELCOME ADVICE MEDICAL SOCIALHU-
MAN ETAL STOP REGARDS AMOS ETAL KNOW IMPOSING YOU BUT
UNDERSTAND HANGUP STOP WIRE COLLECT INFO HARPIES HERPES
HIPPIES URGENT STOP PLEASE HURRY STOP MUST REACH DECI-
SION BASED ALLFACTS BEFORE SPRING THAW STOP PROBLEMS
PROBLEMS STOP LOVE MONA

"That must have cost a bloody fortune," I said.

"What does it mean? Does it mean what I think it means?"

"It means the faun is both domesticated and for all practical purposes out of action."

"They can't make love?"

"Nope."

"And what does he have?"

"The word is herpes. That I remember from premed."
"Get the dictionary."

her-pes n (L. fr. Gr. herpēs. fr. *herpein* to creep—more at SER-
PENT): any of several virus diseases characterized by the for-
mation of blisters on the skin or mucous membranes—*her-
pet-ic*, adj.

"He has herpes. He is herpetic. Or, here, *herpes simplex*, same
difference. It's interesting that it goes back to the Greek."
"Jesus God, what in the world waits in the wings to snag at
us," Lisa said.
"Plenty."
"He has blisters?"
"On the skin or mucous membranes."
"Stop, Harry. Don't run it into the ground. You sound so clini-
cal. It's a person we know. You sound gleeful."
"I don't sound gleeful, Lisa. And we don't know the person—
at least, you don't. It's Mona's stud."
"Are they catching?"
"How the hell should I know? Mona didn't say she was her-
petic."
"Boy, you squeeze the juice out of a word, don't you."
"It's not my word. I didn't make it up. I didn't give the faun
herpes. I am sitting here dead tired coping with this, which is all
I can do. And frankly I don't understand why. What has it got
to do with us?"
"Not us. Me. Mona asked me to ask our doctor, not us. And
don't think I'm not going to do it. I'm doing it first thing in the
morning."
"Good. Do it. But don't you think if it's been around since the
Greeks that Italian doctors are on to the latest herpes poop? Mona
is an expatriate, but when the chips are down it's the old Stars

and Stripes. Very typical. Your faith is where your money comes from."

"You reduce everything to money."

"That's not what I said. Look, cool it. Mona's faun of the moment has a few shoddy mucous membranes, right? He'll probably get over that. He's strong-willed, I mean he never worked a day in his life and survived. So he has the odds going for him. The thing that's bothering Mona is the part about his being domestic all of a sudden. Settled. Sitting around. She bought a faun and she got a hippopotamus and that's what's bothering her. And there's no cure for that. It's really pretty funny when you think about it objectively, which you can't do because you think that Mona is you with wings."

I had used that line on Amy Pokko and it was too good to waste.

"Me with wings? That's insane."

"It bothers you more that Mona's seminal fairy tale is tainted than it does that you have no nails left. You couldn't scratch a back if your life depended on it."

"I'm sick, right?" Lisa said. "Psychotic, right?"

"I never said that."

"Well, I can't help feeling deeply for Mona and for John. How would you feel if the tables were turned?"

"I wouldn't expect you to cable the story of my herpes across the Atlantic Ocean."

"You'd love it if you had those things. And I know exactly who'd be to blame."

"Now you've got yourself suffering from my herpes. You've got some mind on you, Lisa. Your head would make a hell of a transplant."

"You don't have to pick up on everything I say. Can't you have the sensitivity to see I'm all keyed up over this? Mona broke up a marriage to have John come live with her. She had a terrible childhood. She needed some fire in her life. And look what happens. The girl must be so lonely. So lonely."

"If she's lonely she'll find another faun. And if she's tired of fauns she'll relate to John as a mortal with herpes."

But the idea of lonely Mona, overwhelmed in Rome by as insurmountable a problem as the Emperors faced at the first rumbling of Christianity, pleased Lisa more than any glib solution.

She mellowed again, as she had before the tea.

"Darling, you must be dead tired, what with Amos and the party and Mona and all. The best thing for you would be some sleep."

"I am exhausted. Throbbing."

"Look, get undressed for bed. I'll clear the dishes."

"Take the garbage out."

"I notice that Amy Pokko ate three bananas."

"I'll go down in the morning."

"No problem. We can have eggs."

"All right. I didn't get any fresh bread, either."

"Just go to sleep. Go on."

Lisa sighed and went into the bedroom. I sat on the sofa reading Mona's cable. I confess the idea of the temporarily indisposed faun gave a certain lift. And Mona's conundrum, in a time when the world is falling into a jigsaw, did not bother me too much. And the whole event had given Lisa something to think about beyond Amos's last sneeze and the budget.

"Harry, are you coming to bed?"

The Lord works in mysterious ways. Especially in a marriage. There was a definite break in the weather.

I am awed and amazed at those satellite pictures Tex Antoine shows on television—those that spread-eagle the continent and detail storms, clearings, clouds and soft sunlight.

"Harry, look in on Amos."

"I will."

"See that he's covered."

"I will."

You can see all America from miles in the thin air and know that it will rain in California, snow in Nebraska, be gray in St. Louis and fair and warmer in New York. The changes can be predicted, too. To date, nobody has come up with little satellites to spin over individual heads. We must take things as they come and accept the surprises.

"Harry, I'm freezing in here," Lisa said. "Don't mess up the blankets."

"I won't," I said.

And I was careful not to. Not in that climate. It was a climate that had been missing from the apartment for days.

"Thank you, Faun," I whispered. "And good luck."

"What, Harry?"

"Nothing, honey," I said. "I was talking to myself."

THE TOY

Thg thing that caught Harry Harper's eye was his own toy. There it was in the window, intact, complete to the scratched initial he had put on the truck's side twenty years before.

"That's my toy truck," he thought to himself, and it was a combination of words he had not used in some time. "What a world," he thought. "The coincidence is crazy enough. But crazier is the fact that here I am in my thirties and my toy is already in the window of an antique shop. Only in America."

Harry decided to buy the toy, though it was marked at twenty dollars. Why not? Antique toys were camp and in. He could put it on his bookshelf at home or even on the coffee table in his office. It was a beautiful toy, made of heavy steel, and they don't make them that way anymore. It really was a piece of sculpture.

Harry went into the antique shop. The store was small and dark, crowded with objects. His eyes were still filled with sun from the street and he saw everything in shadows.

"Yes, can I help you?"

A little lady in a black dress with an embroidered collar and lacy sleeves took shape as Harry's eyes cleared.

"You can," Harry said. "I noticed a toy in the window. It's marked at twenty dollars. It has some nostalgic meaning to me and I am interested in buying it. But I wonder if you can come down a little."

"We are having a sale," the lady said easily and amiably. "It has been marked down by ten percent."

"Well," Harry said, "that's fine. Fine."

226

"Would you like it wrapped as a gift?"

"Why not?" Harry said. He remembered when the toy had been wrapped as a gift on his tenth birthday. "Yes, sure. Thanks."

"While I wrap," the lady said, "you might wish to browse."

"I must confess that I'm not an antique buff," Harry said. "It was just that the toy had special meaning."

"I understand."

The lady went to the window and lifted out the red truck. Harry smiled to see it close up. It was his, all right. He marveled at the road it must have traveled to intersect with his own road at that time, in that place.

"Excuse me," the lady said, and took the truck to the back of her shop. Harry heard paper rustling.

While he waited he did browse, and something else caught his eye.

"My God," Harry said out loud, "my God. That lamp there is made from my old ice skates."

Sure enough, there was a lamp with a base made from ice skates that had belonged to a child, bronzed, mounted on wood and electrified. There were initials on the skates, preserved in the bronze casting, "HH," just where he had carved them in the leather.

Then Harry saw his old sled hanging from the ceiling. How could he forget it? It was his sled, it certainly was.

Harry felt a sudden dizziness. He bent over and felt his head reel, and then the spell passed. He came up again with a clear mind. And he looked around the shop in amazement.

There in a corner on the floor was a baseball glove, and it was his glove, no doubt. And in a case, a tiny spoon and fork which he remembered lifting cereal with, and a little wooden toilet seat, and clothes and frayed books, and a crib and junior bed and more toys, all his, all from his own past.

"Miss," he said, "miss, can you come out here, please?"

"Yes," the lady said. "I'm still wrapping. My hands aren't

what they once were. And I want to do a nice job for you."

"These things," Harry said, "where did you get them?"

"From many sources," the lady said. "Traveling to the country, people coming in, auction sales, exchanges with other dealers."

"But everything in this store is mine, was mine, once belonged to me."

"How fantastic," the lady said. "The puppets too?"

"Puppets?"

"There, on the wall."

Harry turned to the wall, which he hadn't noticed before, and saw his mother and father, long dead, hanging there, and his friend Louie who died in World War II over Germany, and his first girlfriend and his Uncle Henny and his Cousin Bessie, all long gone.

"Sweet God," he said. "Sweet God."

"Oh," the lady said, "hear that racket. There is nothing like an advertisement in the *Times* classified to bring them out."

There was a clatter outside the shop. Harry looked and saw a swarm of ladies pressing their noses against the door and windows.

"I'm glad I locked the door," the shopkeeper said. "It's my annual sale. Ten percent off. I suppose I'll have to let them in."

She went to the door and Harry watched, then said, "Wait, please wait," but the door was already opened and the ladies pushed in, swarmed over the counter and tables, grasping and examining and choosing.

"No," Harry yelled. "No." He shouted with such violence that his voice cracked and the noise of the ladies stopped abruptly. Everyone gave him their attention.

"These things are mine," he said.

"Now, young man," the lady in black said, "it's true you were here first. And you do have certain rights. But the rules of our sale limit purchase to one item, one to a customer."

"Impossible," Harry said. "There are many things—everything."

"Everything is in working order," the lady said. "I can understand your enthusiasm. But I have lived by my rule for fifty years. During the annual ten-percent sale it is one to a customer, no more, no less."

The ladies protested that Harry had no right to any special consideration and the shopkeeper said, "Now girls, hold your horses. Fair is fair."

In the meantime Harry rushed about the store, touching, crying, wiping his eyes with his hands and moaning.

"Please hurry," the shopkeeper said. "Time is money."

"I can't. . . ."

"You must. These girls have hair appointments, things to do."

Harry sat in the center of the floor sobbing his heart out.

"Now," the lady in black said. "Now."

"I can have anything?"

"Ten percent off."

"Well, give me the truck then," Harry said.

THE EGG OF THE GLAK

To the memory of David Hikhoff, Ph.D.
May he rest in peace. Unless there is better.

SPRING NIGHT. THE CAMPUS QUIET. THE AIR SOFT BREATH. I stood at my post, balanced on stiff legs. The fountain, a gift of '08, tinkled under moonlight. Then he came, trumpeting like a mammoth, stomping, tilting, staggering, nearly sitting, straightening, roaring from the back of his mouth, a troublemaker.

"My diphthongs. They monophthongized my diphthongs. The frogs. The frogs."

Echoes rattled the quadrangle.

I ran to grab him. It was like holding a bear. He nearly carried both of us to the ground.

"Poor kid. You poor kid," he said, waving short arms. "Another victim of the great vowel shift. The Northumbrian sellout." He cried real tears, hundred proof, and blotted his jowls with a rep tie. Oh, this was no student drunk. This was faculty, an older man.

"Let us conjugate *stone* in a time-tarnished manner. Repeat after me. Repeat or I will beat you to a mosh. *Stān, stān, stānes, stāne, stānas, stānas, stāna, stānum.*"

230

"Easy, sir," I said.

"Up the Normans," he shrieked. "They loused my language. Mercian, Kentish, West Saxon and Northumbrian sellouts. French ticklers. Tell your children, and their children's children, unto the generations. Diphthongs have been monophthongized. Help."

"I'm trying to help," I said.

"Police."

"I am police."

"Victim," he said, whispering now. "Sad slob."

How many remember what happened a thousand years ago? If it were not for Hikhoff, I would know nothing of the vowel shift, though it altered my life and fiber. For it was this rotten shift that changed our English from growl to purr.

Look it up. Read how spit flew through the teeth of Angles, Saxons and Jutes in the good old days. Get facts on how the French came, conquered, shoved our vowels to the left of the language, coated our tongues with velvet fur.

For Hikhoff, the shift of the vowels made history's center. *Before* was a time for the hairy man, the man who ate from the bone. *After* came silk pants, phallic apology.

"From Teutonic to moronic," Hikhoff told me. "Emasculation. Drought in the tonsil garden. No wonder so many strep throats in this town of clowns."

Sounds. Hikhoff's life was sounds. The sounds that make your insides wobble. Sounds of chalk screaming, of power saws cutting wood, of forks on glass, scrapings, buzzings, the garbage disposal chewing, jet wails, dentists drilling, pumps gurgling, drains sucking, tires screeching, ambulance sirens, giants breaking wind, booms, bangs, clangings, ripping and tearing, nails scratching silk.

Softer sounds too. Music and musical boxes, bells, chimes, bottle players on "Ed Sullivan," all that, all noise, but mostly noises that make you squirm. His favorite: people sounds. Body sounds, sounds of talking, squishing, words, singing, cajoling, cursing, ordering, asking, telling, excusing, insisting. That is why the great vowel shift meant so much to him.

"What those concupiscent Gauls did to me," he said. "They shriveled half my vocal cords. They denied me my voice."

Hikhoff liked to rasp and sputter. His lungs were organ bellows for rolling R's and CH's that choked to the point of dribble. He listened to himself with much pleasure. He played himself back on a tape recorder, reading from *Beowulf* or Chaucer or the *Prose Edda*, which tells of the Wind Age and Wolf Age when the Sun swallows Earth.

"Aggchrrr, don't talk from your nostrils. Nose talkers are bastards. Diaphragm. Lungs. The deepest tunnels. Use those. Form your words slowly. Shape them in your head. Let them out of the mouth like starved animals, hot smoke rings. Speak each sentence like a string of beautiful sausages. Show me a mumbler and I show you a turd. SPEAK OUT. SAY YOUR PIECE. YOU WILL NOT ONLY MAKE OUT BETTER BUT DO A SERVICE FOR THE ENTIRE HUMAN RACE."

Hikhoff. We became friends. I don't kid myself. At first he had motives, improper designs. All right, think what you think.

"A despondent, disappointed soul." "A bitter person, a cynic." "A lump of rage." "A bad influence." I have heard all that said, and worse. To me, Hikhoff was redeemer, beloved comrade. I close my eyes and there he is in full detail.

Hikhoff.

Body like a cantaloupe. Little head, big jaw. A wet mouth gated by purple lips. Heavy in the breathing. Short arms and legs. A funny machine, an engine liberated, huffing, puffing. Like the power cabs that pull trailers and sometimes go running without their loads. The amputated heart. They move on diesel oil, Hikhoff on food. Fueling always. Always belching gas. I loved him. I miss him.

"Cousin North," he once said in a mellow, huff-puff voice when he finished panting and scratching after a chase around his coffee table. "I accept your repressive shyness. Lord, god king of fishes, you are too young to know what trouble a man's genitals can give." Then, pointing at the top of his paunch, "AND I HAVE NOT SET EYES ON MINE IN FORTY YEARS."

Ah. I knew what trouble, since I was then twenty, not ten. But Hikhoff was making jolly. We had become friends when I carried him home that spring night. Now, later in the turning year, he invited me to dinner. A feast. A groaning board. While we digested, he tried to make me.

He wooed me. First, by throwing peels to the garbage disposal, which he called Mr. Universe. They were swallowed, chopped to purée. Next, he wined me with Liebfraumilch. Then he chased me, the engine with legs, roaring prevowel shift verses about clash and calm, stimulated by, and frustrated by, my agility.

"I am sorry, sir," I said in a moment of pause. "I do not go that way."

"Alps fall on your callow head," Hikhoff screamed so storm windows rattled. But we came to an agreement. Back to normal when his pressure dropped, we talked frankly.

"Sir, Dr. Hikhoff, even if I were interested in deviations, if that's how to put it, I could just not with you, sir. You are a cathedral to me, full of stained light, symbolic content. The funny thing is that I love you, but not that way."

"Distinctions," Hikhoff said a little sadly. "If you have a change of heart someday, let me be the first to know. Wire me collect. For the meantime, we will continue to be friends. You have a good head. A good head is a rare and precious stone."

We continued to be friends. I, who had taken a temporary job as campus cop to audit free courses, stayed on to become captain of the force. I kept taking courses and would still be.

Once each week I went to see Hikhoff and we dined. He did not fail to steam a little after the mandarin oranges with Cointreau, but he never attacked me again. He was well controlled.

We talked of life and poetry. I was writing then. He read my

works, sometimes translating them into Old English. He criti-
cized. He had faith in me, encouraged me.

I wrote of life, courage, identity, time and death. These subjects delighted Hikhoff. He was a grand romantic, full of Eden,
pro-Adam, pro-Eve, pro-Snake, pro-God, pro-Gabriel, anti–the
whole-scene. His self-image wore a cape and carried a sharp sword.
He believed in battle bloody and reunion soft. To sum it up,
Hikhoff had a kind of kill-and-kiss vision.

The important thing was to keep the winds stirred, the debris
flying.

"Churn the emotions, but do not turn them to butter," he said.
"Not with drugs or booze or mushrooms that give a pastel mirage.
Use life, Harold. Be a life addict. Generate your own chemicals,
your own trance and dance. Hikhoff the Absolute has spoken."

Our evenings were fine for me and I hope for him. I was like
his son; he said so. He was better than my father; I say so. I could
have gone on that way a hundred years. But the carpet was pulled,
as it usually is.

One night when we were sealed by winter, I got a call. I was
not sleeping when it came, but on the edge of a dream. The
dream was forming in swirls of snow. The telephone bell was a
noisy bug, and I fought to crush it. Finally I got up, naked and
shivering in the cold room. I knew there was trouble.

The first thought was of fire. Or dormitory suicide. It was not
the season for panty raids, and rape was obsolete up there.

"Hello, yes, hello?"

"Harold North? Is this he?"

"He. Yes."

"This is Miss Linker at the Shepherd of the Knowing Heart
Clinic. On Kipman Place."

"Yes."

"A patient, Dr. Hikhoff, is asking for . . ."

The night was frozen. Ice gave a glitter, a gloss like the shine on photographs. I remember smoke coming from the sewers. It fogged the street. It was pleasure to hear the car skip and start, to think of spark plugs flaming.

By the car clock it was three. I keep my clock ahead by forty-five minutes; this is a silliness, having to do with sudden endings. I have a stupid idea that if destruction should come, I would have nearly an hour to go back and make ready.

They let me go right to his room. He was critical, a mound in the white bed with side bars pulled up. A nurse leaned over him, and he moved his tongue in and out, side to side, as if she were a canapé. He was delirious, saying words in clusters, words melted together like candies left in the sun. They gave him oxygen. He took gallons, emptied tanks.

I cried.

The nurse shook her head "no."

She reached a verdict. There was no hope except for the pin-point dot of light that always flares. He had suffered a massive stroke, an eruption. Lava poured into his system and slowly filled him with black dust.

The nurse gave me two letters. They were marked FIRST and FINALLY. I put the envelopes in a pocket and stayed there by the bed. I heard a train whistle which meant five o'clock. The whistle was for Hikhoff. He opened his eyes, ripped off the oxygen mask, slammed the nurse away and with his fists, sat up, saw me and said, "Touch. Touch."

I took his head in my hands and held him. The round head was a basketball with frightened eyes. "I will write thick books," he said. Then the eyes went away. Hikhoff was dead.

The white room filled with his escaping soul, cape, sword, all. The window was open a crack, and out the soul went into cold air.

Hikhoff's body was cremated after a nice funeral. In his will he requested that his remains be scattered in campus ashtrays. They were not. Instead, they were sent to his family in a silver box. They should have been used as fertilizer for a tree, an oak, something with a heavy head of leaves and thirsty plunging roots, a trunk for carving on, branches to hold tons of snow.

After the funeral I went into seclusion.

I wished for time to think of my friend and to shape him into a memory. He was easy to remember, not one of those who fades with the first season change. I could not only see him but hear him and feel the vibration of his ghost. I had him down pat.

When I was sure of keeping the memory, I read the letter marked FIRST. It was tempting to read FINALLY first and FIRST finally because I suspected Hikhoff of throwing me a curve. But I thought no, not with death in his mind. Hikhoff would do the obvious because the corrupted obvious is purified in the face of death.

Dear Harold,

When you read this I will be dead, which seems ridiculous. Know that I look forward to meeting you again in some other world. At such time I will continue the education of your shade. If there is corporeal immortality, I will persist in your seduction.

Be that as it may. There is a favor I request of you. Naturally it is an idiotic request and very demanding. You have, of course, the option to refuse, maybe even the absolute need to refuse.

In this noble hamlet, Crap-Off-the-Hudson, there lives a lady who runs a store called Poodleville. This lady, a combination of estrogen, the profit motive, and a green thumb for animals, has come into the possession of a fantastic find.

It is the egg of a Glak.

No such egg has been seen for years. It is quite probably the last and final Glak.

The egg was brought to her by a relative who served with a radar unit in Labrador. I saw it in her shop, when I went there with the thought of buying a parrot. Thank God, the egg was sitting near a radiator. Harold, I believe that this egg is fertile.

I have since paid this lady to heat her egg. The hatch span of the Glak is seven years and four days. I sought information from our late Dr. Nagle, of Anthropology. He set a tentative date for the Glak birth in middle April of next year.

Harold, the Glak is officially EXTINCT; so you can imagine the importance of all this! (That is the first exclamation point I have used since Kaiser Wilhelm died.)

I do not anticipate anything happening to me before then. I never felt worse, which is a sign of excellent health. But should I be struck down by a flying manhole cover or a falling bowling ball or the creeping crud, and should you have the agonizing duty of opening and reading this letter, please do the following:

1) Go to the Upstate Bank and Trust. You will find an account in both our names containing $5,000.

2) Contact the lady at Poodleville, a Miss Moonish. Pay her $2,500 for custody of the egg, per our agreement.

3) Take the egg, suitably wrapped, and nurse it until the ides of April. Then you must transport the egg to the one place where the Glak is known to have thrived; i.e., upper Labrador.

4) WARNING BELLS. While Dr. Nagle, of Anthropology, is deceased, I believe he told his son, John, of my find. I also believe, from certain twitchings of Nagle's right ear, that the old man had dreams of glory, that he fantasized a lead article in American Scholar entitled "Nagle's Glak." The driving, vicious ambition of anthropologists is well known. What then of their sons? Beware of the young Nagle, Harold. I have a premonition.

5) Due to this implicit Nagle threat, I urge you to act with dispatch.

Harold, ersatz son, I know this appears to be a strange request. Think carefully what you will do about an old fool's last testament.

If you cannot help me, shove the whole thing. Take my money and spend it on pleasure. Throw my letters into the garbage disposal. Sip Pouilly-Fuissé while singing "Nearer, My God, to Thee."

Break champagne on your head and sail on. Do what you must do.

Harold, writing this and still to write FINALLY (to be opened only if by some miracle a Glak is born, and born healthy) has left me quivering. I feel as if I have swallowed a pound of lard. Thoughts of my own death fill me with sadness, nourishing sadness.

Goodbye, dear Harold. May the things that go clump in the night bless you.

Yours in affection,
David Hikhoff

I put down FIRST, repocketed FINALLY, blew out the candles and sat there in the dark.

Hikhoff died in February, a month hardly wide enough to hold him.

That February was cold as a cube. It straddled Crap-Off-the-Hudson like an abominable snowman with icy armpits and a pale, waiting face. No wonder Hikhoff chose cremation, a last burst of heat. The only reminder that the world sometimes welcomes life came from struck matches, steam ghosts from pipes under our streets, the glow of cigarette tips. It was as if nobody smiled.

My decision to honor Hikhoff's request took a frigid week. In that week I purchased a tiny glazed Hikhoff from a student sculptor who made it in memoriam. The little Hikhoff was a good likeness, orange and brown ceramic the size of a lemon. I carried it with me like a talisman. Morbid, I know, but it helped me make up my mind.

So, for a few hours, I owned five thousand dollars. There *was* an account at Upstate, and a vice president there who expected my visit. If there was an account, there was probably an egg. And, very likely, a Nagle. Still, I was suspicious of Hikhoff, who had a great sense of humor, a capacity for the belly laugh, and the belly for the laugh.

There was also Harold North's choice.

Hikhoff himself, Hikhoff the far-seeing, dangled the golden carrot. I could use the money for play. I, who lived like a hermit, had no grandiose ideas of frolic. But each bill could translate into time. I could go to Majorca; I could write until my fingers were stubs, without a care.

Glak. Damn the Glak. Some of the finest creatures are extinct, have gained stature through oblivion, have won museum fame. Great green things with tails the size of buildings. Hairy fellows with pounds of chin and strong eyes. Flying dragons that dripped acid. Elephants with tusks that could spear dentists. Why not the Glak? Extinction is nature's way. Did this world need a Glak? Who suffered by its disappearance? Is anyone, anywhere, Glak-deprived? There was no real choice. I had to do Hikhoff's post-mortem bidding. We had consumed too much together; I had taken so much for myself of every portion. Could I point my rump at his last request?

Yes, naturally I visited the library. Even before my trip to the bank I looked up the Glak. There was not much to be learned. A tall cranelike bird with a raucous croak resembling *glak glak*. Famed for its mating dance, which involved a rapid twisting of the dorsal plume in a counterclockwise direction. Habitat the subarctic regions of eastern North America. Dwindling Glak population noted in the 1850s. Classified extinct 1902.

Glak, glak. Hikhoff once said he thought maybe the vowels stayed there and we shifted. Glak, glak to tweet, tweet. Could I care less?

In the bank I looked at the five and three zeroes while patting my ceramic Hikhoff, which was stuffed in the left-hand pocket of my mackinaw. When I noticed the Upstate vice president watching my patting hand, I took the Hikhoff and placed it on the table.

"It's a Hikhoff," I said.

"A Hickhoff?"

"The man who left me this money."

"You carry it around?"

"On special occasions."

"That's a nice sentiment. It could start a trend."

I had the money placed in a checking account.

The next thing I did was to find Poodleville in the telephone book. I called and was answered by a voice which could have been a person or an unsold beast. The voice was thin and high, air deprived.

"I am Harold North. I believe a Dr. Hikhoff suggested . . ."

"I've been expecting your call."

"Can we meet?"

"Assuredly. The sooner the better."

Poodleville caters to a genteel clientele, even for Crap-Off-the-Hudson. The shoppe (their spelling) is located in an ancient part of the city, a residential area, a nest of strong, well-built homes, each with some land, some trees, a gate. These are the houses of people with ancestors who settled that part of the land, and of those who came later and found luck smiling. The houses are impressive. Each is a fortress, guarding special privacy. Each has seen many bitter winters.

Through the large windows of these grandfather houses I could see splendid toys, like chandeliers of crystal, paintings in gold-painted frames, pewter tankards, silver samovars, thick drapes, balconies with railings, curved staircases, wooden panels. Each house was an egg in itself with its own source of warmth, cracking out life now and then which ran for a car or a waiting cab.

Bits of movement, footprints not yet covered over by the new snow, smoke trails rising from chimneys animated the neighborhood in slow motion. Winter had the streets under siege. They had a cemetery quality. I could easily imagine Hikhoff waddling behind me, a specter spy observing my movements, enjoying the tranquillity of snowbound luxury.

Poodleville had been built out of the bottom floor of a brownstone. There was hardly a suggestion of commerce, much less of the usual cluster of dogs, birds, fishes, cats, hamsters, apes and even ants. No puppies solicited behind the glass. The window was tastefully decorated with a picture of a memorable poodle champion with the arrogant snout of one who is making his mark in stud. There was also a pink leash and a stone-covered collar.

When the door opened, a bell jingled. The animals sounded off. There was a jungle smell under Air Wick. But even inside, the mood was subdued.

Here was my first glimpse of Elsie Moonish. She stood near the tropical fish, looking at an x-ray by bluish light from the tanks. A canary sang on a shelf above her head. Three or four dogs banged their heads against bars painted in candy stripes. A myna bird slept, and near it a single monkey swung around on its perch, squeaking like a mouse.

Miss Moonish never turned. She kept looking at the negative. I assumed it was a poodle spleen or parakeet kidney that held her.

She was not what I expected from the curdsy voice but an attractive, plumpish, fortyish lady, with her hair, black with gray rivers, in a Prince Valiant cut, a desirable lady, though her legs were on the heavy side.

I wondered if she heard me come in. She must have if she had eardrums, since the warning bell rang and the animals reacted. I made no sound except for a wheeze when I breathed, since I was coming down with a cold.

One wheeze got to Miss Moonish. It was a tremendous snort that sounded as if it came from Hitler's sinus. I think she was waiting for it as an excuse to register sudden surprise. Even the beasts shut up, not recognizing that mating call.

"My pancreas," she said.

"Pardon?"

"I was concerned about my pancreas. But it seems to be in fine fettle. Care for a look?"

"Not before dinner," I said.

"They say I am a hypochondriac, which is to say I fear death, which I do. I love x-rays. What a shame radioactivity is harmful."

"Always complications," I said. "I'm Harold North."

"Ah. Not the other."

"The other?"

"The Nagle person."

Her myna bird woke, blinked, and said *person person person*.

"You have spoken with the Nagle person?"

"Not too long ago. Your competitor. Poor Dr. Hikhoff. I read about his demise. What was it, a cerebral artery? Beautiful man. Such a tragedy."

I noticed why Elsie Moonish spoke thinly. It was because she hardly ever inhaled. She took air in gasps and kept it for long periods. By the end of a breath her voice nearly vanished. How hard it must have been for Hikhoff to deal with her.

"All this fuss over an egg," she said. "Remarkable."

"Speaking of the egg, may I see it?"

"At these prices I would scramble it for you, Mr. North."

First Miss Moonish locked the front door of the shop, though it did not exactly seem as if the store would be swamped with customers. Then she led me back past animal accessories, foods, a barbering table covered with curly hair, to a little door. Behind the door was a staircase leading up.

Over Poodleville, on the first floor of the brownstone, the Moonish apartment had elegance, but with the feeling of leftovers. The room had high ceilings, stained-glass windows, columned archways and plush furniture, all a bit frazzled. There was a rancid dignity. I was directed to a blue tubby chair with the arms of a little club fighter. I sat and waited.

She went into another room, the bedroom as it turned out, and came back with a cardboard box. It was the kind of box you get from the grocer if you ask for a carton to pack for the painters. Written in red (by lipstick) on the top it said FRAGILE. KEEP

WARM. I expected more, a glass case or ebony, but there it was, an old tomato carton.

Elsie Moonish took out a pound of old newspaper, then a ball wrapped in velvet. Carefully, but not too carefully, she unwrapped the egg and there it was. Just an egg, a few inches bigger than a chicken's, dotted with violet splotches.

To make it sound as if I were in on this from the start, I said, "Uh-huh. There it is all right."

She gave me the egg and I examined it. It was warm and seemed to be in good condition. As soon as possible, I put it back in the velvet nest.

"Dr. Hikhoff sat where you are sitting," she said, "for hour after hour. He called the egg his family. He was quite involved."

"He was."

" 'There are chills in this room, drafts,' he would say. A very protective man."

"Definitely."

"Mr. North, perhaps it's time to talk business, a crass thing in face of the occasion. But life goes on."

"Business," I said. "Per Dr. Hikhoff's instructions, I have in my pocket a checkbook, and I am prepared to give you a draft for twenty-five hundred dollars."

"Mr. North," she said, "that's sweet," fitting the egg back into its box.

"Think nothing of it."

"Mr. North, let me say that I feel like the queen of bitches, forgive the expression. But the Nagle person called this morning with an offer of forty-five hundred dollars, all his money in the world, and for the very same egg."

"But you promised Dr. Hikhoff . . ."

"Mr. North, what is money to me? Time? Health? It's only that hypochondria is dreadfully costly. Doctors charge outrageous fees; it's a disgrace. Let me show you something."

She took the egg back to her bedroom and returned with a large book, an album.

"Browse this. My x-rays. Five years of x-rays and some of friends and family. There. My uterus. Fifty dollars. My coccyx. Fifteen or twenty, as I recall. Heart, lungs, the lower tract. Do you have any idea of the cost?"

Looking at her insides was embarrassing for some reason, on so short an acquaintance. If medical magazines had centerfolds, she would have done well. Her organs were neat and well cared for. After finishing a flip of pages, I actually felt as if I had known her for years.

"Miss Moonish," I said, "I will level with you, cards on the table, face up. Dr. Hikhoff left me with a certain amount of cash. Enough to pay you, live a little, and get Glak back home."

"The Nagle person was so insistent," she said. "Willing to risk all."

"I'll match his offer," I said, "though it will mean hardship. *Plus* one dollar."

"Marvelous. I'm so relieved. It's thrilling when two grown men meet in conflict. Especially the moment, Mr. North, when their bids are equal, when they have exhausted material resources. Then they are thrown back on primitive reserves. Spiritual and physical qualities. The *plus*, as you said. The *plus-plus*."

"You lost me."

"Your money, Mr. North, or Mr. Nagle's money. They add up to the same thing. So the bids erase each other. Two men yearn for my egg. Each has offered gold. Now *other factors* creep into the picture. The *plus-plus*. You know, I hesitate to give up this situation. I lead a dull life, Mr. North."

"What you said about *other factors*. What other factors?"

"The city is frozen. Everything strains under tons of snow. I will tend my shop, care for my pets, cut poodle hair, and so forth. I will eat, sleep, wait out the dull months. Despite my x-rays, I feel hollow inside at this time of year. Like an empty jug. An empty jug yearning for—how shall I put it—honey. I want honey, Mr. North, the honey *plus-plus*. Memory."

"Are you suggesting, Miss Moonish, to a total stranger, anything in any way directly or indirectly involving the possibility of what the students call 'body contact'?"

"You have a quick mind, Mr. North. You have a frankness. Being around nature, I, too, am a to-the-point person."

"Miss Moonish, I work as a campus cop. I write poems. I read a lot. I hardly have a social life. I am not exactly a bulldozer. In fact I am a sexual camel. I can go for miles without. My sex is my work. I sublimate. And I don't know you well enough."

"I find you charming, Mr. North."

"And then there is the Nagle person. A terrible amoral fellow from what I gather. Suppose, for the sake of discussion, you find the Nagle's *plus-plus* more charming."

Elsie Moonish stood up and did a slow turn, stretching.

"It's my Glak. I'm in the catbird seat. The Glakbird seat. The Glak-egg seat. I'm absolutely enraptured by the entire chain of events."

"All right, five thousand, though now I am including my own small reserve, retirement money. Five thousand dollars."

"Are you offering an additional four hundred ninety-nine dollars *not* to make love to me?"

"Yes. Yes and no. It's nothing personal."

"It feels personal. Or is it just the price of your own dear insecurity? You don't want this little competition to be decided on the basis of your . . . ability?"

"It's not that."

"It is that."

"Maybe it is."

"Find courage."

"Something is chirping downstairs, Miss Moonish. Maybe a prowler . . ."

"You are the prowler. Prowl."

Damn Hikhoff. What is my debt to you? First a vow. Now, if you take things seriously, my most precious possession. For a Glak?

"I like involvement," I said.

"Who doesn't? Who among us doesn't? But there is a lot to be said in months with r in them for love without possession. The most painful kind of human contact. Transients welcome. Exciting, infuriating. The ultimate act, but without the owning. It teaches a lesson, Mr. North. It renews the lesson of separation. It reminds one of the magic of flesh in winter. Fusion and nonfusion. It builds immunities against the terrible desires of spring."

All that on one exhale, and I thought she would burst from decompression.

"I'm no philosopher," I said.

"Philosophy is in the tip of the tongue," she said, "the small of the back, behind the ears, where the legs meet the trunk, inside the thighs, behind the knees, on the mountain peaks, in the valley. The demilitarized zones."

"I fear my own rust," I said. "Lust. A Freudian slip. I'm not calm."

"Come," said Miss Moonish.

Naked, Elsie Moonish was very nice, though I had a tendency to see past her skin to the insides. We stayed together for hours fusing and nonfusing, loving without possessing, beating the winter odds and strengthening the blood against spring. Our music came from the animals downstairs, and her bed could have been grass. We were in the country. Elsie was wet and ready again and again. I was a fountain of youth, to my amazement. It had been so long.

"How long, Harold?"

"Two years."

"Who?"

"A coed doing a paper on police brutality."

"I hate her."

Then too soon, she said, "Now I have reached the point where I want you to stay. So go."

"Once more."

"No."

"Plus-plus."

"Go."

We took a shower together. She soaped me and said she liked my body. I told her, soaping her, that the feeling was mutual. She said, while I dressed, that I should telephone tomorrow.

I went out into the cold, shaking like gelatin, blowing steam. I would have gone back, but she locked the shoppe behind me.

Back home I saw that I had been broken and entered, ransacked. The room was upside down. The only thing taken was the letter FIRST. Luckily, I had FINALLY with me. I called Elsie Moonish right away, but got only a buzz.

A Nagle who would rob is a desperate Nagle, I thought. How would he deal with the owner of the egg? I worried for Elsie. Then for myself. He might deal very well. I never had seen the Nagle. Maybe he was a football type, a walking penis.

I sat worrying about the Nagle's secondary sexual characteristics, and would have stayed in that trance of doubt had it not been for my cop brain, which saved me. Here I was following the rules, waiting to hear if I won the egg, while an unleashed Nagle of no principle was running loose. What a passive idiot I was. By the time I bolted into the snow, Elsie Moonish could already be inside a camp trunk on her way by American Express.

I caught a cab to Poodleville, and none too soon.

As we pulled up in front of the shoppe, I saw a man hurrying along down the street. He was carrying a large parcel, too small for a camp trunk but large enough. While I paid the driver, not before, it came to me that it was the Glak box.

That very moment a window flew open upstairs from Poodleville. I saw Elsie, wrapped in a wrap, lean out, look from side to side and shout, "Glak snatcher!"

I flew after the fleeing Nagle, my shoes skimming on glossy pavement. The Nagle ran holding the Glak box before him and would have gotten away but for fate. The old part of town is as hilly as Rome. From nowhere a fat child on a sled came swooshing down the street and caught the Nagle at his ankles. His legs opened like a scissors. The egg box soared through the air. The sledder went crashing; the Nagle collapsed in a lump.

I intercepted the box in midair. Then I fell, tail down, box up, on top of the skidding sled and went with it down the Poodleville hill. The sidewalk was frozen glass. The sled broke Olympic records. The world blurred. I caught a glimpse of Miss Moonish as I went by, then saw the branches of trees and gray sky. Down and down I went, and heard the twing twing of bullets around me.

The Nagle was firing and getting close. Fortunately, the sled jumped the sidewalk and hustled along in the gutter. There was no traffic, and clear sailing. I felt a hot flash. I was hit but not dead.

Down I went, about a thousand miles an hour, toward the railroad tracks. I heard a whistle and clang up ahead. The traffic blinker turned red. The zebra-striped bar that stops cars came down. I headed right for the crossing, shot under the roadblock, hit the track, saw the front of the freight, a smoky Cyclops, locked my arms on the box, left the sled, turned upside down, and came down in a snowbank with the train between me and my enemy.

Forgetting pain, I grabbed my box and climbed into an empty car. So this is it, I thought. My body will lie here and roam the United States, a mournful cargo. I bawled. There was so much work still undone. Here I was cut at the budding.

A brakeman found me in the Utica yards. I was in the General Hospital when I woke.

"Do you have medicare?"

"Ummm."

"You are here mostly for exposure and shock. But not entirely. To state it unemotionally and simply, Mr. North, you have been perfectly circumcised by a 22-caliber bullet. Are you sure this was not some kind of muffed suicide attempt?"

"Hikhoff," I raged aloud. "If the Nagle were a more accurate shot, I would have collected your ashes, reassembled you and kicked you in the ass. I have always been intact from cuticles to appendix, and now this. What trauma you have caused."

They tranquillized me.

Soon I learned that when they brought me to the hospital, they brought my egg too. It was in a hot closet near my bed. What damage the excitement might have done to the Glak I could not know.

Poor Glak, I said in a whisper. What if you are born slightly bent? Forget it. Let the world know you have endured hard knocks. All survivors should carry scars, if only in the eyes. Be of good cheer, Glak.

Hikhoff would have enjoyed the sounds of the hospital. Pain sounds, fearsome in the deep darkness. Baby sounds full of good rage and wanting. For those sounds, my companions in the night, the vowels have not shifted. And the sounds of the loudspeaker calling Dr. this and Dr. that, and Dr. Mortimer Post when they do a dissection, and the sounds of the trays and televisions, the visitors, the wheeling carts—all these sounds would interest Hikhoff, for there is the honesty of a white wall about them. Hikhoff, but not me.

Joyfully, I left the hospital an ounce or two lighter, none the worse. I carried my box with new enthusiasm. The Nagle's bullets motivated me. I had a stake in this adventure now, a small but sincere investment.

There were six weeks to endure (it was March) before the egg would pop, assuming it would pop at all, and Labrador to reach on a limited budget. And a Nagle to watch for, a fanatic Nagle who would surely pursue us. Clearly, the first order of business was to find a hideout, an obscure off-the-track place where a man and his egg would be left alone.

I searched the classifieds. Two ads caught my eye. One of them was addressed directly to it:

H.N. KNOW YOU ARE IN UTICA. ALL FORGIVEN. CAN WE TALK? AGREEMENT CAN BE REACHED PROJECT G. RIDICULOUS TO CONTINUE HOSTILE. DANGEROUS TO WAIT.

Dangerous to wait. So the Nagle had traced the destination of the train. Smart man, and a compromiser. If there had been no shooting, no tampering with my equipment, however slight, I would have answered his P.O. box. And why not? He was his father's son, acting on correct impulses. Hikhoff was not even a blood relation.

But, with soreness when I walked, I was in no mood to negotiate.

The second ad was for a room in a nice, clean, well-heated house with a good view, kitchen privileges, housekeeping, good family on a tree-lined street near transportation and churches of all denominations. The price was right. I called the number and, yes, the room was vacant.

The house was welcoming. There was a small garden where a snowman stood and even an evergreen. I rang the doorbell, self-conscious over my package, which I held in my arms since the steps looked cold. I tried to take the attitude that this was a pregnancy and that I was blooming and entitled.

The box made no difference to Mrs. Fonkle, who owned the property. Probably there was a buyers' market for rooms up there.

I told her I was a scientist, but not the kind who makes bombs. I was dependable, safe, well-mannered, a person who asked only tidbits from existence, not noisy, good-natured, involved in breeding a new kind of chicken big enough to feed multitudes. Mrs. Fonkle liked, but worried over, the idea of big chickens.

"How big?" she said, and I held out my hands three feet apart.

"Some chicken," she said, laughing herself into a red face.

The first night she invited me to dinner.

The Fonkles were a mixed grill. Mrs. Fonkle had been married once to a pencil of a man, a man who lacked pigmentation. He was dead now but left a daughter behind, a girl in her mid-twenties who was pretty, all angles, intense and full of gestures.

Mrs. Fonkle's present husband, a plumber, was a side of beef, medium well. Her daughter by him was a dark, soft affair, just nineteen, filled with inner springs that pushed out.

At dinner, there were comments about science and the mushroom cloud and how the world was better before. The daughter of Husband One, Myrna by name, said, "People are beginning to realize that war accomplishes nothing."

"So how come everybody is fighting?" Cynthia said.

"Two things can stop wars," I said. "First is discovering life from another part of the sky with a big appetite for all kinds of people, regardless. Second is the hope implicit in the fact that nations good at sex are bad at marching."

"Tell me, are you a married man?" Mrs. Fonkle said, handing me seconds.

"No. I have no family. I am married to my work."

"She's getting personal," Mr. Fonkle said.

"In a house where doors are left open," Mrs. Fonkle said, "I'm entitled to a few questions."

Mrs. Fonkle's house was truly a house where doors are left open. Even me, a paranoid now, watching for shadows of the Nagle, took to leaving my bolt unclicked.

The first week went well. You could say an intimacy grew between me and the family. I had never lived so close to people.

I spent my days writing. At night I checked the egg and took walks. My Hikhoff sat on a dresser, on top of a doily, and he too seemed serene. But problems arose.

One evening, an ordinary evening, I came in from my dinner. As always, I examined the egg. It was trembling, shivering, moving. I thought *earthquake, catastrophe.* But nothing was shaking the egg. It was the egg itself moving around, rolling a little.

I put the box closer to the radiator, and the jumping slowed. Then I did what I knew from the beginning I would have to do. I sat on the egg.

I put it on a pillow, put the pillow on a chair, stripped to my underwear and gently sat on the egg, holding most of my weight with my arms.

The jumping, squiggling, shivering stopped completely. So there was a Glak in there. And it was chilly, protesting. It wanted its due, namely body heat, and who could blame it?

Look at me now, I said to my Hikhoff, a full-grown man warming eggs with his rear. Look what you did to me. Is it for this that you fed me and pissed and moaned about our feminized century? Finally you have put me into hatching position. Hikhoff, barrage balloon, how you must be laughing.

Falling in with the folksy quality of Mrs. Fonkle's, I had left my door half open. In thin PJ's, holding a turkish towel, her hair covered with a cloth to hide curlers, her feet bare, wearing no makeup on her dear bony face, Myrna came to check my health.

"Are you OK, Harold?"

"Fine," I said. "A little overexposed. I'm sorry. I should have closed my door."

"Oh," Myrna said. She threw me her towel. I covered my kneecaps. "I could swear you made a sound, a kind of clucking."

"Chicken thoughts," I said. "I was thinking out loud."

Her entrance and my surprise must have dropped my pressure and temperature because the egg began again, jumping under me. It had a lot of energy. I had to hold tight to keep myself in the chair.

"You're catching cold," Myrna said, coming into the room.

"No, I'm fine."

"Give me your pulse," Myrna said. I gave her.

"A hundred fifteen beats a minute?"

"Normal for me. Normal."

"Something is bothering you, Harold." Myrna sat down on my bed. "Talk to me. I'm a good listener."

"Nothing," I said. "Besides, Myrna, if your mother walks by and sees you sitting there in your sleepies, what will she think? What?"

Myrna got up with her serious face and closed the door. She came back to the bed and stretched herself, her chin propped on hands. She made herself at home.

"You are suffering," Myrna said. "Don't deny it."

"Better you should go," I said.

Myrna was very attractive in those PJ's. They were sad cotton PJ's with no class, covered with blue flowers, a thing little girls wear. When she moved they tightened around her breasts, small volcanos. They held her bottom nicely, too. For a slender lady she was well built. That long, lazy body was a winding road.

"Is it your stomach, Harold?" she said.

"No. Yours."

"Don't be a glib. Come sit here and talk to me."

"I can't move."

"Why?"

"Don't be alarmed. Don't shout. Myrna, I'm sitting on an egg. You might as well know. I'm sitting on a large egg."

"Harold?"

Like a fool I told her everything. Everything. Everything. The dam broke. I was amazed by my own need to confide. Always a loner, I dropped my guard with a thud. That is the danger of human contact. It breeds humanity.

When I finished the tale of the Glak, Myrna cried.

"I can't speak," she said. "In some ways, this is the most wonderful story I have heard since 'Rapunzel.' Harold, dear Harold, my impulse is to cherish you, to hold you and give you back heat. I know it's wrong. I know that. I know your work is its own reward, and the thing you are doing for Dr. Hikhoff is beautiful and contained in itself. But I have the impulse to take you to me, to be naked with you, to recharge you with all the sun I stored up on Lake Winnapokie last summer. Bring the egg here. Let me give."

Am I made of aluminum?

Myrna, Glak and Harold fell together and again the winter was kept outside.

Even the egg was radiant. If you have never seen a contented, happy, and secure egg, let me tell you it is a fine experience. Dear Myrna, half rib cage, half air, generated fire like a coil. Her nerves practically left her skin. She gave like a sparkler.

Before going to her own room, Myrna promised to come regularly, on a schedule, and to help me with my egg and my own thawing. I felt marvelous. I had a friend, a lover, a bed partner interested only in nourishing.

The next morning, I woke rested, nicely sore as after a ball game, restored and ready for anything. I sat on the side of the bed and the egg came toward me. First, it thumped, then jiggled, did a half-turn, then rolled right up to my thigh.

"Look," I said, "enough is enough. Hear me, Glak, I will do my part and take good care, but this rolling stuff has got to stop. I need time for my own pursuits."

I made a nest for the egg, using the pillow again, and put it under the blanket. Then I went to wash my face, shave, and brush my teeth.

Bright as a penny, tingling with menthol, on the way back to my room, I heard what sounded like the Great Sneeze.

It was Cynthia who stood, blowing into a handkerchief, in my room, at my bed, holding my blanket, looking at my egg. She was wearing a quilted housecoat over her nightgown, her long hair tumbled down, her dark face darker than usual.

"Harold," she said, "we have something to talk about."

"What are you doing home?" I said.

"I have a cold."

"Where's your mother? It's drafty in here."

"Harold, why is there an egg in your bed?"

"I didn't lay it, if that's what you think."

"I don't know what to think."

"Look, Cyn, your father is a plumber, he's got a plunger. I'm in science. I have an egg. There's a perfectly logical explanation."

Hearing my voice, the egg began to turn circles. That's one smart, responsive Glak, I thought, but the incident shook Cynthia, she so young, and she cried like her sister, only wetter.

"Oh, don't weep," I said. "Please."

"A man shouldn't sleep with an egg."

"There's a quote from the Old Testament. Who are you to judge me?"

"It's perverse. When Ma hears about what's going on in this house . . ."

"Cyn, why, oh why should Ma or Pa or any lady be involved? Cyn, older people get nervous about such things. They think right away, suppose it hatches and is some kind of nutty meat-eater. Cyn, please, this whole episode demands silence. If you've ever kept your cool, keep it now."

"It's wrong for a man to sleep with a big egg."

Standing there, she manufactured commandments. It was informative to watch her, though. She breathed in heaves. Clouds practically formed over her head. Her toes nearly smoked. So totally involved, so passionate, she was different by more than chromosomes from Myrna. Plumber blood shot through her pipes. Her valves hissed. You could see needles rise on gauges and warning lights flash.

I had to tell her something. You owe it to your audience. Myrna had the whole truth. It seemed somehow disloyal to tell Cynthia the same story.

"Cyn, this egg is my responsibility. A lot of lives depend on what happens in this room. Because this egg is no ordinary egg. It is an egg found in the wreckage of a strange and unidentified crashed aircraft, a UFO."

"Harold, stop."

"Cyn, on my heart. Probably the whole thing is nothing, a hoax. Maybe there really is a big chicken in there. I may even be a control.

"There are forty-two agents like myself in forty-two rooms with forty-two eggs like this. None of us knows if he has the space-egg. To throw off the competition, Cyn. Standard procedure. The point is, this egg may just be the one. The thing. Cyn, you have got to keep this to yourself."

"A thing in our house?"

"A nice thing. A vegetarian. We know that much by tests. Lettuce, carrots, parsley, like that. By computer calculations, a furry, sweet kind of beast like a rabbit. A bunny. Nice."

"Beast? Why did you use the word beast?"

"Well, a furry bunny is a *beast*, Cyn. It's still a *beast*."

"I don't know what to say."

"Nothing. Go about your business."

"How come our house?"

"IBM-selected. Strictly impersonal from a juggle of IBM cards with punched classified ads. Out of the way. Small city. Quiet. Unlikely discovery. IBM didn't figure on you, Cyn. I mean, it's obvious if this got out there could be panic."

"Harold, I do not believe you. And to me what matters is what I know, which is that you personally are sleeping with a lousy egg while youth flies."

"Where does youth come in? And what do you know about youth? You're too young to know beans about youth."

"Look at me. Do you see the bags under each eye? Do you know how sleepless I have been for a month because of you in this house?"

"Me?"

"Yes. And now you tell me about lettuce-eaters from the movies. I don't want to know anything, Harold. I hate you and I hate your thing."

The egg rolled again. Cynthia could not contain herself. She grabbed a dustpan and began to swing. I got my hand under the flat part just in time. She would have splattered my Glak all over the neighborhood.

We struggled and it was not all violence. We tangled as people do, and it came to pass that Cyn ended up with her back to me, my arms around her front, and she threw back her head so I drowned in perfumed black hair. She was a buttery girl, a pillow, who gave where squeezed but popped right back to shape. Now she stopped the battle and cried again. I turned her and comforted her. What could I do? Send her out yelling?

As we fell together onto the sturdy bed (it was maple), Cynthia tried to crunch the egg with a leg this time. I thwarted her, then put the Glak on the floor where it jumped like a madman.

Love was made that morning.

"Harold," she said near noon, at which time her mother was expected from the supermarket, "I don't care who or what you are. All I care about is that I come first and not some turkey from Mars."

"OK, Cyn, my honor. And the egg business is between us."

"Don't say between us. I'll break the bastard if you ever so much as pat it in my presence."

"I didn't mean between us, I meant between-us. Hush-a-bye. Our business."

"Hush-a-bye yourself. Make me sleepy again."

Within an hour I had swollen glands. They were heaven's gift. I would have preferred measles or mumps, but the glands would do. I needed time, and Cynthia's cold, a splendid virus that made me sweat, chill and shake, gave me time.

With Myrna offering fire, with Cynthia openly hostile, competing for egg-time, and me being only one human being, I needed time, time, time.

I refused to recover. But my illness did not protect me. The sisters were stirred by helplessness. The nights were much. First Myrna would come and soon fall asleep. I pulled blankets over her. Cynthia liked the bed's far side. She blew fire in my ear. One Fonkle slept; another awoke until the weest hours. I was destroyed.

I had nothing left for the Glak. I was spent, an icicle, so cold and uncaring I could have sunk the *Titanic*. The Glak leaped in deprivation and threw covers on the floor.

"Harold," Mrs. Fonkle said to me one gray morning soon after, "something is going on."

"What?" I said weakly, coughing a lot.

"A woman with daughters is a woman with all eyes. And such daughters. I think they like you, Harold."

"Fine ladies," I said. "Cute as buttons." I put a thermometer which was not even oral in my mouth to prevent further speech.

"And my intuition tells me, Harold, you like them. But *them* is not Myrna and *them* is not Cynthia. You follow my mind? Harold, your blanket is shaking. Are you all right?"

"Mmmm." I tried to hold down the egg with my hand.

"What is life but decisions," Mrs. Fonkle said. "A time for fun and games, a time for decisions."

I was expecting this inevitable confrontation and prepared. With the thermometer still plugged in, I dived, without warning, under the pillow. I howled. There in readiness, was a can of Foamy. I squirted the Foamy around my whole head, mouth, face, eyes and hair. To cancel the whoosh of the lather, I yelled like an owl. Then up I came like a sub, from the depths of the Sea of Despair. Mrs. Fonkle was torpedoed.

My wet white face, waving arms, kicking feet, jumping quilt, had a fine effect. A cargo ship by nature, hit on her water line,

Mrs. Fonkle slid slowly under waves without time for an SOS.

After carrying her to her room and leaving her on her bed with a wet rag on her forehead, I went back to my own room. My thermometer was on the floor, its arrow touching the silver line at normal. I quick-lit a Pall Mall and heated the mercury drop. At 104.6 I was happy and left it in a prominent place, wiped myself clean, got back in the bed and awaited commotion.

Should all the air-raid sirens and dystrophy ads and cancer warnings we go through be wasted, a total loss? How much has society spent to keep you alert, Harold North, pumping adrenalin, listening for vampires? Use your training. Deal with challenge. I lay there waiting for my next idea.

Coma. A beautiful word, and my answer. Coma.

When I heard Mrs. Fonkle rise finally, I put myself into a coma. In a self-created and lovely blue funk I lay there, smiling like Mona Lisa, stroking my egg.

Naturally enough, she called the doctor.

"And the blanket was jumping during all this?"

"Like a handball . . ."

I heard them in the hall. Mrs. Fonkle came with him to my room. I stayed in my coma while the doctor stuck pins, took blood, gave needles, checked pressure.

Later, in a miserable mood, Mrs. Fonkle stormed back alone, pulled at my blanket while I pulled back, and said I was a cheat, a malingerer, a fraud, a lecher.

"Dr. Zipper says nothing is wrong with you. Not even athlete's foot."

I never would have given Zipper the credit. He actually found me out.

"So, Mr. North, name the game."

"Darling," I said, "darling, darling and darling." I planted a kiss on Mrs. Fonkle's thyroid. "I hope you are on the pill," I said. "I hope at least you took precautions." I looked lovingly at her while her eyes rolled, a slot machine making jackpots.

"You never did," she said.

"I didn't. We did."

"It never happened."

"Old speedy," I said. "When again? Tell me. Come on. Tell."

"It never happened."

"They're not kidding when they say like Mama used to make," I said.

"Pig," she said. "An unconscious lady."

How I hated myself. If I could, I would lie down on spikes, I thought. Well, maybe something in her will be flattered. Maybe she will feel good that a young man was inspired to do her some mayhem. Let her think of me as a crumb, a nibble, a K ration on the road to Social Security.

It was Myrna who brought supper on a tray.

"Harold," she said. "I have thought you over. In your present weakened condition this egg business is too much for you. Psychologically, I mean. You have got to think of keeping for yourself, not of giving. Darling, we are all so worried. Even Mama is in a state of distraction. She served Daddy three portions of liver tonight. You have got to get well. Let me take the egg. I will keep it cozy while you recuperate. Let me take it to my room, at least for the nights. Harold, please say yes."

Why not? If Myrna, who had embers to waste, said she would care for the Glak, she would care for it. This was a trustworthy lady. And my blanket would no longer bounce.

"I agree," I said. "Thank you, dear one. Thank you."

Myrna beamed. Then and there she took the box, put back the angry egg, and carried it to her bedroom. Transporting the bundle she hummed a lullaby.

"Now," she said, removing my empty tray, "use all your energies to heal. Save everything like a miser until you are better."

"I will save," I said, nearly crying from good feeling.

To do her duty, Myrna retired early, even eagerly. I think for the first time in her life she locked her door. When the house settled down, Myrna asleep, the Fonkles watching television, Cynthia came with dessert.

"Hello, Jell-O," she said.

"Hello Jell-O to you, angel."

"Harold, I have had some second thoughts."

"At this late date?"

"Harold, that stinking egg has got to go. It's draining your strength. Government or not, I am going to bust it to pieces. I never liked it, but I lived with it. But when the time comes that the egg hurts you and keeps you from total recovery, then it's time for a change. I want your permission to smash that egg because permission or not here I come."

"Let me think on it."

"Think fast. You know me. The first minute I catch you with your eyes closed—splat."

"I'll think fast. I must weigh personal gain against my sworn . . ."

"I have stated my intention, Harold."

I thought fast. Not bad. Why not let Cynthia eliminate the egg, at least, some egg? It would remove her desperation, apprehension and combativeness. Not to mention her curiosity if she ever discovered that the Glak was already gone.

After doing with my Jell-O what I have always done, that is, slicing around the cup and putting the saucer over it and turning the whole thing upside down so that the Jell-O comes out like a ruby hill, Cynthia removed the dishes.

"I am going to the movies," she said. "Have your mind made up, Harold, by the time I get back. And by the way, you eat Jell-O in the most disgusting sensual manner. I'm dying to be with you."

I kissed her nose.

What a marvelous family. Even Mr. Fonkle was roaring with laughter downstairs, so happy with the "Beverly Hillbillies."

The TV which occupied Mr. and Mrs. Fonkle with slices of

flickering life was in the living room. The living room was removed by a dining room from the kitchen.

On the balls of my feet, I went down and slipped into the control center of the house. There I opened the fridge and removed three eggs. Why three? Cynthia knew the egg of the Glak was big. In fact, by then it had swelled to the size of a small football. Big eggs make big splashes.

I tiptoed upstairs, walking in my own footprints. In the room I took Scotch-tape strips from the dresser drawers where they held paper to the wood. With what glue was left I pasted two eggs together. Praise be, there was only enough tape for a pair. I cut my pinky with a blade and speckled the pasted eggs with A-positive. There was enough left, before clotting, to do the third too.

I waited with my egg bomb under the blanket in the Glak's former place. The third egg went under my pillow on an impulse.

The arrival of the specialist surprised me. Mr. Fonkle showed him in.

"Harold," Mr. Fonkle said, "this is Dr. Bim. Dr. Zipper called him in for consultation. It seems you are a puzzling case, a phenomenon to medicine."

Dr. Bim nodded. I replied in kind. If Zipper was sure I was faking, why this? Playing safe against malpractice, I thought, and I looked to my Hikhoff for confirmation.

"Feel well, Harold," Mr. Fonkle said. "We're in the middle of a hot drama. Excuse me."

Dr. Bim went to wash his hands, then came back and closed the door. After drying, he put on white cotton gloves.

"I never saw a doctor do that," I said.

"We all have our ways," he said. "Now to work."

Dr. Bim pounded me with hands like hammers.

"Now, close your eyes and open your mouth," he said.

I closed hard and opened wide.

"When I tell you, Harold, then look. Not before. Depress the tongue. Hooey, what a coat."

"Aghh."

"Keep the eyes closed."

"Broop."

"Now bite hard."

My mouth shut on the barrel of a gun. My eyes popped open.

"No noise," he said, and kept the gun close.

"Nagle, I presume. How did you track my spoor?"

"By checking room-for-rents in the papers on the days after you left us, Harold. By asking around. From the zip code on a certain letter to a certain lady who sells poodles."

"You are nobody's fool. Nobody's."

"Thank you," the Nagle said, appreciating my large heart. "It's a shame we couldn't come to a more civilized agreement. I hope, Harold, that you comprehend my motivation. Take my father, a man who spent his whole life contributing bits and pieces. Imagine, fifty years of droppings, footnotes in *American Scholar*, a few *ibids* and some *op. cits*. Nothing to make headlines, never once. Then one day in comes your fat friend Hikhoff carrying a genuine, fertile Glak egg. 'Tell me, Dr. Nagle,' he growls in that meretricious voice of his, 'what do I have here?' Harold, at that moment, in the fading evening of my father's life, the sun rose. On the brink of shadow, my father saw blinding rays. Understand?"

"Yes. It's not hard to understand."

"Do you have any concept of what a fertile Glak egg means to an aged anthropologist?"

"A small grasp."

"Immortality. For the first time my father begged. For what? For halfies. No more. Not fifty-one percent, just fifty. The Hikhoff-Nagle Discovery is how he put it. Hikhoff laughed at him."

"The egg was full of meaning for Dr. Hikhoff," I said.

"I swore at the funeral, Harold, that my father's memory would be based on more than just mummy swatches from the graves of second-string Egyptians. Now I fulfill my vow."

"Nagle," I said, "are you in this for your father or for your own need to up the ante on your ancestors?"

"How would you like a loose scalp?"

"Sorry. But I am vow fulfilling, too. You have read the letter marked FIRST."

"And tonight I will read FINALLY."

"Impossible," I said, "that letter was lost. When I woke up in the hospital after you . . ."

The Nagle scratched his ear. "It could be," he said. "Does it matter? What can FINALLY be except more of Hikhoff's Old English ravings. Virility of the vocal cords, which was the only place he had it."

"Have some taste," I said. "The man is among the dead."

"Let FINALLY blow along the Utica-Mohawk tracks. The egg is what matters."

"We could go partners," I said.

"Ha. You are a gutsy one, Harold. Too late for partners. Now give me the Nagle Discovery. Any hesitation, reluctance or even a bad breath and you join Hikhoff for choir practice."

He was a nice fellow, the Nagle, with a face like Don Ameche, not the killer type, but you never know.

"The egg is here under my pillow," I said.

My luck held. The Nagle had never seen the egg before. He lit up when I showed him that pink-splotched pullet, balancing it in his palm.

"Slow and easy," I said, with wild eyes.

"It's been a pleasure," he said, tucking the egg in a towel and putting it into his medical bag. "Maybe when this is over and done with, you and I can sit and play chess."

"I would like nothing . . ."

Pong. I was hit so hard on the head I flew half off the bed. I saw Ferris wheels turning at different speeds. I tumbled too, spinning like a bobbin. Then later, there was another crash. A gooshy sound, a wetness. I woke.

"Bye, bye. Poor thing," Cynthia was saying, lifting my blanket, observing the destruction.

"What, what, what?"

"Harold, it had to be this way. Even that specialist said all you needed was complete rest. Better the egg should never see light, even in the free world, than you should die in your prime."

Cynthia never noticed the Scotch tape in the goo. She was so self-satisfied.

The next days passed smoothly.

Myrna had my Glak. Cynthia had her pleasure unshared. The Nagle was accounted for, squatting on his chicken. Mrs. Fonkle avoided me like doom. Mr. Fonkle, served like Farouk by his wife, brought cards to my room and we played.

Out of respect for her promise and a sense of my need for quiet, Myrna came gently only to report on the Glak. It was hopping all the time now, making tiny sounds. She described the sounds as like chalk on the blackboard, and I knew how happy Hikhoff would be if he could hear, as maybe he could.

While Myrna warmed Glak, Cynthia warmed Harold. Her vision of recovery was not based on abstention.

My only discomfort came from Mrs. Fonkle, and it was mild. Out of suspicion, she fed her daughters garlic and ox tails and other odoriferous, glutenous foods that made their lips stick or filled them with protective cramps. I kept Tums and Clorets at bedside.

March went like the best kind of lamb. The windows unfroze. A bird sang on the telephone line. I had to move again and make plans again.

How did Chaucer say it? *Whan that Aprille with his shoures soote the droghte of March hath perced to the roote.* Like that. Up I came like a crocus.

Now it came time for partings and farewells. Cynthia was easy to leave, so easy it hurt. When the month turned, she met a podiatrist of good family. Her prospects improved. When we had our confrontation, she brought knitting along. In the tense air she knitted like a factory. A sweater for him.

"I am called back to D.C.," I said. "And will be punished."

"Punished, heh?"

"Forget it. Nothing painful. Chastised is more the word."

The thought of my punishment made it easier for Cynthia to say goodbye. Really, she had never been the same since the breaking of the egg. I think she thought less of me for not breaking it myself. Who can fathom a woman's heart? While we talked, she compared me to her podiatrist and found him better. The mystique of new weather.

"No reason to prolong this suffering," I said. "I will always remember you and what we had together and how you sustained me."

Cynthia dropped a stitch but caught it. Her reflexes had gained from our acquaintanceship.

It was harder to leave lanky Myrna.

"I know you must go," she said, "I know and I won't make scenes. Do you plan to return?"

"My life is a question mark," I said honestly. "What can I say?"

"It won't be the same without you two."

"Or for me. Ever."

"Send an announcement if it hatches. Nothing too fancy. A simple card."

Mrs. Fonkle, who had taken to charitable activities, said a swift goodbye. She was full of dignity and adorable poise. Such an ego.

The air was balmy on the day I left the Fonkle home. I had a new suitcase, the pudgy executive type, and in it my Glak had room enough. The egg was practically a bowling ball now, strain-

ing to pop. The Fonkles stood in a family group when I entered
the cab. I waved and wished them well. I was full of emotion,
with watering eyes. They did so well by me and mine.

We live in a time of shortening distances, except between people. How easy it is to reach the most remote corners of the imagination. A person like myself can go from Utica, New York, to
Labrador for $120.35 by bus and by plane. The facts made me
swoon. Utica to Labrador. We are only hours from the place
where the world ends.

To reach Labrador you go first to a travel agent. You tell him
you wish to visit Labrador. He does not flinch.

"Where," he says, "Goose Bay?"

"No," you say, having studied maps and folders. "Maybe the
Mealy Mountains."

"We have a special on the Mealys," he says.

"Or Lake Melville," you go on, "Fish Cove Point, White Bear,
Misery Point, Marys Harbour, Chidley on Ungava Bay, Petit-
sikapau Lake, Nipishish, Tunungayualuk or perhaps Gready. I
haven't made up my mind."

"Go to Goose Bay," the agent says. "From there you can go
any place."

"Can I jump off to Kangalaksiorvik Fiord?"

"In the Torngat region?" he says. "Naturally."

By intuition I had already chosen Kangalaksiorvik Fiord as the
place where my Glak would be born. Not that Canadian citizenship could not be gotten closer, but Kangalaksiorvik felt right.

"The scenic route," the agent said, stamping tickets. "By Greyhound from Utica to Syracuse leaves 10:50 A.M., arrives Syracuse
12:05 P.M. Leaves Syracuse 2:30 P.M., arrives Montreal 10:20 P.M.
You have a bite, see a picture. At 4:00 A.M., Air Canada flies out,
and at 7:20 A.M. you are in Goose Bay, for a total cost, including
economy air fare, of $120.35 plus a little tax."

"Then?"

"Then in Goose Bay ask around, hire a charter, and zoom you are in Kangalaksiorvik. The Torngats are lovely this time of year."

From the agent's convenient uncle I bought ten thousand dollars in travel insurance. My policies were divided between Myrna and Cynthia, deserving souls. At long last, with my Hikhoff snug in a pocket and my Glak bag in my hand, I headed for the terminal. On the downhill slope of responsibility, time is sweet.

For me a bus ride is only slightly removed from sexual intercourse. Since a child, I am prone to vibrations, put to sleep, handed the same dream. In the dream I drift in a washtub on a silver pond. This pond is populated by stunning things, all color and light, who knock themselves out for my amusement. I look forward to this dream like a friend.

My bus dream began and expanded to include my Glak. Each time the bus bumped or took a hard curve, the pond produced a three-headed lizard who nuzzled my nose. His triple grin woke me. I reached to see if the egg was intact, then, assured, slept again.

The bus went smoothly, as did my transfer to Air Canada.

There was some worry about how my Glak would like flying, especially under someone else's power, but there was no problem. The egg did not jiggle, except for takeoff. Since there were empty seats, I belted the Glak beside me and reclined my chair. The silver pond is strictly an automotive fantasy. In planes I dream of crashing.

Here in the clouds over Eastern Canada, I was allowed no repose. Behind me sat a couple who were touring the world. I had seen their luggage, a mass of labels, in the terminal. Now, on the way to Labrador, I deduced from their talk that they were running out of places. After Saskatchewan, there was nothing left.

"See there, in small print," the man said, showing a guidebook. "See there, a fellow named Bjarni discovered Labrador in 986. Imagine. Bjarni the son of Herjolf. See there, he sold his boat to Leif Ericson, who later used the identical craft in his explorations."

"How do they know?"

"See there, it's in the guide. Helluland, land of stones."

"Where?"

"Fish and fur are the two major industries."

"Oh."

Labrador did not sound bad. There were trees, according to the guide, conifers, birch, poplars, spruce, lichens, moss, red azaleas, blue gentians, even white orchids. And they had chickadees, geese, ducks, lemmings, lynx, wolves, ermines, martens, otters, foxes, seals, bears, owls, red gulls, and Patagonian terns. There were some Eskimos, the ones not shot by fishermen, Algonkins, Nascapees, Englishmen and Scotch. Not bad for a bird. Activities, company, a little conflict. A nice subarctic community.

It was a foggy morning. Helluland, land of stones, fish, furs, etc., lay like a lump. Our plane began its descent. I could see no ermines or white orchids, only patches of smoke and the lights of the Goose Bay Airport. No wonder Bjarni unloaded the ship.

"Are you sure we haven't been here?" the lady said.

"See there," said the man, "it does look familiar."

Familiar it looks, like your own subconscious laid out to dry. Goose Bay may be a fine place. I don't know. I checked my egg in the airport men's room. There was a crack in the shell, the tiniest fissure, not the kind that swallows grandmothers in Sicilian earthquake stories, more like a hairline. But it was there. If I were a first-time mother, a primigravida as they say, with a broken bag of water, I could have acted no worse.

I collared the first Lab I saw and screamed at him about renting a plane to Kangalaksiorvik.

"Matter of fact, there's a plane leaving now. Pilot is by the name of Le Granf. He currently drinks coffee in the coffee place. You will know him to see him by his enormity. Also, he has one arm."

I found Le Granf in the coffee place, and there was no missing him. In a red and black mackinaw, he looked like a science-fiction checkerboard. Built in blocks, head, chest, middle, legs, he was made from squares. His one arm held a pail of coffee, black.

"Mr. Le Granf?" I said.

"Yas," he said, a Frenchman monophthongizing his diphthongs, "who are you, Quasimodo, the hunchback of Notre Dame?"

"I am Harold North," I said.

"Beeg news. Vive Québec libre."

You basically insecure vowel shifter, I thought. You son of a bitch. It's your plane.

"I understand that you pilot a plane up to Kangalaksiorvik."

"The world's puke."

"I've got to get up there."

"Why? You have a yen to bug seals?"

"Why is my business."

"True. How come this rush on Kangalaksiorvik? I got passenger for there. OK. We fit you in for a hundred dollars."

"Done."

"I swallow this sweat, we go."

Le Granf gulped the coffee and we went. We walked to a hangar in front of which sat something which must have been an airplane.

"Meet Clarette, the old whore," said Le Granf. "My saggy express. The snatch of the wild blue. You change your mind to go?"

"No."

"Stupid. My passenger is not here yet. Get in and we wait for him."

We climbed into Clarette's belly. There were four seats, two at the controls, two just behind.

"Clarette has a terrible cough," said Le Granf. "I worry for her tubes."

He pressed a button and the propeller turned. Puffs of smoke shot from the nose. The cough began, a hack.

"Phew. Not good."

I stopped noticing because Le Granf's other passenger arrived. It was the Nagle carrying a duffel bag. We saw each other head-on, and both of us made the sound of old doors closing.

"Acquaintances," said Le Granf. "Then we have stimulating conversation of the past."

I was sitting next to Le Granf, but when the Nagle came aboard, I did the prudent thing and shifted next to him in back. He put his duffel bag in the storage space and saw my executive suitcase.

"Are you armed?" I said.

"Don't make nasty personal jokes," said Le Granf.

"I was talking to my friend," I said.

"Ah."

"No, of course not," said the Nagle. "What are you doing here, Harold?"

"Same as you. Same as you."

"But I have the egg."

"You have a chicken."

"I get it," the Nagle said. "The goal-line stand. I admire your persistence, Harold."

"You have a chicken, Nagle."

"Sure, Harold. I have a chicken."

"Where is this chicken?" said Le Granf. "Include me in the discussion."

"Go ahead, tell him," I said.

Le Granf informed the tower that we were ready for takeoff by yelling out the window. Then Clarette fought her bronchitis, and slowly we were moving.

"She will rise," Le Granf said. "We will have our jollies."

She rose, after a fashion, and the Nagle told Le Granf his story of the Glak. I must admit, he presented his case objectively, as he saw it, keeping all things in proportion.

"So, well, then one has a chicken and one a Glak?" said Le Granf, after I explained the complications. "Marvelous."

I began to feel oddly ill. I got violent cramps. I had flashes. My stomach swelled. In a flash of insight—the kind Hikhoff taught me—I knew I was feeling the symptoms of labor. This condition is not unusual in emotional kinds like myself, but still it is embarrassing.

"So," said Le Granf, "tell me. Which of you poppas is the real father, that I want to know. What kind of educated man would fornicate with a feathered friend?"

"Nobody fornicated with a feathered friend," I said.

"Love is love," Le Granf said. "But a bird."

"Fly the plane," I said, doubled over with pain.

Le Granf found a bottle of brandy and passed it around.

"I have heard tell many strange tales under the Northern Lights, you bet," said Le Granf, "but two men infatuated with the same pigeon, oh boy!"

"Ignore him," said the Nagle.

"Tell me," I said, "what made you pick Kangalaksiorvik?"

"The *galak*, I suppose, which sounds like Glak."

"I never noticed that."

"And you followed me all the way up here with nothing but the chicken story, Harold? I keep expecting you to play a trump card. Are you waiting until we land to hit me on the back of the neck?"

"Follow you? Why should I follow you? What you have there in the sack is a rooster, maybe a hen, but no Glak."

"Harold," said the Nagle, "I hope I find a friend someday as loyal to me as you are to Hikhoff."

Bouncing like an elevator, Clarette flew us to the dead heart of winter, over fields of blue ice.

The Nagle and I fell into bemused silence. Under my pains, I had thoughts of Hikhoff, out of place, out of time, out of focus, tossing vowels like darts at the passing parade. Was Hikhoff him-self involved in a pregnancy, kindled by food? Could it be that he felt himself with child, some kind of child? Were Hikhoff's bellows labor pains too, for an invisible offspring? The Glak. Some son. Some daughter. Some product, at least, of Hikhoff's perpet-ual pregnancy.

Le Granf sang dirty songs about caribou and snowshoe rabbits. They helped pass the journey.

"There it blows," said Le Granf. "Look down. Nothing, eh?"

Clarette lost altitude, such as there was, as Le Granf searched for a landing place. He flew us off to the left of what seemed to be a settlement, circled, dipped, banked.

The Nagle and I grabbed for our luggage. We both had red faces, flamed by the moment of truth.

"Nagle," I said, "I feel sorry for you. You will soon stand chin deep in snow and discover at the moment of triumph that you have carried a fryer to practically the North Pole."

"Really, Harold. Do you plan to hit me?"

"No violence from me," I said. "The violence is done."

Le Granf found a spot, a clearing in the woods. Clarette settled into it as if it were a four poster, a remarkable landing, one-point.

The deal with Le Granf was for him to wait.

The Nagle's egg was as ready as the Glak's. Neither of us an-ticipated more than a few minutes. Outside in the absolute cold, the Nagle and I wrapped scarves around our faces. We lugged our burdens toward a place near trees.

"This is it," I said.

Like duelists, we stood back to back. We bent to our bags. Out came the Glak egg, hopping to my hands. It was hot as a muffin. More fissures lined the shell and more showed all the time. The egg was more like a web.

Le Granf stood near the plane out of decency. He could see how serious we were and hummed the wedding march.

The egg broke in my hands.

I was holding a blinking, stringy thing with stubs for wings and fat feet.

"Hi, Glak," I said.

"Hi, Glak," the Nagle said to his chicken.

You would think my warm hands and the furnace of my affection would have meaning to a Glak barely sixty seconds old. No. Already, it strained for escape, looking at me as if I were a Nazi.

I put it gently on the frozen turf. It did what it was supposed to. It waddled, fell, slipped, staggered, stopped, stretched and said *glak* in a raucous manner.

Cheep, said the Nagle's chicken, and he said, "Did you hear that?"

I paid him no attention. My Glak, *the* Glak I should say, was examining the world. It took a step toward the forest, but hesitated.

"Come here, Glak," I said to the wasteland.

Glak.

Cheep.

The Glak did not come back. It took a baby step toward the woods, then another.

I moved after it, but stopped. There, in the land of stones, I heard Elsie Moonish's dictum on love without possession, the act without the owning.

I without Glak, Glak without me. We were both our own men. Poor Glak. Already it speared looks here and there in a jerky search for its own kind. Were there any others? Would it find them? Did we do this frazzled thing a favor or the worst injustice?

"Goodbye, my Glak," the Nagle was saying. His chicken had taken a stroll, too. The Nagle began snapping pictures of it for the record. I had no use for the record, and Hikhoff had written nothing of Polaroids.

"Glak," said my Glak, more raucous than before. And there it was, Hikhoff's croak, as prevowel shift as they come.

The Nagle snapped away at his impostor, a yellow tuft.

Then the newborns met. The Glak and the chicken felt each other out, shrugged, shivered, took a look at Labrador and walked off together into the primeval forest.

"A Glak and a chicken," I said to the Nagle, who rolled film. "Some team. Chickens, at least, are not extinct. Glaks do not yield their drumsticks so willingly. Maybe hope blooms here in the snow."

Off went the birds. What could I say? Could I give wisdom? Could I say, "Call Fridays"? Could I say, "Read *The Snow Goose* by Gallico and drop in to show gratitude on Christmas"? There was nothing I could say. With a bird, just-born is the equivalent of a human adolescent. There is a definite loss of communication.

"Come on, crazies," said Le Granf. "Clarette is oozing oil."

Polite to the end, the Nagle and I offered firsts at the door. We were subdued. Le Granf started his rubber-band motor.

"Wait," I said, climbing out, running back to the nursery where two shells lay open like broken worlds.

"Moron. Come on," said Le Granf.

I put my Hikhoff on the ground, facing the trees.

At Goose Bay I said to Le Granf, "Monsieur, you are a reindeer's udder." Nothing.

I said, "Sir, you are an abortion." Puzzlement.

I said, "Pierre, your missing arm should goose the devil." Double take.

I said, "Laval, you are a lousy pilot with a greasy plane."

He hit me on the head. I hated to use Le Granf that way, but I needed the jolt. I felt better, much better, purged. It was the Nagle who picked me up.

"Nagle, what do you plan to do now?" I said. "Myself, I plan to go someplace where a pineapple can grow. Someplace where the sun is the size of a dinner plate. I am going to get salt water in my mouth."

Still reeling, I thought, *who needs me most?*

E. MOONISH SYRACUSE, NEW YORK OFFER PLUS-PLUS IN SALU-
BRIOUS CLIMATE STOP ALL EXPENSES STOP PLENTY HONEY STOP
PLEASE REPLY COLLECT STOP LOVE STOP HAROLD NORTH

After cabling, I went with the Nagle for a drink. While the drinks were being brewed, I excused myself, left for the john and read FINALLY under an open bulb.

Dear Harold,

Bless you and keep you. Also thank you. Harold, enclosed is a check for $1000. Write poems. Also here is my recipe for a grand roast Glak:

Take Glak, place in pan, cover with butter and slices of orange. Spice with garlic salt. Add paprika and pepper. Line pan with roasting potatoes and tender onions. Place in preheated range 450 degrees. Cook thirty minutes per pound. Serve hot. Suggest lively Gumpolskierchner '59 for a sparkle.

Best regards,
David Hikhoff

"It was delicious, delicious," I yelled to Hikhoff. "Boy, you have some weird sense of humor."

Hikhoff, roller of r's, chamber of guts, juggler of opposites, galloping ghost, A.E.I.O.U., now sleep well.

So it was that I entered my puerperium, which is gynecological for the time of recovery after delivering, the time of postpartum elation. Of life after birth.

Format by Vivian Ostrow
Set in Electra
Composed and printed by York Composition Company, Inc.
Bound by The Haddon Craftsmen, Inc.
HARPER & ROW, PUBLISHERS, INCORPORATED